ACROSS BOTH SIDES
OF THE MIRROR

Copyright © 2023 by Bianca Pensy Aba

ISBN: 979-8-218-15372-4 (paperback)
ISBN: 979-8-218-15573-5 (ebook)

This edition first published in 2023

Published by Bianca Pensy Aba
www.biancapensyaba.com

ACROSS BOTH SIDES OF THE MIRROR

A Novel

BIANCA PENSY ABA

Pour ma maman, Salomé Aba, an exceptional woman.

Anyone who swims far enough into the ocean could have the fortune or misfortune to meet her. She captures men and women, arbitrarily. If they fit her fancy, she will allow them to go back to shore unscathed. These people will usually receive their heart's deepest desires: riches, luck, fertility, healing, etc. The ones who do not meet her favor will disappear into the waters, their souls spoken for.

She is often seen with her golden mirror and a snake around her neck. She enjoys admiring her own beauty. To lure people in, she sometimes lets her mirror drift near the shore. If anyone takes it, she haunts their dreams until they swim back to her to return it. Then, their fate is in her hands.

When in the possession of a mortal, the golden mirror carries her powers. Anyone who owns it gets an opportunity to take control of their reality. The ones who cannot do so leave their souls up for the taking.

Mami Wata, la Sirène.

CHAPTER 1

Nova pushed the snooze button for the third time; she did not want to wake up. A few minutes later, she felt her bed vibrate again. She immediately searched for her phone with one hand while the rest of her body was still resting under the cover. There it was, under her pillow. She looked at the time: 8:20 AM. This time, she had to get up. She did not particularly enjoy her job, but she still needed to show up on time. Rushing to get ready in the morning had become normal for her.

As she sat up, she began to mentally prepare. Untwisting her hair would take no more than ten minutes. She would brush her teeth while she was rinsing her body in the shower. Thankfully, she didn't need to think about what she had to wear. Her pink and blue uniform was facing her, hanging on her closet door. She could read the logo from across the room: "Fit Gals and Pals". She hated that name. She thought about the numerous times the phone rang, and she had to answer, "Thank you for calling *Fit Gals and Pals*; how can I assist you with your fitness needs?" Every time she answered that phone, it was a reminder of where she was in her life. She was approaching her third decade with the lingering sentiment that her existence was devoid of purpose and direction.

Waking up in a frenzy every day to sell gym memberships to reluctant prospects was not what she had pictured her life to be when she graduated from college seven years ago. She was hoping to be in the phase of her life where she was doing something she was passionate about. But she had allowed time to go by and had never paused to figure out what that was.

One thing she was certain about was that she should have been at the stage where she had things somewhat figured out. Yes, the normal hardships should be expected; but things should not be this way. She should be coming back home after a wonderful day at her dream job, or at the very least one she enjoyed. Then, she could immediately dive into a schedule filled with all her exciting hobbies. At the minimum, she should know what her passions and interests were, what made her eyes light up. Instead, her reality was her brushing her teeth in the shower while making sure her hair did not get wet under her shower bonnet.

Nova knew she would have to take the tollway today. Traffic was always crazy on I-4 around this time. Normally, it would have taken less than fifteen minutes to get to work. But with traffic, that could easily double. She looked at the time as she slid her feet into her black sneakers: 8:36. She took a quick look around her apartment to make sure everything looked okay before she shut the door behind her. Mercifully the road was clear, so she got to the gym right on time.

"Hey, Jeff!" Nova waved at her manager upon entering the building.

He nodded back at her without looking away from his computer. The only times she ever heard him speak in elaborate sentences were when he was interacting with clients or during their occasional meetings. He was not necessarily rude. He was merely not interested in anyone. He didn't make any effort to mask his disinterest with small talk. Nova liked that about him. She had always appreciated people who were honest and genuine, no matter what it looked like. She could not extend the same appreciation for her coworker, Paul. She was convinced that he could make the list of the top ten most obnoxious people in a hundred-mile radius.

"Hey, Paul. How is it going?" she greeted him without looking his way.

"Living the dream! You know how I do, girl. I already sold two memberships and I ain't even had breakfast yet," he said loudly, rubbing his blond hair in every direction.

"That's great. Good for you." She clocked in, making a point to keep looking away from his direction.

Who had that much energy every single morning? Not her. It was not so much the enthusiasm that annoyed her. It was his having seemed to always act as if he was the lead in a play, which by default made her his reluctant audience. She remembered the day she came back from her trip to Miami to visit her parents. She still had her box braids and her skin complexion had gotten a couple of shades deeper. She was expecting to get comments about her new hairstyle. Typically, she wore her medium-length hair in a twist out or afro; thus, coming back on Monday with braids down her back would garner some comments. She did not mind them. But Paul always had to go over the top.

"Okay, look at you!" he yelled as she walked toward her desk.

"Hi, Paul," she said. She quickly sat down to take any attention away from her.

"You are rocking those braids! Looks like you were in Miami living it up!"

"Thanks." She stared at her computer screen, hoping that he'd understand that she did not want to engage.

He did not. "And you are looking even more chocolaty than before. I love it!" He was waiting for her to react.

"Thank you. I need to catch up on some work now, I guess," she said curtly.

Paul was a good salesman. Though, Nova was convinced he most likely wore the prospects down with all his talking during the walk-throughs. She believed that most of the time, they purchased the membership to shut him up.

As for her, she was fine at her job. Growing up, she had gotten countless doors slammed on her face, so brushing off "noes" had become second nature. Sales had come easy to her. Unfortunately, she did not enjoy her job very much. She felt odd having to convince people that *Fit Gals and Pals* was the best gym around whenever she did not believe it herself. They did not have as many amenities as most of the other gyms. They did not have an indoor pool like most of their neighbors, and a lot of their equipment was dated. And frankly, they were overpriced for what they were offering. But Nova had gotten used to it. She had been working there for four years, and she was making just enough money to afford living alone. And to be fair, the gym had some decent traffic. The job was just so damn repetitive. The prospects would come in, and she would first give them a walk-through inside the facility. Then her least favorite part, the dreadful questionnaire.

"Please describe your current exercise routine."

4

"How often are you looking to train on a weekly basis?"
"What are your health and fitness goals?"
"On average, how many hours of sleep do you get every night?"
"What is your occupation?"
"How physical is your work?"
"Are you married or single?"
"Do you have any kids?"
"How would you rate your daily level of stress?"

She never knew what to expect as responses to those questions. Some people would express how much they were annoyed they had to answer them by giving very brief answers. She preferred those people since it made the whole process move a lot faster. But others would reply to each question with their life story. She did not dislike those consultations, yet it was becoming increasingly harder to appear interested. All the answers eventually sounded the same.

To summarize: life happened, and that was the reason they could not focus on their wellness and meet their health and fitness goals. She found it a bit ironic that the very thing that would assure them a better quality of life—their wellness—had taken a backseat as "life was happening" to them, thus, leading to the deterioration of the overall quality of their existence. The more she thought about it, the more she realized that she did not differ from those people. Although she was in good physical shape, life had happened to her as well. The reason she was not where she wanted to be at this stage was simply that life had happened. She had fallen victim to the monotony. The routine was comforting but also crippling. The life she wanted to live only existed in her imagination, while her actual reality was subpar.

Nova walked to the front desk to wait for her first appointment to come in. Her first prospect was a walk-in booking. Typically, those consultations were quick. Most people who walked in to book an appointment had already decided that they wanted to sign up for a membership. The consultation was just a formality. As she was waiting at the front desk, an overweight middle-aged woman walked in at 10:00 AM.

"Hi! My name is Alicia. I'm here for the gym walk-through with Nova," the lady said looking at both Nova and the front desk receptionist, not sure who would answer.

"Hi, Alicia! I'm Nova," she said, extending her hand for a shake.

"Nice to meet you, Nova!" Alicia shook it.

"Likewise. So, let's get started. I will first give you a walk around the gym, and then we will sit down to go over some questions. After that, we can discuss all your options," she explained in a professional and friendly tone.

"Sounds great!" Alicia replied, looking around the facility. She was obviously overwhelmed by all the machines and the sweaty people walking in every direction.

Nova started her walk-through the same way she had done countless other times. Sentences were now pouring out automatically. She did not need to make any effort to think about what to say next. Words continued to spill out to describe the different gym's sections she was showing to Alicia. When Nova led her to the free weights station, she could tell that Alicia was intimidated. She probably had little experience working out in a gym. She would need some assistance to get started. Alicia was the perfect candidate for personal training. This meant an additional commission for

Nova as well. She knew how she needed to proceed.

She continued the walk-through with confidence. "This room here is for our group classes. They are included in the cost of the membership, and all the dates and times will be listed on our website." She was almost certain of what Alicia would say next.

"I think I might need some one-on-one attention. I have not really worked out since…goodness, high school? Time really goes by fast. Wow."

That was what Nova wanted to hear. She had timed it perfectly. They were approaching Hakeem, the personal trainer. He knew the drill. He had helped her close many sales following this exact routine.

"I completely understand that. It is a great idea to start with a personal trainer to get a good foundation and avoid setbacks or, even worse, injuries."

"Oh absolutely! With three little ones running around, I don't need any injuries." Alicia laughed through clenched teeth.

Nova smiled in response. They were now next to him. "Hakeem, I would like to introduce you to one of your new members, Alicia. She will very likely need to start her fitness journey with your assistance and expertise."

"Very nice to meet you, Alicia," he answered, then he shook her hand. "We are honored that you have trusted us to help you with your wellness. Any questions that you have, please do not hesitate to ask. We are a family here."

He smiled at both Alicia and Nova. He was undoubtedly aware of the effect that his smile had on women. They both smiled back like they had just hit puberty, enthralled. Hakeem was as handsome as it was fit, with the most gorgeous smile

7

Nova had ever seen. She always found a route to walk her prospects toward him at some point during her consultations. Whether they needed a personal trainer or not, ninety percent of the time they would sign up for the membership if they were introduced to tall-glass-of-water-Hakeem. Frankly, she could have sold most people without his help, but she was looking forward to his smile every day. He was not the only reason she still worked there, but he was a good excuse to stick around.

As expected, Alicia signed up for the unlimited membership. Before she left, she confirmed that Hakeem would be her personal trainer. Nova smiled and nodded. She couldn't help but think about Alicia's reaction when she realized that she had not worked out since high school. At that moment, Nova sensed her longing for her past. She could still remember her youthful days, but those moments now only faintly existed in her memories. Time went by so fast. Life was meant to be lived in the now, not in the hopefulness of a potential better future.

"Look at you! One shot, one kill!" Paul shouted when she walked back to her desk.

"Thank you. She was a walk-in, so it was pretty straight forward."

"Oh yeah, those are super easy! I think I'm at one hundred percent close on my walk-ins so far this month."

She quickly acknowledged his comment and looked away, searching for Hakeem. He was walking by the other side of the sales cubicles. He looked her way and made a hand gesture signaling he wanted to find out if the prospect had signed up. She smiled, nodded, and gave him a thumbs up. He gave her a thumbs up back and walked away. That was the extent of their interactions. As quick as those exchanges were, they made her day. Yes, she had a huge crush on him. Yes, she knew that he did not feel the same way. He was nice to her, but their relationship was merely professional for him. She had caught him looking her way a few times. But he always waved when that happened, not in a flirty way, just in a friendly manner. She felt like he was out of her league. So, she was okay with simply getting a few smiles and occasional pats on the back whenever she introduced him to potential new members.

The clock mercifully struck five to free her. "Bye Jeff! See you on Monday." She waved goodbye to her manager. She exited the building, and he nodded goodbye without looking up.

The weekend was finally here. Nova was especially looking forward to this one because she had plans to meet with her two closest friends for drinks. It had been close to two weeks since she had seen them. She was convinced they were both doing so much better than she was. She hated that she had become the person who compared her life to others, especially her friends. And as much as she did not want to think about it, she knew that she was the loser of the group.

Tadhana, who preferred to go by Ana, was a brand strategist for a retail company. She was a year younger than Nova. She recently had gotten in a new relationship with a guy who worked in the accounting department of her company. Nova could never remember his name; Ana always had a new fling. She was sharp and career driven. Nova admired how hard working she was and how much effort she had always put into reaching her goals. She wished that she had half of her drive and fierceness. Ana was the one she went to whenever she needed to get practical and frank advice.

Kameela was lightyears more mellow. She was the serene one, into all things spiritual and astrological. Every time Ana or Nova dated, Kameela always made sure their dates were astrologically compatible with them. They both found hilarious how intense she always got when she went over her predictions. Kameela had tied the knot with Josh the week of her thirtieth birthday. They had dated for three years and had been Mr. and Mrs. Williams for a few months. She was a stay-at-home wife. Nova wished she were half as carefree and zen as Kameela. She had been wondering if her friends wished they had any of her qualities. Honestly, she was not even sure what they were anymore. Her two friends were so secure in who they were. And there she was, twenty-nine years on the planet and what did she have to show for it? Hopes and dreams unknown to herself.

Nova shooed her negative thoughts away and let the excitement to get ready for her night out with the girls take over. She was not only looking forward to seeing them, but she was also looking forward to going out to have some drinks. She finally had an opportunity to dress up and look cute. She rarely went out. She chose a mid-length red flowy dress with a sweetheart neckline. She paired it with her favorite black heels. As she looked at the mirror, she couldn't help but smile. She had forgotten that she could see herself as beautiful and deserving. That image in the mirror, that was the woman. That is who she wanted to be: confident, sexy, and bold. She stared at herself for a moment. She inhaled to take her own reflection in. It was imperative she took control of her life. Soon.

She arrived at the restaurant half an hour later.

"Well, hello, Lady in Red!" Kameela welcomed Nova the moment she walked in.

"It is so good to see you!" They hugged for a while. Kameela liked to stay in the hug until the cadence of their heartbeats matched. Nova loved that about her.

Kameela stood five feet and ten inches above the ground, with beautiful honey-brown skin which took the bright light of the restaurant perfectly. Her face was framed by her long earthy locks. She gazed at Nova with her warm smile. "It has been a couple weeks, catch me up!"

They sat down on the red bar stools. "Well, there is not much to catch you up on. *Fit gals and Pals* is the same old thing. Jeff and I's conversations' word count is still under two hundred and fifty." They both chuckled.

"What about that cute coworker of yours?" Kameela put her hands under her chin and leaned forward with a beam.

"Hakeem?" Nova asked. Kameela nodded, holding a wide grin. "That man is not interested in me. He has been working there for almost two years, and he has never shown any sign of interest. He is totally out of my league," Nova said, looking down and away.

"What are you talking about?" Kameela gasped in shock. "You are freaking gorgeous! And you are also smart and funny! He would be lucky to even get a date with you."

"That is so sweet, thank you. But honestly, I feel like my life is at a standstill. I am nowhere near where I should be at this stage. The problem is: I don't even know where I'd rather be." She sighed.

"Give yourself a break! You have great friends." She pointed at herself. "You have a good job. You can afford to live alone and at your own pace." Nova sensed some envy in her delivery, almost as if she wished to have the freedom she believed Nova possessed. "I really think you should start meditating more often. I think that your solar plexus chakra has a lot of subconscious blockages." Her tone ended concerned.

Nova smiled at her answer. She loved the girl, but she could never go to her for pragmatic advice. She always had to go to the chakras, the stars, and whatever else she believed in. She could not wait for Ana to walk in so she could speak about the physical world and get feedback applicable to reality.

"I heard chakra, what did I miss?" Ana giggled on her way in. She walked toward them with her arms open for a group hug.

She looked more petite and toned than the last time they met. She had a small yet strong frame. Her porcelain skin and her silky dark hair, now cut in a short bob, made her look even more youthful and lively. They both stood up to embrace her. It felt so good to be together. The server came and took their orders. Kameela ordered a glass of pinot grigio, her favorite. Nova went with her go-to strawberry margarita.

"I'll have an old fashioned, thank you." Ana winked at the server. "So, catch me up, guys!" She turned back to Nova and Kameela.

"To summarize, Nova feels like she is not where she wants to be in life, and I was telling her that some of her concerns could be addressed by unblocking her solar plexus chakra," Kameela explained in one breath. "But you guys don't want to listen to me. So, what is your take?"

"I actually think her closed third eye is the problem." Ana chuckled. Nova laughed quietly.

"Ha. Ha," Kameela said with a straight face.

"I'm just kidding! I actually have been meditating more often, and I must admit that it has really helped me relieve some stress," Ana continued in a more serious manner. Kameela nodded in agreement and looked at Nova with raised brows, as if it was confirmation that she should follow her advice. "In addition to unblocking your solar plexus chakra," Ana said, then winked at Kameela, "you should also think about creating a vision board. I know it might sound cheesy, but it works. It is important to visualize your goals in order to reach them. Then set up short-term goals and reward yourself every time you reach one. Baby step girl, you got this!"

"Thank you, you two are the best!" Nova answered, teary eyed.

They both put their hands over hers for support and encouragement. At that moment, Nova realized how lucky she was to have Ana and Kameela in her life. They had met their freshman year of college and had been friends ever since. Although they could not hang out as often as they used to, she still thought of them as the only family she had.

"Speaking of vision boards, one of the goals that I had on mine this year was to get promoted," Ana announced. "Ms. Manola was promoted a couple of days ago as a fucking brand manager! The youngest one in the company, might I add!" she screamed. "I've been waiting to tell you guys because I wanted to do it in person. Finally, all these years of hard work are paying off." She wiped the tears rolling over her grin.

"That is amazing, congratulations!" Kameela screamed. She jumped to hug her. "You so deserve it! You have been working your butt off!"

Nova followed with a milder, although still enthusiastic congratulations and hug. She was genuinely happy for Ana. However, as much as she was proud of her friend, she also felt envious. It was another reminder that whilst both of her friends were getting to check all their boxes, she was looking at hers unchecked. Her life, unfulfilled. But now was not the time to lament. They toasted to Ana's promotion and caught up for the rest of the night. As they parted ways, they promised to meet again soon.

CHAPTER 2

She woke up the next day feeling energized by her conversation with the girls. Today was a new day, and she wanted to make the best of it. Her plan was to deep clean her apartment. Then, she would go to the mall to treat herself to something nice as a reward. She had nothing specific in mind. Whatever she would see that she liked—as long as it was within her budget, of course—she would buy. She deserved it! Whether she liked her job or not, she had been working hard for the past few years, and she had never stopped to smell the roses. Ana was right, she needed to reward herself for achieving short-term goals, no matter how small they were. Creating a vision board felt a little bit overwhelming, but small rewards for accomplishing short-term goals were feasible.

She had not deep cleaned in a few months. Her apartment stayed clutter free for the most part. She kept two light blue throw pillows on her off-white sofa. Her walnut coffee table was only decorated with an empty vase. Her bedroom only contained the essentials: a bed, a dresser, and a mirror. The more she cleaned, the more she realized that she had a lot of stuff she needed to get rid of, especially in the kitchen. Her fridge was filled with expired items. And the more she threw unnecessary stuff away, the more physically and emotionally lighter she felt herself become. She turned on some meditation music on her phone and continued to clean. Kameela was not wrong; the music brought immense peace.

"Maybe my solar plexus chakra is blocked," she whispered with a quiet laugh.

She finished wiping all her furniture and reached her bedroom mirror. It was leaning against the wall. She smiled at her reflection. She did not have the same feeling she had the night before. Was it just about the outfit? She did not want to only feel good when she was all made up and dressed up. She looked at the mirror more intensely. She noticed that it was smeared with her fingerprints. She grabbed her glass cleaner and wiped it vigorously. When getting up, she accidentally used the edge of the mirror for support instead of the wall. She watched as her mirror fell flat on the ground. She slowly lifted the frame to uncover the glass, shattered.

"That's just great," she cried out.

She was not superstitious, but the past few years had not been the best. She did not need another potential seven terrible years. It was a cheap mirror she had gotten at a random store, so she did not care it broke. It was just an annoying inconvenience. Now, she would have to go somewhere to get a new one when her original plan had been to go to the mall and have a fun shopping day. After sweeping the broken glass, she sat down to take a breather.

Perhaps she could buy a really nice mirror instead of the kind that just broke. She could barely see her full reflection there. She had to choose not to see her face or her feet whenever she looked at herself. The only way she could ever see herself fully was through a mirror's reflection. Why not get a fancy one? That could be the nice purchase she made for herself. It did not have to be expensive. She preferred thrift stores anyway. She knew that she could find a nice, unique floor mirror at one of the neighboring ones. In the novel spirit of spontaneity, she decided to drive around until she saw an interesting antique shop.

It was nice riding around with the window down and the wind blowing on her face. The air smelled like fresh grass. She had to do that more often. She glanced left and right while her jazz playlist delivered slow and sultry tones. She spotted a thrift shop on her right. She could read the engraved name from the distance: *Magique Antiques.*

"Perfect!" She decided when she pulled in.

"Welcome to *Magique Antiques*," an elderly woman greeted as soon as she stepped inside.

"Thank you," Nova answered, already looking around, distracted by all the items surrounding her.

The shop was eclectic. Lots of woody furniture, ornaments of all sorts, cool-looking jars, beautiful paintings, silverware, glassware, clothes, sports equipment, etc. Everything was unique and seemed to have so much history. She saw some costumes that looked like they belonged on the set of the Great Gatsby next to a photograph of the New York Skyline. She had lived in the neighborhood for a couple of years, but she had never noticed the place. The faint smell of pumpkin pie made her feel cozy. She continued to walk around, led by her curiosity. Things were not organized in a particular manner. Every corner was filled with fun and quirky items. One was a small figure of Santa Claus sporting a mohawk. She laughed and continued to explore in awe. At last, she discovered a dozen floor mirrors randomly placed next to beach ornaments.

Almost immediately, her attention was drawn to an ornate gilded oval-shaped mirror. The golden frame was made entirely of lotus flower-shaped designs that were in different blooming stages. It had to be taller than Kameela, probably five foot eleven, and close to three feet wide. Nova was not a mirror connoisseur, but she still recognized that this one was outstandingly beautiful. She stood in front of it and looked at herself, immobile. She had a strange feeling. She did not quite comprehend it. It was odd to admit, but the mirror had a certain gravitas that simultaneously intimidated and captivated her. She walked closer to the mirror and extended her hand to graze the sleek, clear, and unblemished glass. Before her finger could meet the surface, a voice rose behind her.

"Beautiful mirror, isn't it?" said the lady that welcomed her in.

"It really is. I wonder what its history is. Do you know by chance?"

"Not really, dear. I believe it is originally from somewhere in Central Africa. It is my dearest item here. You would get it for a steal."

Nova looked at the price tag: one hundred and eighty-five dollars. That was way more than she would typically spend on…anything, really. But today was a new start, and she wanted to do something nice for herself. Her initial budget was two hundred dollars. She was not planning on spending that amount on a mirror alone. Yet, she felt like she really needed to get this one. It was not just a purchase. It would mark a new beginning for her. Moving forward, she would be kind and generous to herself. Buying this mirror was the start. Plus, the lady was right; this mirror was probably originally worth four times that price.

"I'm sold," Nova said.

"Fantastic! We do provide free delivery for purchases over one hundred dollars, so we will get this to you before the end of the day."

They both walked toward the front to complete the transaction.

"That's awesome! This place is great. I'll definitely come by more often to see what you guys have."

"Thank you, dear. And let me know how the mirror works out for you," the lady said with a mild grin. Nova nodded. That was an odd statement. She was sure it would work fine since she could see herself in it. She provided her address for the delivery. "Expect the mirror anytime between 5 and 6:30 PM today," the woman advised.

"Perfect, thank you so much. Have a great day!"

"You are welcome, dear. We will see you soon!"

Nova stopped by the nearest grocery store on her way back home, since her fridge was emptied from her deep cleaning. She was aimlessly roaming around the aisles. She wanted to get home a few minutes before the mirror delivery. As she strolled past the fresh vegetable section, she noticed a guy. He had an athletic frame. His hair was neatly wrapped in a bun. The sheen of his olive skin was competing with the gloss of his mane. Normally, she would not find a guy with a bun attractive, but it suited him. It was the third time she had seen him in an aisle she had walked past. It was probably a coincidence. Or was it? *I'm looking cute today, maybe he is interested but is too shy to approach me*, she thought to herself.

She walked in his direction. She would not talk to him.

19

Instead, she would get close enough to give him a chance to approach her. She was a few feet away, so she faced the opposite direction. That way, he would not notice how nervous she was. She giggled at the thought of what she was doing.

"I did not realize green peppers were so funny," a deep voice rose with a melodic accent.

Yes, her plan worked! She took a second to compose herself before turning around. "The red ones are even funnier," she replied with a broad smile.

He smiled back. "That is one way to consume your daily five fruits and vegetables." They both chuckled at the corniness. "I'm Naveen, nice to meet you."

"Like the Disney prince?"

"Yes." He smiled. It was obvious that he had heard that countless times.

"Nice to meet you too, Naveen. I'm Nova."

"That's a beautiful name. I have never seen you here before. Do you live in the neighborhood?"

"Thank you. And sort of, a bit further south. I usually go to a different grocery store."

"I see. Well, I'm glad you decided to come to this one today." He held a grin.

"Why is that?" She beamed. She was surprised at how relaxed she was. Typically, she would have been overwhelmed with shyness. She would have probably mumbled something under her breath as she quickly walked away, like a puppy caught doing something they weren't supposed to do.

"Well, I think you are beautiful, and I would like to take you out for drinks and get to know you better," he said with a drip of sweat rushing down his right temple.

"I'd like that."

Naveen exhaled quietly when he heard her response. She smiled, endeared by his nervousness. Normally, she would not have engaged with a random guy at the grocery store; but at this moment, she had this unexpected panache. She was not sure where it came from, but she would take advantage of it until it went away. Frankly, she could hardly believe that he even approached her. Kameela and Ana made a point to tell her how beautiful, smart, and funny she was, every chance they got. But they would say that: they were her friends. Initially, she wanted to believe them, but as the years went by, she believed it less and less. Yet at this moment, as she was exchanging phone numbers with Naveen and remembered how she felt when she looked in the mirror the day before and earlier at the antiques shop, she felt like she was slowly starting to miraculously regain the confidence that her past had held hostage.

"Well, Nova, I will text you within the next couple of days so we can arrange to meet for drinks sometime next week."

"Sounds like a plan."

She couldn't stop smiling. Her day turned out to be unexpectedly good. A new fancy mirror on the way and a potential date on the horizon. She turned the music up the moment she got to her place. She sang along and twirled around endlessly like she used to do when she was a young girl who loved to dance. The music was so loud that she almost did not hear the doorbell ring. She turned it off and paced to the door. She looked through the peephole and saw two men holding her mirror wrapped up in cushion foam. She opened with a formal grin. The kind that only attempted to mirror a genuine smile by displaying one's teeth.

"Delivery from Magic Antiques for Ms. Nova Wright," the two men said at the same exact time.

"That's me." She let them in.

They carried the mirror inside. It looked larger and heavier than when she saw it in the shop. "Where would you like it to be placed?" The younger one inquired, panting.

"In my bedroom, please."

She led them through her bedroom and pointed to where she wanted them to put it. They placed the mirror where she requested and unwrapped it carefully. It looked even more beautiful than she remembered. The gild had a regal sheen. The lotus flowers seemed more open than before. She was satisfied with her purchase. She thanked the two men and grabbed a ten-dollar bill for them. They walked out and thanked her in return for her business. They both had a strange look on their faces. She couldn't tell whether it was exhaustion, irritation, or something else. Perhaps she should have tipped more? She shrugged the question off. The antique mirror was hers now, unbroken and whole.

She walked back into her bedroom. The mirror looked majestic. It looked like it belonged in the palace of an eighteenth-century duchess, and not in her seven hundred square foot, barely decorated apartment. Though it was only occupying the space against the wall; the energy around it filled the room. She undeniably felt drawn to it. She walked closer to it. She stood in front of it to examine her reflection. She had such an intense feeling every time her eyes met her vision behind the glass. It was hard to explain as she did not understand herself. It felt like a sort of invitation. She shook her head to snap out of the odd sensation. She had a more eventful day than usual. She probably needed to rest. Yes, that was it. That was all. She took a final glance at her reflection and walked outside of her bedroom.

She called Kameela to tell her about her grocery store encounter. Over the years, she had gotten closer to her. Ana was just so busy with work that it was hard for them to connect as often. She admired her friend's work ethic, but she wished that she had more time to nurture their friendship.

"Hey, girl! What's up?" Kameela picked up after a couple of rings.

"I'm great," Nova answered, high-pitched.

"Who is he?" Kameela immediately inquired, matching her excitement.

"You are good!" She giggled. "So, I met this cute guy at the grocery store today."

"What's his name?"

"Naveen," Nova said, still giddy with excitement.

"Nova and Naveen, how melodious! Let me get my wine glass out! Go on."

Nova knew for sure that she was grabbing her fancy glass with the letters P-R-A-N-A spelled around it. "He is so cute and funny! So, we exchanged numbers, and he is going to take me out for drinks sometime next week."

"I'm so excited for you! It has been so long since you have been on a date. I'm happy you are putting yourself back out there," Kameela replied. Nova heard a gulp before her friend continued. "Make sure to get his sign so I can let you know how compatible you guys are," she requested with a serious, almost professional tone.

"I'll make sure to get it. What signs am I supposed to be compatible with again?"

"How many times are we going to go over this? You guys really don't listen to me, huh?"

"I'm taking notes. Tell me one last time, please." Nova decided to take notes this time. That way, she could work all the details she remembered into conversations with Kameela every time the opportunity presented itself. Nova wanted Kameela to feel listened to as Kameela attentively listened to her.

"Alright! Since you are a Pisces, you are most compatible with other water signs: Cancer and Scorpio. You can also pair well with Earth signs, mainly Taurus and Capricorn."

"Cancer, Scorpio, Taurus, and Capricorn, I got it. I'll let you know what he is, and hopefully, it's a match."

"Yes, I can't wait to hear all about it."

"Enough about me. How are things on your end?" Nova could immediately sense the change in Kameela's energy the instant she asked her question. It was the way her voice lowered.

"Things have been kind of rocky with Josh lately. He is ready to start a family, and I'm not. As soon as we got engaged, he insisted that I become a stay-at-home wife so I could easily transition to become a stay-at-home mom. I'm so thankful that he is taking care of me, you know, but sometimes I feel bound. Since he is taking care of everything financially, he is also making most of our decisions. And I trust him…but I feel like I'm losing myself, you know." She paused. "Maybe I'm overreacting. I mean, Mercury is in retrograde, so I think it is really having an especially negative effect on me."

Nova didn't know what advice she should give. Her longest relationship was less than a year, back when she was in college. How could she potentially know how marriage worked when she had not even been on a single date for months? She tried to think of the best standard response, the kind of generic advice that was appropriate for almost any romantic hardship. "Did you try telling him how you feel? I think you should communicate those feelings to him. He loves you, and I know he will do anything to make you happy."

Nova had met Josh less than a handful of times. One time at their engagement party and the other one at their wedding. He was quiet, but he always greeted Nova and Ana with a nice hug. A hug which meant he knew Kameela loved them. Thus by extension, they mattered to him too. He was always very nice, though he avoided small talk. Nova was not exactly sure what he did for work, something in finances, she reckoned. Kameela and he were so different. He was the pragmatic type who only dealt with numbers and facts whilst Kameela made her decisions based on her senses and the stars. Opposites attracted indeed. Nova noticed that he always looked at her with so much warmth, like she was this delicate flower that he was in charge to water and shield.

"You are right. I have been going back and forth in my head when I simply need to tell him how I feel. Every time I tell him that something bothers me, he corrects it. He is so attentive, my sweet Virgo man." Her pitch went up one octave. "Thank you, Nova."

"Of course! All these years of you talking me off the ledge. About the time I come through for you."

Nova felt good at that moment. Useful. Purposeful.

***

Almost a week had gone by before Nova heard from

Naveen. For a moment, she thought he simply was not interested. Their little interaction was a routine activity for him. Flirting with random girls and getting their phone numbers was a way to boost his ego. She was just another victim.

She had felt lonely during those few days. She hated the fact that her happiness was suddenly depending on some random guy texting her. The only times she felt a sense of relief were when she looked at her new mirror. She felt better, as if things were falling into place. It was still hard to make sense of it but looking at herself gave her a boost of confidence. In those moments, she sensed there was hope that she could be who she wanted to be, live the life she wanted to live. Even though she was not sure how, looking in the gilded mirror made her feel like things would fall into whatever rightful place they belonged to, in due time. But as she walked away and further from the mirror, she went back to her old self, helpless and stuck. She stared at herself in other mirrors to see if that feeling would be generated as well. Nothing happened.

"Girl, you've been flexing in front of the mirror the past couple of days. Making some gains?" Paul had commented.

"I'm trying to," she lied.

She hoped no one else had noticed her new obsession with staring at herself, especially Hakeem. She did not want him to think of her as some superficial girl who was infatuated with her own reflection. But he had waved at her the same way he always did. He had not noticed simply because he only looked her way to greet her or when she walked toward him with a new prospect.

She rushed home every day to stand in front of her

mirror. As soon as she saw her reflection, she felt rejuvenated, confident, and fearless. The feeling was intoxicating. It strengthened the longer she stared at her reflection. But it went away the longer and further away she was from it. "**Hey Nova! I hope your week is going well. I'm sorry I didn't reach out sooner, but I have been swamped at work. Let's do drinks tomorrow evening if you are free?**" Naveen added a smiley face emoji at the end of his text message.

She couldn't contain her grin when she read his message. He had not forgotten about her. She was not just some girl he had flirted with to boost his ego. He wanted to see her again. She replied almost immediately, forgetting Ana's advice. "I always wait at least forty-five minutes to an hour to respond. They need to know that I have a life, and I'm not sitting around waiting on them." The reason that advice was not applicable was that Ana had a life, Nova on the other end did not. Not yet.

"**Hey Naveen! No worries, it has been a busy week for me too.**" It had not. "**I'm free tomorrow after 8 PM. Just let me know where,**" she responded with a matching smiley face.

She was free before eight. Really all day. But she wanted to sound busy, to create the illusion she had exciting things to do outside of waiting for a stranger's text. She wished in that moment she did.

"**Awesome. Let's meet at 9 PM at The Route, their drinks are excellent!**"

She texted Ana and Kameela as soon as she confirmed to Naveen she was looking forward to their date. After her phone call with Kameela, she had let Ana know via text message that she had met a cute guy at the grocery store. Ana had expressed some excitement and had asked her to keep her in the loop. She was overwhelmed with her new job responsibilities, but she loved her new position.

"Guys, the freaking Route! I don't even know what to fucking wear. I have never been to such a fancy place."

Nova only used cuss words when she was very excited or really upset. Her parents were zealous Jehovah's Witnesses. She had a very strict upbringing that limited her interests and social interactions. She had walked away from her parents' congregation and belief system when she moved out for college. She only had (because she could only have) witnesses as friends until she met Kameela and Ana. She always remembered the first time she heard Ana use a swear word. "Why would you not round up a damn grade? He is so fucking annoying. Now I have to beg him for some stupid extra credit."

"Somebody is excited!" Ana texted back. **"You are a fucking hottie. He will be wowed no matter what you wear!"**

Nova saw bubbles forming next to Kameela's name, announcing her response. **"I agree! Red and orange are your colors though. OMG, you should totally wear orange to awaken your sacral chakra and boost your confidence and sexual energy!"**

Nova and Ana separately texted each other laughing faces. Nova agreed that red and orange were her colors, but she did not need them for a confidence boost. She had her lotus flowers golden framed mirror for that. She thought about telling her two friends about it. But how could she even explain it? She felt good when she looked at herself in the mirror? They would just wave it off and respond something along the lines of, "You go, girl! You should feel good! You are hot!"

Sometimes she felt like they were overcomplimenting

her because they knew how insecure she was about the state of her life.

She ended their group conversation by agreeing she would wear an orange dress and let them know how the date went the next day. She listened to Nina Simone, *I'm Feeling Good* on repeat as she was getting ready for her date. She loved that song. And she was feeling good indeed. She sang along as her off-the-shoulder burnt orange dress was carefully laid on her bed, ready to be worn. Her open-toed heels were resting on the floor, prepared to reveal her polished white toenails. Her make-up was subtly accentuating her cheekbones and her nude lipstick highlighted her plump lips. She had watched countless makeup tutorial videos to master her soft glam look.

She walked closer to her new mirror to examine her outfit. She did a little dance, which caused her to have a flashback of her younger self. A little girl who was lively and unrestricted. Little Nova had turned into this amazing woman in the mirror. At that moment, she felt incredibly good. Things felt right. She suddenly felt an intense pull to kiss her reflection. So, she leaned forward and did.

The exact moment her lips met the glass, she physically felt time stop. It felt like her own heart had paused. Any sound around her seemed to have been sucked into a sort of vacuum. Everything looked blurry. The shapes of her furniture and everything around her were indiscernible. The only thing she could see was the glow of the golden lotus flowers framing the mirror. The widening and opening of the petals. It seemed that the words that could best describe the situation belonged in a language that she didn't know how to speak but inherently understood. She felt like she was transported, yet she felt still. She had no control over what was happening, but it felt incredible. She did not want to fight that liberating feeling. She closed her eyes, not knowing what she would see when she would open them.

When she finally opened her eyes, everything looked the same. Nothing in the room was different. Her bed was still at the center of the room, against the wall. Her drawer still stood to his right with a framed photograph of Kameela, Ana, and herself on top. Her walls were still painted the same forgettable white. She examined the mirror itself: it looked the same…except for the lotus flowers. They seemed to face the opposite direction. Had they always faced that way? She was not sure. They probably had. Of course, they had. Though, she unquestionably felt different. She had felt that way when she looked at the mirror for a while. This feeling was more intense. It lingered. Almost as if it was not a feeling but her state of being. She looked at her watch. 8:40 PM. She had to go. She did not want to be late for her first date with Naveen.

CHAPTER 3

"Wow, you look unbelievable!" Naveen said. He promptly pulled Nova's chair out. He looked very handsome with his navy-blue buttoned shirt and his hair in a neat bun. She remembered how nervous he was when he had asked for her number. She enjoyed the way his eyes lit up when he looked at her. He was jumping from one topic to another. He mentioned how busy his work had been between noting how quickly the weather was warming up.

"So, what do you do for work?" Nova asked after taking a sip of her strawberry margarita.

"I'm a software engineer for an IT company," he answered. "What about you?"

Normally she would have felt rather unaccomplished when explaining that she was a sales representative for *Fit Gals and Pals*. But then, she felt confident and proud. "I'm a sales rep at *Fit Gals and Pals*. My job is to meet new people every day and get them started on their wellness journey." She was surprised by her own answer. Not only because she said it, but because she believed it.

"That's awesome. You know I have been looking for a new gym, and it sounds like you know your stuff. I might swing by some time to look at what you guys are offering."

"You totally should! But enough about our jobs. Do you

typically pick up girls at the grocery store?" She smiled like a mischievous kid up to no good. She was internally astonished by her own boldness.

He smiled while shaking his head. "Not at all, actually. I just thought you were beautiful. Plus, you looked like you had such a great time hanging out with your veggies. I just wanted to know more about you."

They continued to chat for the length of the evening, barely noticing the crowd evaporating out of the restaurant.

"What is your biggest pet peeve?" he said.

She rested her chin under her hand to think. "Hmm, let me see," she began. "I got it. People who chew and drink loudly."

He laughed. "Classic." He took a sip of his drink and swallowed it noisily.

"Don't!" She tapped his forearm lightly and laughed.

He chuckled. "Sorry, I had to."

"What about you?"

"The loud chewing and drinking are definitely on my list, too," he said. She nodded approvingly. "And people who don't use turn signals."

"You better get used to it, my friend. You are in the land of the Florida Man."

They both broke into laughter. "Goddamn, Florida Man!" he yelped.

She giggled, then asked, "What is the funniest headline that you have seen?" She could hear her heartbeat speed up with excitement. She loved how light and easy things were with him.

"That is a tough one. Hmm, let's see." She was looking at him. She enjoyed watching the way he frowned his brows, carefully searching for his words. She enjoyed the smell of liquor and grilled food floating around them. "Okay, it's so hard just picking one, but this one had me laughing for an entire day. *Florida Man was arrested for calling 911 after pet ostrich was denied entry to a local strip club at 9:15 in the morning.*"

As if they had coordinated it, they laughed out loud at the same exact time. Tears rolling down their eyes. When Nova regained her composure, she spoke between residual laughter. "That's so good, but this headline is missing an alligator and some random naked guy running around in the background."

The cackles resumed. When they both settled down, Naveen shared some of the worst dates he had been on when he decided to give online dating a try.

"I got catfished one time. I got there and looked around for my date. Then, this elderly lady waved at me. I was shocked! I didn't know people did that."

She chuckled at how genuinely astonished he was at the concept of catfishing. His earnestness was endearing. She liked him. She hoped that he felt the same. The sparkle in his eyes made her believe he did. She thought about her own romantic history. She did not have any dating horror stories. Her last relationship was her sophomore year of college. He was a senior, and she was a sophomore. They dated for about nine months, and it ended shortly after he graduated. They tried to make it work long distance, but it was just not worth the hassle. They were not in love. Come to think of it, Nova had never been in love. The way people described being in love felt unfamiliar to her. She had strong feelings for the guy, but she received confirmation it was not love when Kameela spoke about Josh. She had felt nothing neighboring anything she described. Perhaps Naveen could be her first love.

"I had such a wonderful time," she said when they walked outside the restaurant.

"Me too." He continued, "Maybe we can go to another bar. There is one a few blocks away that closes late." Nova was flattered by the offer. He did not want the night to end.

"I would have loved to, but I have to be up early tomorrow."

She was surprised by her own answer. A part of her wanted to say yes and spend more time with him. A part of her wanted to show him all her amazing qualities at once, so he could see how special she was. Someone worth caring for. But a stronger force spoke out, assertive. A force convinced that by living now, he will long for her and want even more.

"I understand," he said softly. "We should meet again soon. What are you doing next Wednesday?"

"I don't think I have anything planned as of yet, but I will let you know for sure on Monday." Who was this woman? This person confident in all her answers. She was not hopeful that things would work out in her favor; she knew that they would.

"That's perfect! I'll start looking for some nice spots for us to meet."

They ended the night by exchanging a warm hug. Nova would not have minded staying in it a lot longer.

***

Naveen met with his friend Golibe the next day. They had been hired by their company around the same time. They had similar backgrounds. They both migrated to the United States over a decade ago. Naveen was from India. Golibe was from Nigeria. They had similar stories regarding the cultural

34

shock they had felt when they initially moved to America. They bonded over their experiences as immigrants and the similarity of their upbringings. Their parents gave them two options: doctor or engineer. And here they were, making them proud by living the lives expected of them.

Golibe had been dating a girl who was originally from his hometown for about three years. She had asked Naveen to call her Ada, short for something else. Naveen understood. Thankfully, his name was easy to pronounce for people of almost any background. Especially since Disney had used it for one of their princes. Thus, he did not have to explain how it needed to be enunciated countless times. He mostly had to suffer through the terrible prince jokes.

Golibe had been trying to set him up on multiple dates since his breakup with Michelle, about a year ago. Naveen had dated her for a little over two years. He had even looked for rings. A couple of weeks before he was ready to propose, he stopped by Michelle's condo to surprise her with Chinese food and wine. They had the keys to each other's places. As he walked in, his eyes uncovered the shattering truth: the woman he was ready to propose to, on top of another man on her living room couch. He was heartbroken, yes. But he was even more insulted that she would do that there. She knew he had the keys to her house. It was infuriating that she did not care enough to hide her affair better. Perhaps she did in the beginning? How long had it been? He did not ask. He said nothing. He placed her key on the counter and left.

Golibe had finally convinced him to sign up for online dating apps. "Dude, you need to get with the times. There are some nice girls on the app. You know that is where I met Ada, right? And you can just swipe away and set up your dates from your couch. It's so convenient!"

"Bro, are you recruiting for them?" He laughed at his friend's excitement.

Naveen eventually signed up for the same app that Golibe had been using when he met Ada. He went on a handful of dates. He started some okay conversations and was hopeful at first. A couple of them stopped responding after a while. He was perplexed, not sure what he did wrong and why they would not just tell him they were no longer interested. And then, the infamous catfish encounter. That was the last straw. He deleted the app.

He was so excited to tell Golibe he had met this beautiful and lively woman at the store. He had waited to see how the first date would go before sharing the news with him. Their conversations began with the usual complaining about the never-ending changes at their work.

"I'm so over these meetings. It's a complete waste of time," Golibe said.

Naveen nodded in agreement. He then quickly shifted the conversation to what he wanted to talk about: their romantic lives. Well, mostly his.

"How are things with Ada?" he asked.

"That girl already wants marriage, oh," Golibe said. "It has only been three years. I love her, but I'm not there yet. I need at least another year or two."

"Did she directly ask you?"

"No. But every time we go out for dinner, she manicures her nails, dresses extra nice, and inspects every dessert as if a ring is supposed to be hidden in it or something."

They both erupted in laughter. "Sounds like I need to start working on my best man's speech," Naveen said, still cackling.

Golibe sucked his teeth in disapproval. "Eh! Please joke about something else. I'm only thirty years old. I'm not ready for a lifetime commitment."

Naveen shook his head, amused. He then changed the subject to what he had been looking forward to talking about. "I met a girl, and we went on a date yesterday."

"What? Slow down! Why didn't you tell me about it before you went?" Golibe asked, almost rising from his seat.

"I just wanted to see how it went and if it was even worth mentioning."

"You are mentioning it, so tell me about her! Nav, I'm happy that you are even putting yourself back out there."

"Go, she is amazing," he said. "I just thought she was very pretty the first time I saw her. But when we met for drinks, she not only looked gorgeous, but she also had a certain je ne sais quoi about her."

"My boy is already in love, oh! Did the je ne sais quoi led to the Voulez-vous couchez avec moi?" Golibe inquired in his best French accent.

Naveen furrowed his brow and shook his head. "Bro, it's not like that. I just want to get to know her first. I really think this could be something."

"Well, cheers to that!" Golibe raised his glass.

***

When Nova got back home from her date with Naveen, she first looked at the time: 12:36 AM. Wow, a four-hour first date. Time indeed flew by when one had fun. She could not wait to text him on Monday to confirm that she was free on Wednesday. She felt good about how the date went, she felt good about their potential future together, and most importantly she felt good about herself. She walked into her bedroom, toward what she now thought of as her confidence booster: the stunning gold-framed lotus flowers mirror.

A feeling of warmth enveloped her the closer she got to it. And like she did before she left for her date earlier, she leaned forward to kiss her reflection. This time she did it as a thank-you for the confidence boost. Admittedly, she also wanted to confirm that whatever happened earlier had been a figment of her imagination.

However, the moment her lips met the glass, she was again confronted with the stillness of time. Her heartbeat halted. She could not see things around her clearly. Then a static motion. She felt like she had been shaken, yet it seemed like not a single muscle of her body had contracted. She opened her eyes fearfully.

Her bed was still against the wall. The dresser was still standing where it should. Everything looked the exact same, yet again. Well, no. The lotus flowers seemed to have gone back to their original position. Or had they never moved at all? She needed to get some rest. It was probably close to 12:45 AM. She looked at the time on her watch to confirm: 8:44 PM.

"What the hell?" she whispered. Something was probably wrong with her watch. She checked the time on her phone: 8:44 PM. "What is going on?" she said louder.

She turned her TV to check the time: 8:45 PM. She sat on her living room couch, silent. Not sure what to think or do. She stayed seated with her eyes closed for a while, hoping that when she opened them, time would have fixed itself. A few minutes went by, and her phone vibrated. A message from Naveen. He probably sent a text to make sure she had made it back home safe.

"Hey Nova, how far are you? I can order something for you if you'd like."

She was still seated but felt dizzy. It felt like the ground beneath her feet was shaking. She did not know how to process what was happening. All the logical explanations were no longer an option the moment she received the message from Naveen. She had just spent almost four hours on a date with him. She had not imagined that. A possibility crept in her mind: the mirror…was it somehow…responsible? She could not believe that she was entertaining that thought, but it was the only explanation which made sense.

The feeling she had when she first saw it at the antiques store. The sensation that rose when looking at her reflection, as if her reflection was not merely reflecting her but looking back at her with intent. What happened when she kissed the mirror must have been some trigger, perhaps? The flowers faced opposite directions when she kissed the mirror the first and second times. The way she even felt when she was near the mirror: invigorated, like she was someone else. A better her. The *her* she wanted to be. Was that it? Kissing the mirror paused time and transformed her into a better version of herself?

Let me know how the mirror works out for you. That is what the lady from the antiques shop had said to her. She knew something. Whatever happened with the mirror, she must have known about it. Nova needed to go there first thing in the morning to get answers.

"Hey, is everything okay?" Naveen texted her a few minutes later.

Regardless of what was happening with the mirror, Nova

knew that she liked Naveen. She wanted to see where things would go with him. She owed that potential happiness to herself.

"**Hey Naveen! I'm so sorry.** One of my friends needed my help," she lied. "**I'm on my way now, please order a strawberry margarita for me. I'll be there in a few minutes!**"

"**No worries, hope your friend is okay. Drive safe.**"

The moment she got to the date; Naveen was wowed like he had been earlier. "You look amazing!" he said.

"Thank you." She smiled timidly. Her mind was not present. She was thinking of all the questions she would ask the antiques shop lady.

"Is everything okay with your friend?" Naveen asked, frowning.

"What?" she muttered. What was he talking about? The instant her question left her lips, she remembered that she had lied to him to justify her late arrival. "Oh, she is fine now. Thank you for asking."

They talked about the weather and his busy work schedule, like before. Nova felt like it was an out-of-body experience. As he was talking about his week, she realized that the energy she had earlier, her vibrance was gone. She was not sure whether it was due to the shock that she was feeling or the fact that she was feeling like herself, without whatever boost the mirror had given her earlier. She was hoping with all her being that it was the former. She could tell that Naveen felt the difference too. He was still interested in her, but his energy was different. Their conversation was missing the lightness and laughter of their previous interaction. Obviously, he did not know the previous reality, but at that moment, things felt flatter. Nothing lingered in the air with warmth and intrigue. This moment felt like the reality she had been living all these years, the one she desperately wanted to escape.

"Do you typically pick up girls at grocery stores?" she blurted out.

She was trying to mimic the way she had asked him earlier, hoping to entice the same passion from Naveen. But the moment the words came out, she realized that her question did not sound flirtatious, it sounded critical.

"Uh no, I just thought you were beautiful."

"Well, I'm glad you did this time," she replied. She held a smile to lighten the mood again. He smiled back.

He asked her what she did for work. This time she described her job as something she was doing for now and that she did not enjoy. All her panache had gone away. He nodded in understanding. After he shared his catfish story in a more concise way, they both took a sip of their drinks. She did not bring up the Florida Man. She did not want to do it the wrong way and make things even worse. They were both silent for a moment.

"Well, we should probably head out. The place will close soon," he said.

She felt like a dagger had been willed against her chest with cruel precision. Earlier, he wanted more. He suggested that they should go somewhere else that closed later, so he could spend more time with her. Now, he wanted the night to end.

"Yes, we should," she said.

He hugged her goodbye (too quickly) with no promise to meet again soon. "I had a good time. Please text me to let me know that you made it home safe."

She agreed and walked away quietly. She felt mixed emotions. On the one hand she was sad the date had not gone as well as it did earlier. But on the other, she felt like she could simply go back to the mirror and let it take her back wherever Naveen was already looking at places for them to go on Wednesday. Frankly, her focus was to get to *Magique Antiques* first thing in the morning to figure out what the hell was going on.

CHAPTER 4

Nova walked into *Magic Antiques* at 8:00 AM on Sunday morning. She had barely slept the night before. She had so many questions. She was confident that the lady from the shop was the only one who could answer them.

"Welcome to Ma—," the elderly lady greeted. She paused the moment she recognized Nova.

"What did you sell me?" Nova immediately yelled out, slamming the door behind her.

"It's good to see you again, dear." She smiled as if Nova had given her a hug.

"You knew! You told me to come back to let you know how the mirror worked out for me. Well, something weird happened, and I need to know what's going on!"

The lady calmly walked toward the entrance. She turned her open/closed sign, so the closed side faced the street. She sat on one of the couches that she had for sale and pointed to Nova to sit on the brown leather matching one next to it. Nova sat quietly, glaring at her.

"First, I'd like to introduce myself, darling. My name is Carole."

Nova nodded so rapidly it was hard to tell that her head had moved at all. She did not care about her name. She wanted answers. "Please, Carole, tell me what's going on."

"The mirror that you purchased is not ordinary, darling."

"Yes. I was able to gather that much."

"Did you kiss your reflection or wink at it?"

"I...kissed it," Nova said, breathless. Carole knew. "What is going on?"

"Well, dear, I don't have all the answers, but I will try to be as helpful as possible." She paused and inhaled. "Kissing or winking at your reflection is the initial trigger. You essentially get transported to a sort of alternate reality on the other side of the mirror. On that side, you become the person you have always wanted to be, essentially what you believe is the best version of yourself. Everyone else is the same version of themselves on the other side."

Nova could not think clearly. This revelation challenged everything she thought was factual. She was not at all ready to examine the implications of what she had heard. So, she strictly focused on getting all her questions answered.

"What about time? It happened yesterday. I was on the other side for a few hours, but when I came back to the real side, only minutes had gone by." She had gestured air quotes when saying "the other side", still in disbelief.

"It seems like an hour spent on the other side of the mirror is the equivalent of a minute in reality. I don't know the science behind it, but that is how time works when you travel across both sides."

Nova found the use of "science" misplaced. There was nothing scientific about the entire ordeal. She wished that it were, so her world could go back to making sense. "So, if one minute spent here equals one hour on the other side, and I have spent eight hours here..." She took her phone out to calculate the conversion. "Eight hours times sixty minutes equals four hundred and eighty minutes, so that is four hundred and eighty hours divided by twenty-four hours, which is twenty days." She paused for a moment. Her eyebrows were so frowned that they were almost touching. "So, the eight hours I have spent here is almost three weeks on the other side?"

Carole was looking at her silently, waiting for her to finish. "Dear, it doesn't work the other way around." She smiled, unflappable. "Time only passes in the true reality when you are on the other side. Time only exists on the other side when you are present. If you are not there, time is still."

Nova gasped. "I see. So, if I go back on the other side, things will simply pick up where they were when I left?"

"Precisely."

They both did not speak for a moment. Nova was taking things in. Carole was gazing at her with an expression difficult to read. "Why me?" Nova asked at last.

"Darling, I'm sure that you are very special, but you were not chosen for this," she began, slowly letting her words out. "Whoever came in to purchase this mirror, then kissed or winked at their reflection, would have gotten the same experience. Well, only people who are content and happy with who they are do not. They simply end up with a very stylish mirror since they already see who they want to be in it. But anyone who is not happy with who they are and believe that they are not the best version of themselves gets transported to a sort of alternate reality where they become who they have been yearning to be."

Nova nodded rapidly, ready for her next question. Hearing she was not "the chosen one" was not surprising. She had accepted the fact that she was not special years ago.

"When I came here the first time, you told me that it was originally from somewhere in Central Africa, is that true?"

"I believe so, though I'm not a hundred percent sure. The history of the mirror is mostly unknown. However, it is believed that it was found drifting somewhere near the coast of Central Africa."

"How did you end up with it?"

Carole did not answer for a few seconds. It was the first time she looked somewhat perturbed. "I have been on the other side as well. I almost lost myself. Dear, I must warn you; it gets very addicting. You could get stuck." Her voice sounded deeper, grave. Given how calm she had been thus far, it was concerning.

"How?"

"The people who have spent a full twenty-four hours, an entire day on the other side of the mirror, have essentially returned to the real world in a state of coma. My belief is that they continue to live the life they were living on the other side in their unconscious mind. They chose not to wake up from that alternate reality. I believe they have chosen to stay there because it was easier to live there than their true reality. Darling, you must remember that life on that side of the mirror is not real. The mirror can be a useful tool to show you the way to become who you want to be. However, the moment you know the way, you best stop using it. Dear, you will have to be brave and decide to step out into reality. You must have the courage to live the life you want to live in the real world."

"Did you almost get stuck?"

"Yes, dear." Carole was silent for a moment. The air felt heavier. "This mirror is now a part of my life for that very reason. It always finds its way to me. Every time someone chooses to stay in it or gets rid of it; it finds its way back to me."

Nova tapped her right foot against the wooden floor. "I need to think about whether I want to continue to use the mirror. It sounds quite destructive. I might need a few days to decide if I even want to return there at all."

Carole smiled absently. "The moment you trigger the mirror for the first time, you start the cycle. If you do not travel to the other side for twenty-four hours, you will lose the ability to go there altogether. I should also add that you can only use the mirror once a day on each side. So, you will have to stay there as long as you deem necessary each day. Just make sure to come back before the twenty-four-hour mark, and you will be fine. Don't ask me why, dear. I don't know any of the whys. I just know some of the hows."

Nova sighed. "Anything else that I need to aware of?"

"Nothing that I can think of at this time, darling. There is more you might discover on your own. What I shared with you is from my own experience and experiences of others before you. You will have your own journey. And who knows, you might learn even more than I was able to share with you today."

A thought suddenly crossed Nova's mind. "What if I did not kiss the mirror again and stayed on that side for twenty-four hours, thinking it was my true reality? I would have fallen into a coma?"

"This is one of the many mysteries. Somehow, everyone kisses or winks at their reflection again after they have spent some time on the other side the first time, before the twenty-four-hour mark. We all knew that something was different,

47

and we all felt compelled, almost pulled to mimic what we did originally, to make sure all the strange happenings had been imagined. Everyone who had spent a full twenty-four hours on the other side of the mirror had willingly chosen to do so, knowing the consequence."

"I see." It was a lot more than Nova was prepared to take in. Perhaps, she needed to talk to someone close to her before she decided how to move forward. "Can I tell someone about this, or do I have to keep it to myself?"

"You can tell whoever you choose to. However, the moment you decide to stay on the other side or stop using the mirror, the person you have talked to about the mirror, and whoever else they might have told, will lose all their memories related to the mirror." Nova sighed at the revelation. "You can come back any time, dear. I know this is quite a lot to digest. As long as you have the mirror, it is my responsibility to make sure things go as well as possible for you."

"Thank you," Nova finally said with a timid smile. Carole appeased her by giving her some insight. "Thank you for answering all my questions."

"You are welcome, dear. Now, this is something I have to do on the side, but I still have to make a living," Carole said in the most casual and playful tone she had used so far. She stood up and walked toward the door to turn the open/closed sign around. A couple of people were waiting outside. She let them in and apologized for the late opening.

"Have a good day, Carole." Nova waved goodbye.

Carole waved back. Nova felt uncomfortable with the extended length of time that Carole stood still to watch her walk away. She could still feel the woman's gaze when she got in her car and drove off.

***

Nova had been laying on her bed for a few hours with her eyes wide open. A hundred thoughts were running through her mind. They were going so fast she could barely identify them. She sat up, to hopefully calm herself down. She turned some meditation music on, eyes closed. She breathed in and out the way Kameela had taught her. In, clarity; out, fear. She stayed still and repeated her breathing for ten minutes: in, clarity; out, fear. She opened her eyes. The mirror was facing her: majestic, inviting, and warm. Her mind was made up: she would use it until she figured out how to translate who she was on the other side to her lived reality.

What was the harm, anyway? The rules were clear. It would be easy. She would spend exactly twenty-three hours on the other side, which was enough to get through her day and night there. She needed to follow a set schedule to avoid any confusion. That would be twenty-three minutes in the real world. She would then get back to reality, where she could apply what she had learned on the other side. She would live her normal life: go to sleep, wake up, go to work, go back home, and back to the other side before the twenty-four-hour mark. She saw no downsides, except the fact that things could get repetitive. But she was used to repetition with her current lifestyle. At least, now, the potential repetitions between both sides would be life-changing in the long run.

She thought about telling someone. The only people she knew who believed in other worlds were her parents and Kameela. Her parents would not understand even if they miraculously decided to speak to her. They would blame it on the devil and her worldly friends who had corrupted her. How ironic. She had rejected her former religious and spiritual

49

beliefs only to end up with a magic mirror. She chuckled at the irony. Perhaps this was a sign to actively attempt to reconnect with her parents. She had had no communication with them since she had left the Jehovah's Witnesses. Perhaps on the other side, she will muster the courage to contact them again.

On this side, Kameela was her best option. But how would that be helpful? No, she would just get in the way. She would not mean to, but she would. Nova needed to do this alone. She needed to figure this out on her own. Maybe if things got out of control—and she did not see how—maybe then she would. But not now. She looked at her bedroom clock. 6:08 PM. The last time she came back, it was 8:44 PM. She would travel at 8:30 PM to spend twenty-three hours on the other side and get back on the real side before 9.

As she finally settled into her new reality, her fear slowly transformed into excitement. This mirror was actually a wonderful chance for her to turn her life around. As Carole advised, she just had to use it the right way and let go of it the moment it had served its purpose. Her mind stopped racing. She felt at peace. She was ready to jump into the promising unknown.

CHAPTER 5

8:30 PM.
Nova approached the mirror with confidence, ready for the magic voyage. Her lips met the glass. Eyes closed. Static motion. Blurriness. Warmth.

She opened her eyes slowly. She looked at the lotus flowers facing the opposite direction. She looked at her bedroom clock: 12:38 AM. She smiled at the accuracy of the magic.

The next morning, she woke up feeling light and energized. Her Sundays were usually slow and quiet. She had to go to *Magique Antiques* on the real side to get answers, but here she had the freedom to do whatever she wanted. Normally, she would stay home, order some food, and binge-watch a show. Sparingly, she would go for a run—mostly when she felt nostalgic about the better parts of her childhood. She enjoyed those things. But she felt like exploring a new spot for brunch today. The normal her would have never dreamed of going out alone to have a bite or even a drink. She was too self-conscious. What would people think? She was so pathetic and lonely that she had no one to grab a bite with? Here, she felt it was empowering and freeing to go out by herself. She could enjoy her own company.

The sun was up, so she put her favorite yellow backless

summer dress on. She had only worn it a handful of times. She untwisted her hair and put some make-up on. Just enough to make people wonder whether she was wearing any. She looked in the mirror and felt confident in her beauty, her worth, and the meaningfulness of her existence. She wanted to wink at her reflection, but she did not want to trigger any reaction from the mirror. She wanted to stay on this side as long as possible.

Sitting at the bar alone was not as awkward as she had anticipated. She ordered a mimosa and chatted with the bartender.

"You should come next Saturday. All the drinks will be half off all day long," he said with a raspy voice and a grin.

She was having an even better time than she had expected. The laughter of the crowd sounded like a song she wanted to play over and over again. The smell of syrup and scrambled eggs filled her up before she even got her food. As she was taking another sip of her mimosa, she felt a tap on her shoulder. She looked back and immediately recognized Hakeem.

"Hey, Nova!" He hugged her. She could count on one hand how many times he had hugged her in the past two years. "I come to this spot almost every weekend for brunch, I have never seen you here before." His voice was a higher pitch than usual.

"Yes, it's my first time here actually. I was in the mood for mimosas, and they are half off here until 4." She held a beam. Her shyness and awkwardness around him were non-existent on this side.

"Good deal! I'm here with a couple of friends." He pointed at a guy and a girl sitting in a booth on the other side of the restaurant. "You should join us."

"I'd love to!" She closed her tab and followed behind him.

"Hey, guys, this is Nova. She is a sales rep at *Fit Gals and Pals*." The two people waved at her. They were both as attractive and fit as Hakeem. "Nova, this is Emily." Emily shook her hand with a tight lip smile that exposed her dimples. "The G-man, George." Hakeem pointed at his very muscular friend.

George laughed at his own nickname then smiled at Nova. "Nice to meet you, Nova." He shook her hand. He had the most vascular arms she had ever seen.

"So, you are here alone?" Emily immediately inquired.

"Yes, I was in the mood for mimosas, so I decided to come here." Nova picked up on some animosity in her voice. It was in the dryness and pointedness of the delivery. She was so glad this was happening on this side. She would have lost her composure in reality and drown into self-consciousness. Here, there was a fluid energy countering her frame that helped her hold it together. It was something in the atmosphere that only she could breathe which gave her an unyielding confidence.

"Wow. You are brave, girl. I could never sit at a bar by myself," Emily said, tucking her wavy auburn hair behind her ear.

"Well, thank you. Although, I didn't think grabbing a drink could be interpreted as an act of bravery."

The guys chuckled. "Nova, what are you doing working at *Fit Gals and Pals*?" George said. "Someone with your charisma should be with us at *Fitness Link*. Our sales reps make bank!"

"Here we go." Hakeem rolled his eyes.

"Seriously. Dude, you know that our gym is superior to yours by any standards. And we have way more traffic. I still don't know why you left."

"He wanted to get away from me," Emily interjected. Hakeem looked away, visibly uncomfortable.

"You are never going to let this go, are you?" George said. He couldn't contain his grin. The whole ordeal was obviously very entertaining for him.

"It's true. The moment we break up, out of nowhere, he has found a better opportunity at *Fit Gals and Pals*. That's an oxymoron." She looked at Nova.

Nova had never particularly cared about her job, but she felt defensive of it then. Admittedly, it was not the best gym. However, for the most part she had had a positive experience there. "To be fair we do offer pretty competitive rates and we have great reviews from our members," she said coolly.

"Exactly," Hakeem said. "I like working there, it feels more like a family. I'm planning on being there for a while." He smiled at Nova, gazing directly into her eyes. He had never looked at her that way. For the first time, she felt like he was not looking at her solely because she was in front of him. He was looking at her because he wanted to see her.

"Do we have a little office romance here?" George asked, grinning. He was looking back and forth at Hakeem and Nova. Nova could feel Emily's intense stare on her.

"No, we are just coworkers," she said, maintaining a polite smile.

"Yes, I thought so. I mean, you are beautiful, but I don't think you are his type," Emily replied. Her cold tone conflicted with her cool, almost nonchalant exterior.

"Although we are just coworkers right now," Hakeem emphasized 'right now', "I find Nova very attractive." He glanced at Emily. The tension of their history was swallowing all the air out of the room.

No one spoke for a moment. "Would you like to order something, ma'am?" The server stopped by their table to check on Nova.

"No, thank you." She was ready to leave. The atmosphere was tense. "It was really nice to meet you guys, but I have to head out now."

She rose up to a collective "Nice to meet you too."

"Think about my offer," George said.

"I will."

"Let me walk you out," Hakeem offered. He stood and let her walk in front of him. The chatter of the room muted the sound of their steps. They walked out quietly. "I'm sorry about Emily," he said the moment they were far enough from the booth. "She is still not over our break-up."

"No worries. I'm sure it's hard to get over you," Nova said with a smirk. Here was the boldness, the reminder she was on the magic side.

"Something is different about you," he said. "I like it…a lot."

She winked and hugged him goodbye. "See you tomorrow!"

He looked at her drive away, motionless.

***

11:38 PM.

Nova's lips met the mirror's glass. She was transported back to the real side at 8:53 PM. Carole was right, it was an exact science. When she made it back to reality, she didn't feel tired or excited from the day she had spent on the other side. Instead, she felt some of the weariness she had felt from her conversation with Carole. She only had memories from the other side. All the physical and emotional sensations she felt were from reality. The moment she traveled back, everything she had experienced from the other side was now abstract. Insecurities and doubts were her companions here. But there was a new hopefulness now. A feeling that soon her life in reality could mirror what she was already experiencing on the other side. She thought about how odd it would be seeing Hakeem tomorrow, having the knowledge from the other side.

She woke up the next morning already missing that fluid energy around her which boosted her confidence on the magic side. She walked into *Fit Gals and Pals* with an extra pep in her step, generated from hope.

"Hi, Jeff!" Her manager glanced and replied with a quick hand raise. "Good morning, Paul."

"Hey, girl! How was your weekend? It was busy as hell here! How did you manage to get the weekends off?"

She wished she could tell him about her weekend. The one when she found out that magic was real. She was dying to share her time on the other side of her mirror with someone. That person was not Paul for obvious reasons. He did not even care about her weekend. He had only asked so he could tell her he had to work. He could not wait to tell her how many people he had signed up for membership.

"I guess I was lucky."

"You should think about working weekends! I signed five people up. Most people are off on the weekends, so it's a better time for them to come to the gym. They are more relaxed and easier to close."

Paul was boringly predictable. "I'll think about it. Good for you though," she said absently. She then looked around.

"Hakeem is not here yet," Paul said.

Her heartbeat accelerated. Her temperature rose. She felt embarrassment circulate through her body. It was like she was naked in front of an unimpressed crowd. He knew. That meant that other people had noticed too. Hakeem was probably aware as well. She wished she could hide and travel back to the other side.

"Why are you telling me that?" She tried her best to mask the emotions overpowering her.

"Nova, it's obvious," he said matter-of-factly, as if he had told her that the Earth revolved around the Sun.

She was silent for the rest of the day. She avoided looking up. She was not sure why she felt such shame and embarrassment. It was not a crime to have a non-reciprocated crush. To busy her mind, she checked her phone throughout the day, hoping to get a text message from Naveen. Hopefully something, anything to bring some light to this side. But nothing happened. Not a message from Naveen. Not an interaction with Hakeem. The day went on aimlessly. She could not wait to travel back there.

When she got home, she created a calendar to mark the times of her back-and-forth travels. She wanted to stay on the magic side as long as possible, but she also did not want to make any mistakes that could potentially cause some irreversible damages. She looked at the time. She had an hour to spare with nothing left to do on this side.

She texted Kameela. **"How did the talk with Josh go?"**

Her phone rang right away. "I'm so glad that you texted

57

me. Your timing could not have been better," Kameela said as soon as Nova picked up. She was speaking too fast. She was clearly distraught.

Nova felt guilty for looking at the time right away. Whatever this was needed to be quick. She had somewhere better to be. "What's going on?"

"I just got in a huge fight with Josh. I'm packing my bags. Can I come stay with you until I figure something out?"

Kameela was so agitated that Nova could picture her brusque movements behind the line. It was so out of character for her. She was always so calm and collected. "Slow down. What happened?"

"Nova, I will explain when I get there. I'll be at your place in about twenty minutes. I have got to get out of here." She hung up.

Nova panicked. This would be more than an inconvenience. How long would she stay here? Perhaps she could talk her out of whatever she was trying to do. She had said she would be here in twenty minutes. It would most likely take her longer than that. Nova would be gone only for twenty-three minutes. She would be back on time to deal with this situation. She felt guilty about how selfish her immediate reaction had been. But she had a good thing going, and she couldn't let anyone come in the way of it.

8:40 PM.

Time for magic. Lips against glass. Paradise.

***

She woke up the next day, excited to go to work. She was curious to see how Hakeem would behave, given their Sunday's interaction.

"Good morning, Jeff!"

58

A quick glance from Jeff. A double take. "Good morning."

She had almost forgotten how deep his voice was. Amazing. Even Jeff had sensed the difference and taken the time to look at her.

"Good morning, Paul."

"Hey, girl! How was your weekend? It was busy as hell here! How did you manage to get the weekends off?"

Apparently, some things were the same. Oddly, she was not as annoyed by Paul here. She found his excitement endearing on this side.

"I had a good weekend," she said. He smiled and rubbed his hair in all directions as if he wanted to create the friction needed to start a fire, to get energized. Nova couldn't help but be amused. She continued, "That's great, I'm sure you got a lot of people to sign up. And as far as my schedule, it was just good timing. They already had a couple of people working weekends when they hired me."

"Nice! I did, yes, a handful of them. You should consider working weekends. There is a lot more traffic. People are in a way better mood and so much easier to close."

"I'll think about it, thank you."

Paul was not that bad, all things considered. Perhaps being on this side made her immune to his obnoxiousness. Or she just needed to not be as cold toward him on the real side. After their exchange, she did not look around to get a glimpse of Hakeem. She did not feel the need to. She was confident that he would find his way to her before the end of the day.

She worked on contacting all her old leads. She had so many to get through. The sales team only consisted of her and

Paul. Jeff helped sometimes, but he was mainly focused on administrative tasks.

"Any update on the hiring?" she asked Paul.

"I know that Jeff has interviews at the end of the week. Hopefully, he hires someone. It is definitely becoming overwhelming with just the three of us. We are holding it down, though!"

She nodded. She thought about George's suggestion: *Someone with your charisma should be with us at Fitness Link. Our sales reps make bank!* She was feeling overworked and underpaid. Perhaps it was time for a change.

Halfway through her day, the new front desk receptionist walked toward her cubicle with a blasé stroll. She honestly could not keep up with the people working the front desk. They were all in their late teens or early twenties and typically only lasted a few weeks. She understood why they did not stay. They were barely getting paid the minimum wage.

"Hey, Nova, there is a walk-in at the front who is asking for you," the new receptionist said while staring at his phone.

She was not expecting any walk-in today. It could have been someone who came in a while ago that she had forgotten about. When she was close enough to the entrance, the silhouette became familiar: Naveen. She was planning on messaging him later today, before she went back to the real side. But there he was, with his hair down and his smile up.

"You look very professional in your pink and blue uniform," he said.

"You were serious about looking for a gym." She grinned and then hugged him hello.

"That and I really wanted to see you. I hope I'm not coming off as stalkerish." He grimaced.

She giggled at his expression. "No, you aren't. And I do not have many appointments today, so this will actually help my numbers."

"At your service." He bent his knees and bowed.

"Well, let me show you around first, and then we can discuss your options." It was amusing to give him the sales pitch.

"Sounds like a plan." He followed behind her. She could feel his eyes tracing all the curves and turns of her body under her uniform. Her skin warmed up in response.

The moment Nova began Naveen's walk-through, she sensed a gaze following them. Hakeem was standing by the treadmills with a client. He was glaring at them. She deliberately avoided looking his way. She walked Naveen toward the sitting area.

"So, what do you think?"

"It is a nice gym. There is a comforting and familial atmosphere."

"Absolutely. I'm glad you picked up on that. Now I have to go over a few questions with you before we move forward."

"I'm all ears."

For the first time in a very long time, she was excited about the part that she typically dreaded the most. This was an opportunity to learn more about him.

"Please describe your current exercise routine," she read.

"Hmm, let me see. I used to go for a thirty-minute jog four to five times a week, but lately, I have been swamped with work. So, I'm doing mostly at-home stuff: push-ups, abs, squats, etc."

She nodded and took notes of his answers. *"How often are*

you looking to train on a weekly basis?"

"Hopefully, four to five times at least." He looked at her with a grin that highlighted most of his teeth.

"What are your health and fitness goals?"

"What do you like? The intense meathead, very muscular type, or the kind of in-shape soon to have dad bod type?" She laughed. "What if I like the meathead, very veiny and muscular type?"

"Then I will be here seven days a week until my forehead vein becomes visible." They broke into laughter. "Ok, no, seriously, to answer the question: being in good shape and healthy is my goal."

"Ok, so forehead vein," Nova continued, ignoring his decision to be serious. She drew a stick figure with a zigzag inside of its circular head. They cackled again when she showed him her art. Hakeem was still gazing at them from the treadmills. She composed herself before the next question. *"On average, how many hours of sleep do you get every night?"*

"Six to seven hours on average."

"What is your occupation?" she read. "I remember this one, software engineer for an IT company, right?"

"You got it." His smile brightened.

"How physical is your work? I'm assuming not much," she teased.

"Don't do that! All that working on a computer is a surprisingly good finger workout."

The laughter resumed. Nova knew that Hakeem was still watching in the distance. *"Are you married or single?"* She leaned forward with her hands under her chin.

"I have been waiting to tell you, but my wife and I think

that you are really cute."

Nova laughed. Naveen did not. It was the first time he looked solemn. "Are you serious?" Nova furrowed her brow.

He laughed out loud. "Of course not! You should have seen your face. Hilarious!"

Nova rolled her eyes and held a chuckle. "Please, could you be serious for the last two questions?"

"I promise, I will." He held his pinky out.

She grinned and locked her left pinky into his before she continued, *"Do you have any kids?"*

"Not yet." A suggestive look.

"How would you rate your daily level of stress?"

"On a scale of one to ten, probably seven. I definitely need a better work-life balance."

Nova could help improve his work-life balance. She pictured their life together, full of laughter and happiness. "Alright, we finally got through them." She shook her head in amusement. "So, the different membership types that we have depend on how often you would want to come. If you are planning to be here four to five times a week, it will be more cost-effective to purchase the unlimited membership."

She was hoping he would get that one, a promise that he would be there almost every day. They could spend more time together. But how would that affect her situation with Hakeem? She still had a crush on him, and it looked like there was finally an opportunity to see what could be with him too.

"I'm going to be honest with you, I just wanted to see you today. There is a nice gym in my apartment complex. I'm going to purchase the unlimited membership because you have done an amazing job showing me around and humoring my childish behavior." He squinted his eyes, appearing more serious. "This is a bit of a drive for me, so I probably won't be coming here much, except to hopefully see you. But I really enjoyed our date the other day and our time today."

"Me too." A warm smile. "Are we still up for Wednesday?"

"Of course. I found a really cool spot downtown. I'll send you all the details Wednesday afternoon."

"Perfect!"

Naveen signed up for the 'unlimited' membership. They hugged goodbye a lot longer than any salesperson had ever embraced a prospect.

Nova was getting ready to leave when the clock hit five. Paul had left an hour ago, and Jeff was doing some inventory count. Earlier, he had confirmed to her that they would hire someone within the next week.

"Hey, there! Closing time?" Hakeem walked toward her.

She had not thought about him much after her interaction with Naveen. "Hey! I haven't seen you all day," she lied. "You must have been booked with clients."

"Yes, today was very busy." Perhaps that was why she did not see him on the real side? "It looks like we got a new member today who is very eager to get started."

"We do?" She knew what he meant but acted oblivious.

"The guy you signed up earlier was completely under your spell. It looked like you were into him too." He attempted to sound casual, but Nova knew there was more hidden behind his cool demeanor.

She had been waiting for a sign, a show of his interest for the past couple of years, but she had never gotten anything. Now that it was happening, she was not sure how to react. On the other side, she did not see him all day. But here he was on this side, wanting her to know that he had been watching. At first, she wanted to be cold. Retribution for all the times when he had not paid her any mind. But that was not fair. He was essentially seeing a different side of her, and he was reacting accordingly. The onus was on her to change her behavior on the real side so he could behave similarly.

"I can't help how people react to my charms." She put her hand on her chest in a theatrical manner.

"Miss Nova Wright," he began, grinning. It was so pleasant to hear him say her full name. "Have you always been like this? I don't know how I missed it."

"I don't know either." She shook her head dramatically, like she was starring in a soap opera.

"Well, now I know, and I want to know more."

"I like the sound of that."

Jeff walked back toward the cubicles. Office romances were frowned upon, so they stopped their banter. Hakeem waved goodbye as Nova exited. When she pulled away from the curb, she caught him still standing by the entrance, watching her drive away.

65

CHAPTER 6

It was almost time to travel back to reality. Nova thought about texting Kameela to check in on her. However, she did not want to deal with that situation on both sides. This side was her heaven. Her escape. Kameela was smart and resourceful, and Josh loved her. Maybe on this side, they would work things out if she did not reach out. Yes, she would stay out of it here. She was not being selfish. She not reaching out would force them to talk things out. Her silence was a good deed.

10:38 PM. Eyes closed. Lips against glass.

***

9:03 PM. Reality.

KNOCK! KNOCK! The pounding was deafening. Nova ran to open the door to stop it.

"What the hell were you doing? I have been knocking and calling for like five minutes," Kameela shouted.

"I'm sorry, I fell asleep." She had expected to get back before Kameela made it to her place. She must have gotten on the road the moment she hung up. If Nova knew that Kameela would have made it there so quickly, she would have shortened her stay on the other side. Actually no. She would have taken some time to think of a better lie. She wanted to stay on the other side as long as possible.

"What? I called you not even fifteen minutes ago, and you knew I was coming," she replied, her voice still echoing with anger.

"I'm sorry, I had a really long day. I'm sorry." Nova had never, in their almost decade of friendship, seen her like this.

Kameela's features softened. Her frown lessened. "No, I'm sorry. I'm misdirecting my anger toward you. Thank you for letting me come here." *You did not give me a choice,* Nova thought. "I promise I will only be here for a few days. I just need some time to think and be away from him."

"You can stay here as long as you need to." She tried to sound sincere. The better part of her was. The selfish part wasn't.

She wanted to be there for her friend, but she also did not want to risk the truth of the mirror to be exposed. This stay needed to be short. Each day Kameela spent in her apartment put her secret in danger. What if Kameela went to her room and kissed or winked at her reflection? She used to be content with her life and who she was, so previously the magic of the mirror would not have affected her. But clearly, she was no longer satisfied. Could she also be transported to the other side of the mirror? She did not think to ask Carole if two people could use the mirror at the same time. The mirror was hers. This was her time to have a piece of the happiness that everyone was raving about. Even if it was not real, it felt real; and that was all that mattered.

"Thank you, Nova."

"So, what happened? I have never seen you like this."

They sat on the living room couch.

"I finally mustered the courage to talk to him about the way I have been feeling, you know. I told him I was not ready to have kids. That I wanted to start working again, even if it was just part time." She paused. Her voice was shaking. "He had the nerve to tell me that is not what he signed up for. He wants a big family, and I'm thirty, so it's about damn time we start having kids." Tears rolled down her eyes. Nova got closer and wrapped her arm around her. Maybe she should have contacted her on the other side. "He has never spoken to me that way. I felt like I didn't know him at that moment. It's infuriating that he thinks he can dictate what, when, and how because he is the breadwinner." She paused again. "And he let me walk out. He turned the TV on and watched me leave." More tears followed, drowning her speech.

"I'm so sorry." Nova was not sure what advice she could give her. "So, what do you want to do?"

"I don't know. I need to think and meditate. I love him, but I don't know. I need a few days to gain some clarity."

"I understand. Take the time that you need." A few days were manageable.

"I will not be in your way, I promise. I'll sleep on the couch, and I'll only go in your bedroom to shower or use the restroom."

Nova had only one bathroom inside her bedroom, where the mirror was. She would be gone almost nine hours a day for work. Kameela would be home alone. The mirror was seductively inviting. Kameela was not in her optimal state of mind. What if she felt drawn to it? She definitely would; it was inevitable. Kissing or winking at her reflection was not far-fetched. Oh god. Everything would crumble. Why now? She had just gotten this miraculous opportunity. Perhaps she should tell her. Kameela was not selfish like her. She would understand why the magic of the mirror needed to remain hers alone. Or would she? How could Nova justify not wanting her friend to have access to a piece of paradise? Kameela's happiness did not take away from hers. No. The mirror was hers to enjoy…alone. Sharing it would make it less special. She needed to feel special. How could she make sure Kameela would not kiss or wink at her reflection? She couldn't simply ask her not to do so. That would be absurd, and it would immediately raise questions.

An idea lit her brain. "You will not be in the way at all. Just worry about getting the clarity that you need." She embraced her tightly and held her in for a long while. "Now, make yourself comfortable while I go in my bedroom for a few minutes and pick some stuff off the floor." She ended with a silly grin to hopefully lighten Kameela's mood.

"Girl, I don't care. You cannot be worse than Josh."

"I care. It's a disaster in there. Just settle in. I'll be right back with a blanket and a pillow."

"Okay. Thank you, Nova. Really."

"Of course."

Nova ran into her bedroom and quietly locked the door behind her. The mirror was so darn heavy. She was dragging it slowly, carefully. She watched each footstep to make sure she did not step on the towel she had meticulously slid under it. Thankfully, her closet was only a couple of yards away. Finally, her walk-in closet would serve a better purpose than storing all the items she had purchased on clearance.

Kameela was taller and thinner than her, she had no reason to get in that room. It was her best bet. She carefully angled the mirror to get it through the door. She could not afford to break it. What would happen if she broke it? Another question for Carole. Just a couple more steps. There. Phew. Her paradise was preserved. She shut the closet door as quietly as she could, storing magic inside of one hundred-something square feet.

She walked back outside. Kameela had not moved. "I hope this is comfortable for you." She handed Kameela her softest blanket and her fluffiest pillow.

"You are so sweet, thank you."

"Of course. It's safe to go in the bedroom now," she said, smiling. "Oh, I broke my floor mirror the other day, so you'll just have to use the bathroom one for now. I'll stop at the store on my way back from work tomorrow to get one."

"Nova, we shared a room in college. It's fine. I don't want to inconvenience you at all."

Well, too late for that. "You aren't. I was already planning to do that. I just wanted to give you a heads-up."

"Okay." She nodded. "I'll go ahead and get my night routine done now. I know you have to be up early for work."

***

The first day with Kameela at her place went by successfully. As expected, her workday was uneventful. Jeff had randomly called her in for a meeting. He had asked her how she felt about her position and her future with the company. She answered briefly and absently: she felt good and was satisfied with her position. It was odd, given that her monthly check-in was not scheduled for another couple of weeks. He also had a closed office conversation with Paul after her. The company probably wanted to make sure that all the employees were satisfied to get ahead of potential resignations. Before they left, Jeff also informed them they had finally hired a new salesperson who would start within the next few days. About damn time.

She didn't care about any of those updates. The most important thing was that the mirror was safe. On her way back home, she had stopped to buy a cheap floor mirror to put in her bedroom for Kameela's sake. Truly, for her secret's sake. She could now focus on helping her friend without having to worry. She walked inside her apartment. Some wavy instrumental sounds and a wonderful smell—a home-cooked meal—welcomed her in.

"If it doesn't work with Josh, I'll start shopping for rings," Nova said. Kameela responded with a hesitant laughter. "I'm sorry, way too soon," she added when she noticed her friend's expression.

"No, no it's okay." Kameela smiled, stirring whatever was in the skillet. "Plus, I saw all the bacon in your fridge. You know I don't date carnivores." She ended with a wide grin.

"Someone got their funny bone back, I see. So, what meatless delicacies are we having for dinner?"

"Roasted cauliflower pasta."

"Yummy," Nova said with a straight face.

"This is a win-win situation: you are providing me with a space to get clarity and I'm providing you with an opportunity to clear your body of toxins."

"Grand," she replied with a faux grin.

They sat at the dining table to eat dinner. Nova quickly checked the time. She still had some time to spare before she had to travel back there. "So, how was work, hon?" Kameela asked with a fake romantic tone.

"Busy, babe. We are understaffed right now so it has

been hectic. Thankfully, they just hired someone who should be starting in the next few days."

"That's good."

Nova took a bite of the pasta. She didn't want to admit it to avoid the vegetarian lecture, but the entire meal was a lot more tasteful than she had expected. "What's up with you? Anything from Josh?"

"No, he is pretty stubborn and prideful. I think he is hoping that I reach out first."

"Will you?"

"Absolutely not. He was out of line."

"So, what if he doesn't reach out?"

"He will. He is prideful but not stupid. I think he knows he was in the wrong." She tried to appear assured, but her tone was uneven.

"I'm sure he will," Nova affirmed.

She was genuinely confident that Josh would contact Kameela sooner than later. He adored her. She remembered their wedding vows when he had declared she was the best thing that had ever happened to him. He would reach out soon to fix things. Kameela would go back home. And Nova would enjoy her paradise without fear again, soon.

"On another note, I spoke to Ana today. Looks like she is really loving her new role. But it is taking most of her time, so she had to break things up with the guy from accounting."

"Well, that works for me. I could never remember his name anyway." Nova laughed. Her laughter fainted rapidly. Her feelings were hurt to hear the news from Kameela and not directly from Ana. She was under the belief that Kameela and Ana's relationship had also drifted apart. Maybe it had? Why was she being so negative? Ana would probably let her know about her ex-lover and her next prey the next time they would talk.

8:22 PM.

Nova had to travel back soon. She had thought of a reason to justify her almost half an hour absence.

She got up and spoke while putting the dishes away, "I took your advice and I have been taking nightly baths with all the salts and essential oils."

"Finally! It has only been an eternity since I first suggested it. How do you like it?"

"It's a-ma-zing! I stay in there for like thirty minutes, it's so relaxing."

"I told you!"

"You were right. I'm going in now, so I'll emerge again in about half an hour." She walked toward her bedroom.

"Girl, make it an hour!"

Nope. That would result in a coma, apparently. Twenty-three minutes exactly. She was already stretching it by staying that long.

"Alright, I'll see you soon." She stood by the door.

"You are just taking a bath; you are not going anywhere. Not need for goodbyes." Kameela shook her head. "Enjoy your bath!"

Nova closed the bedroom door behind her. She turned the water on in the bathroom and lit a lavender scented candle—courtesy of Kameela. She found her old music player and turned some meditation music on. The smell, the sound, the warmth. It all felt nice and comforting. She would get in the tub when she returned. She closed her bathroom door, in case Kameela walked in her bedroom. She was certain that she wouldn't. But in case she did, she would play it safe.

Kameela had been careful to give her enough privacy. And if she walked in the room, with the music playing and the water running, she would not attempt to disrupt it. After all this was her recommendation. She would not interfere with that.

8:43 PM.

She walked inside her closet and turned the light off. She led her lips to the glass.

***

10:38 PM.

She immediately felt lighter when she emerged on the other side. Her first thought was to check if she had any messages or missed calls from Kameela. Time was waiting for her here, so it made sense that her phone had zero notification.

She texted her. "**How did the talk with Josh go?**" Same message, so she was expecting her phone to ring any moment.

A few minutes passed. An hour. Nothing. Perhaps Kameela had talked to Josh on this side since she had not reached out at the same time, and they were working things out.

Finally, her phone rang. "Hey! Is everything okay?" Nova picked up on the first ring.

"No, I got into a huge fight with Josh," Kameela replied. She sounded unmoved, as if she had already found a resolution.

Nova made a show to sound surprised. "Oh no! What happened?"

"I told him I wanted to work, and I was not ready for kids yet. He basically said that he wanted a big family and since I'm thirty, we needed to start working on it now. Basically, going back to work is not an option in his world.

75

So, I left."

She was speaking so calmly. She had obviously talked this situation out with someone else and had some time to cool down. "Where are you?"

"I'm at Ana's."

Nova immediately felt gutted, like someone had inserted a knife at the center of her chest. Kameela only came to her place on the real side because she had reached out at the exact time she was packing her bags. If it were up to her, she would have preferred to have gone to Ana's. *Your timing could not have been better*, she had said. Nova was not her first choice. She was the most convenient and better-timed option. All this time she thought she and Kameela were closer. The feeling might not have been mutual. Although she felt some sadness, she shrugged it off. Whatever was in the air on this side of the mirror with nitrogen and oxygen appeased her. Plus, she also realized she would not have to deal with that situation here.

"Okay. I'm so sorry you are going through that."

"It's okay. I just need some time to get some clarity and act accordingly. Things will be okay. I'll let you know."

"Alright, please keep me posted. I'll talk to you guys soon."

She took a while to fall asleep. The situation was still slightly bothering her. Even on this side, helped by whatever made this reality magical, she was not immune to getting her feelings hurt. She inhaled and exhaled a couple of times. What was the big deal? So, what, Kameela and Ana had grown closer? She still had two amazing friends who were there for each other and always there for her. This was not about her; it was about Kameela. Her friend needed her support during a difficult situation. She needed to be there for her in whatever way she could. She texted Kameela before falling asleep. **"I'm here for you if you need anything."**

CHAPTER 7

"Nova, come to my office please," Jeff said.

Paul watched her walk in their manager's office. Nova almost let out a cackle when she noticed how hard he was biting his lip. An impromptu meeting was typically not a positive one. Thankfully, she had the knowledge from reality. So, she expected their meeting to go as it did on the real side. Merely a brief check-in.

"Door shut?" she asked.

"Yes, have a seat." His office was cooler than the cubicles. He looked more present than usual, sitting straight and making eye contact with her. Things felt more intense. "You have been with the company for about four years, correct?"

He had asked the same question on the real side. "Yes, four years and counting," she replied. She had simply nodded yes there.

"Yet, you have never communicated that you were interested in a promotion. Why is that?"

He had not asked that question on the real side. Though, she had been thinking about it. There, she had been telling herself that *Fit Gals and Pals* was not where she wanted to be when she entered her third decade. She had hoped she would have been at a different stage in her life, a better stage.

However, on this side she felt differently. She knew this was not her end game, but why not take advantage of this opportunity? While she was figuring out the better option for her life, she still had to play the cards in her hands. And come to think of it, they were not so bad.

She could simultaneously enjoy her life the way it was whilst actively working to improve it.

"That is a fair question. Frankly, at first, I did not think I would be here for a long time." A tad of honesty she knew Jeff would appreciate. "But over my time here, my appreciation for this company has grown, and I'm definitely interested in a career path with *Fit Gals and Pals.*" She was embellishing her aspirations to Jeff, so she was doing her best to sound confident and sincere. She was sitting as straight as he was, with her shoulders held back. A promotion meant more money, which could be used toward putting a plan of action for whatever was next for her.

"I'm glad to hear that. You have been doing well here. You always meet your numbers, and we have wonderful feedback from our members."

"Thank you."

"I have hired a new sales rep. She will be starting next Monday. I would like to offer you the assistant manager's position. Your tasks will be the same for the most part, but you will also be helping with some of the administrative stuff. Of course, you will be getting a raise as well. How does that sound?"

Nova was at a loss for words. She was thrilled to be offered the position on this side, but she could not help to think about it not happening on the real side. Why? She would deal with it when she went back. Here, she would enjoy the moment. "It sounds wonderful. Thank you so much for offering me the position!"

"Absolutely. You have been here for four years, and you have been very consistent throughout. I just needed confirmation from you that this is the path that you wanted to be on. You will receive some paperwork from HR before the end of the day, so please complete it before you leave. You will be going over some virtual training the rest of the week to prepare for your new responsibilities. Your new position will take effect on Monday. Please hold off sharing the news, I will make the announcement before the end of the week. Sounds good?"

"Sounds perfect!"

"Well, congratulations!" He got up and shook her hand. His smile was bright, punctuated by one dimple on his right cheek. Jeff had a dimple? *The more you know.* He looked like a proud parent picking up their kid after their first day of school. This day was long overdue, and they both knew it.

Nova closed the door behind her. She fought her hardest to not break into a dance and scream her lungs out. She silently walked back to her cubicle, fighting all her instincts.

Paul looked anxious, frown face. "Is everything okay?"

She could not reveal the news to him yet. "Yes. He was just going over my numbers and he let me know he had hired someone who is starting on Monday."

"That's it? The door shut had me nervous." He wiped sweat off his temples with a napkin.

Nova chuckled at his dramatic reaction. Why did she find him so annoying on the real side? He was harmless. She skimmed through the gym for Hakeem. Her eyes met his stare. He smiled and waved. She wanted to share the news with him. He had helped her with so many of her sales. She could not wait to see his reaction when he'd hear the good news. She also wanted to message Kameela and Ana. However, it did not feel timely given what Kameela was going through. She would give it a few days for things to settle down for Kameela. Then, she would tell her friends. She was also excited to see Naveen tomorrow. She could tell him about her promotion. She was looking forward to spending more time with him.

As she thought about all the people she was excited to share the good news with, her parents crossed her mind. She had not spoken to them much since she had left Miami to go to college in Orlando. She had only visited them once. And that was all it took to calcify the long-paved road that already distanced them. She had intentionally chosen to go to college as far away as financially possible. Going out of state was not an option because she needed to take advantage of the in-state tuition rate. If she could have left Florida then, she would have. She wanted a fresh start.

Her upbringing had been strict, to put it mildly. All the interests she had shown could not be pursued due to their worldly nature. She had to be at the Kingdom Hall at least three times a week. She had to go door-to-door to preach the good news. She could only befriend other witnesses. She was discouraged to ask certain questions. So, she had to find those answers on her own. The more research she did, the less she believed in the faith she had been raised in. Eventually, she stopped believing in all of it, altogether. She had to get away. Learn how to be a part of the sinful world she was taught to distance herself from. But getting closer to the world meant distancing herself from her parents. She loved her parents.

Her mother was nurturing and patient. Her dad was the most hardworking person she knew. They always made sure she had a great structure. But she had never felt close to them. There was no intimacy. Their conversations were merely filled with talking points from the organization. She did not know who they were.

One day, when they were having dinner, she mustered the courage to ask a question lingering in her mind. "Do you believe that exactly 144,000 people from the billions from the past, present, and future will be resurrected to heaven?"

Her parents looked astonished that she would ask such a question. "Of course," her dad replied, short of gasping.

"But there are millions of witnesses."

"The ones who have followed Jehovah's laws and who will not go to heaven will live on Paradise Earth, honey. You know this," her mom chimed in, eyes widened in shock.

"Nova, what is this about?" her dad said. "You have been acting differently for the past few months, and now you are questioning the Truth?" She did not answer. She wanted them to understand that she had doubts.

And they did. Her parents eventually shared their concerns about her to the elders. They did not want their daughter to perish during Armageddon. She was called in for a meeting with the elders. The worst experience of her life. Their questions were intrusive, inappropriate, and invasive. *Have you had any sexual relationships? Have you had any inappropriate interaction with someone of the same sex? Have you watched any pornographic content?* She simply wanted to discuss her uncertainties, but here they were questioning her purity and sinlessness. Before the meeting, she still had an ounce of faith, a hope what she had believed all her life was even partially true. Hope these people were family. The hopefulness was erased by the end of the meeting. She wanted nothing else to do with the organization. So, she expressed her concerns. She was reasserting her voice.

However, that came with consequences. She was now at risk to be marked, if she did not correct her behavior. Being marked meant that she was not a good person to associate with. People could only interact with her when she was at the Kingdom Hall. She would essentially be shunned by members of the congregation, her friends, and even her parents. She decided to take the risk, so she could live the life she wanted to live.

She continued to question things. She stopped going to the Kingdom Hall. Shortly after her continued behavior, she was called in for another meeting with the elders. She did not care anymore. She wanted to be marked to have a reason to leave, to get away. And she was. Her Witnesses friends avoided her. Her parents only talked to her when necessary. It was brutal. The next fall, she left Miami to go to college in Orlando. Going to college was frowned upon by the organization. Her unrepentant sinful behavior accompanied by her pursuit of higher education put her at risk of being disfellowshipped. This would mean that she would be shunned by all her fellow Witnesses, her entire congregation; and worst of all, her parents. They could never speak to her again.

Every time something meaningful happened to her, she thought about contacting her parents. The only way to have a decent relationship with them was to work her way back to be in good standing with the congregation. She had no interest in doing that. She simply wanted her parents to love her for who she was and to be a part of her life. At this moment, she wanted them to be proud of her because she had gotten a promotion at her job. She wanted them to be happy for her because things were finally going well for her. But they would not be. Their disappointment of her would override everything else. She would try to contact them again…eventually, but not today, not here. Nothing would taint her happiness on this side.

9:38 PM. Eyes closed. Lips against glass.

CHAPTER 8

9:06 PM. Back to reality.

She quietly opened her closet door. The sound of the water running was mildly covered by the music playing. She found the drain stopper to fill up the bathtub. She sat inside of the tub and let herself relax for a few minutes. She wanted to give genuine feedback to Kameela about her bath, if she asked. She could feel her stress evaporating with the steam. She knew it would be short-lived, but it felt so good in the moment. Suddenly, a thought rushed through her mind: the promotion. She would have to talk to Jeff tomorrow. He did not offer it to her here. Whatever the reason was, it did not matter. She would simply ask him about it. He knew that she deserved it. He had even wondered why she had not asked. He would probably be pleasantly surprised by her asking. Hope and happiness could also exist on this side. In fact, this was where it mattered the most.

The words of Carole still resonated, *You must remember that life on that side of the mirror is not real. The mirror can be a useful tool to show you the way to become who you have wanted to be.* Asking for the promotion on the real side was a significant step toward applying what she had experienced on the other side to her advantage in the real world. She was on the right track.

After about ten minutes, she stepped outside of the bath

and dried off. Some of her stress had been swallowed by the water disappearing into the drain. She walked outside, lighter.

"How was your bath?" Kameela inquired the moment she saw her.

"It was wonderful. I feel all nice and relaxed." She stretched and exhaled.

"You look nice and relaxed."

Nova nodded. "What have you been up to?"

"You are asking like you have been in there for hours." She raised a brow. "I have not been up to much." She paused, recalling something. "Oh actually, I chatted with Ana for a bit."

The way she said it conveyed that it was something they did constantly…without her. Frequent conversations Nova was not privy to. When did the disconnect happen?

"How is she?" She contemplated asking how often they talked in her absence, but she left those words unsaid.

"Good. You know her: work, work, and more work."

"It seems that I don't," she interjected brusquely. She had not expected those words to come out. They slipped out of frustration from this side, but also from finding out that Kameela had preferred to go to Ana's on the other side.

"What do you mean?" Kameela asked, staggered. She bit her lip while she waited for Nova's response.

Nova initially thought about taking it back, writing it off as a joke. However, she wanted to be honest. She needed to be honest. "If I didn't text you when you were packing your bags after your fight with Josh, would you have come here or would you have gone to Ana's?"

Kameela's face sank. "I love you both equally. You two are my best friends. I don't know what I would have done if you didn't reach out. I'm just thankful you did."

Nova knew what she would have done. She had experienced it. Kameela chose Ana on the other side. That was what she would have done here too if she had it her preferred way. "I think you would have chosen to go to Ana. It's fine."

"What is this about?" Kameela's face tightened with concern.

"I thought you and I got closer over the years. I love Ana but I consider you to be my best friend. I thought you felt the same way, but it seems like you and Ana are closer than you and I."

"Nova, why are you comparing our relationships? I love you both. You two are like family."

Kameela was still not giving her the answer she was looking for. She knew all three were best friends, but she had believed that over the past few years the two had gotten closer. Why did this matter so much to her, anyway? The three were close. Why was it so important for her to be Kameela's best friend? She did not want to admit the reason, but she knew why. She wanted a victory on this side. She wanted to know she was number one on someone's list.

"I'm sorry. I don't know why I said all that. I just feel like I need a win." She looked down.

"This is not a competition. This is friendship. I love you." Kameela embraced her, holding her longer and tighter than usual.

Inside of the embrace, Nova realized that Kameela would obviously give such an answer. Everything was peace, love, and happiness in her world. No insecurities. Plus, the steadfast feeling things would just work themselves out, including the situation with Josh. She had been upset the night it happened, but she had seemed so unconcerned since, confidently meditating her worries away. She could not understand what Nova was feeling. There was no point trying to explain it further.

"I know. I love you too," she replied to wrap up the conversation. She broke off the embrace.

"I think you should try to meet with Ana. I think you guys just need to catch up."

"You're right."

That night, she went to bed feeling somewhat lighter. Although she was not fully transparent, she had expressed her true feelings and had not tried to mask them. She was still saddened that Kameela did not consider her to be her best friend. However, the more she thought about it, the easier it was to convince herself that it was trivial. She would try to rekindle things with Ana. The growing silence between them was not only Ana's fault. It was also hers.

She texted Ana before going to sleep. **"Hey girl, I hope things are going well with the new role. We should grab a drink sometime this week and catch up."**

The next day she woke to Ana's response. **"Hey girly! Totally. Let's do Friday 6ish at our usual spot?"**

Her casual response relieved some of Nova's fears. They simply needed to put more work into their friendship. Perhaps she had overthought herself into feeling like she and Ana were growing apart. Perhaps Kameela had gotten closer to her because she had more availability to talk to Ana when it was convenient for her. She was excited to get their relationship back on the right track. The anticipation fueled her.

That morning, she walked into work with a novel confidence. "Hey, Jeff. Do you have a moment?" Nova said. Was the boldness from the other side rubbing off on her in reality? Or was she confident going in because she already knew that he wanted to offer her the position? Because the outcome was pre-written in her favor. Either way.

"Yes, come in," he replied, brow slightly furrowed.

She sat down. "As you know I have been working here for about four years." Her voice was trembling. "I'm interested in growing with the company and would like to know if there is an opportunity for me to do so." She ended more confident, knowing that the opportunity was hers to claim.

Jeff crossed his arms and gazed at her. "Yesterday I called you in and I asked if you were satisfied with your position. You said you were and made no mention of wanting things to change."

"Yes, but I thought about it last night. I'm interested in a promotion if it's something that is on the table," she countered, less confident than when she walked in.

"Paul told you, didn't he? The paperwork has been signed. I unfortunately cannot change that. I wish you had made your interest known yesterday."

"Paul did not tell me anything. What's going on?"

"Oh." He paused for a second. "I offered Paul the assistant manager position yesterday. I was planning on making the announcement before the end of the week."

Nova was wordless. The moment she was offered the position on the other side immediately replayed in her mind. She wanted to tell him she had been working here the longest and that her numbers had always been consistent. But those words could not find their way out, lost in the maze that were her thoughts.

"I see."

"I was strongly considering you but yesterday during our meeting, you seemed content with your position. I got the impression you were not interested in a promotion. I figured you did not want the additional responsibilities; hence I offered it to Paul who has made his interest for any leadership role known since the very beginning."

This was the most she had ever heard him explain a decision he had made. For a brief instant she felt validated that he cared enough to explain his reasoning. The feeling was quickly washed away by sadness and frustration. This was another reminder she was not chosen on this side, yet again. She let herself daydream about the other side, paradise. She could not wait to get back there.

"I understand."

"Now that I know you are interested in growing with us, I will inform you of all the future opportunities that we have, okay?" He half smiled, which was not enough for his dimple to make an appearance.

"Thank you." She walked out of his office with her head down.

The rest of the day Paul's smirk became increasingly noticeable. How in the world had she found his mannerisms endearing on the other side? He was already unbearable as a coworker. She could not imagine how insufferable he would be given any fraction of authority. She desperately searched for Hakeem's face throughout the day, but he did not look her way at all. Not even once.

Mercifully, a walk-in stopped by. It was Nova's turn to

do the walk-ins' walk-throughs. An opportunity to interact with Hakeem.

She walked to the front desk to greet the prospect. "Hello, I'm Nova. Nice to meet you."

"Hi. I'm Lily. Nice to meet you too." A rather enigmatic smile contoured her face.

Lily reminded her of the sexy female protagonist in any action movie who had a dark past. She had long dark hair which contrasted with her piercing dark hazel eyes. She was both toned and shapely, in all the right places. Nova had to remind herself not to stare. Her guess was that Lily had just moved into town and was looking for a local gym. Or she was trying to get a better deal. With her physique, she was unquestionably an avid gym goer.

Nova quickly walked her through the gym. Lily was obviously very experienced and did not need to be told what the different machines were. She stared at Nova while she was talking about the gym's amenities. Nova pointed at whatever equipment she was talking about, but Lily only looked at her. Her gaze was unsettling. Nova tried to ignore it. She continued her pitch by getting closer to Hakeem for their standard close routine. She did not need his help today. And she would not have minded shortening the walk-through. However, given the day she had so far, she wanted to interact with him and get a dose of his smile.

"Hakeem, I would like to introduce you to one of our new members, Lily," she said when they were next to him.

Hakeem's reaction was delayed. He looked at Lily and didn't stop until he punctuated his sentence. "Very nice to meet you," he said. He shook her hand, then held it for a moment that felt like eternity to Nova. "We are honored to have you as a new member. Please don't hesitate to let me know if you need any help."

Let me *know.* Not *us* like he always said. He wanted her to come directly to him. He had barely looked Nova's way. She did not even receive the smile she had come for. What was she thinking walking this gorgeous woman his way? She was not thinking. She had just thought about fulfilling her overwhelming desire to get close to him. She wondered if this encounter would go the same way on the other side. She was the best version of herself there, so Hakeem was attracted to her. But that did not mean he would not be attracted to Lily. On one hand, she wanted to put his attraction for her to the test by walking Lily his way, but on the other she did not want to risk it. Maybe she would give her a terrible walk-through on the other side, so she would not sign up. That thought made her crack a smile.

"Nice to meet you too. I'm looking forward to getting started," Lily said.

Lily signed up for the unlimited membership. When she left, Nova was confident that something was off about her. She could not put her finger on what. Though, her judgment could have also been clouded by Hakeem being evidently attracted to the dark-haired beauty.

"Nice job, Nova. You are crushing it!" Paul said with even more enthusiasm than usual. She knew that he could not wait for the news that he had been promoted to be revealed.

"Thank you."

As usual, she left as soon as the clock displayed the number five. Her ride home was quiet that evening, but her thoughts were loud. The missed opportunity with the promotion, her friendship with Ana and Kameela, the lack of interest from Hakeem and his attraction for Lily. Oh Lily. Something was up with her. Whatever it was, she did not care to find out, as long as she stayed away from Hakeem. Perhaps she should stop fantasizing about Hakeem on this side. He was obviously not interested. But what was the alternative? She had hoped that something would come out of her date with Naveen, but she still had not heard from him. Sure, it was not the best date, but it was not the worst either. Hell, he had gotten catfished before. Why did he give up so easily? Perhaps he was busy with work? Perhaps she should contact him? The fear of rejection was overwhelming. She could not bear going through it. She needed a break. To get away. She could almost hear the mirror calling her when she walked into her apartment. Her thoughts were interrupted the moment she stepped in.

Move your awareness up to the center of your forehead, between your highbrows: your third eye. Your chakra of wisdom and intuition. Invite indigo, the color of night skies. Let your third eye bathe in indigo and take what it needs: balance, clarity, insight, and discernment.

Kameela was seated on her yoga mat, with her legs crossed and arms resting on the length of her thighs, carefully controlling her breathing with her eyes shut. Nova walked in slowly and quietly to not disturb her meditation. She sat on the couch without making a single noise.

Kameela slowly opened her eyes when she finished. She said nothing for at least thirty seconds. Nova did not speak. She knew better than to talk before her friend "returned to her body", or whatever the lingo was.

"Thanks for coming in silently," Kameela finally said.

"Of course. You don't usually meditate at this time. New routine?"

"Josh called," she immediately said. Besides her mouth, her face did not move. Her expression was impenetrable.

"What did he say?"

"He wants me to come back home." She inhaled. "He apologized for the way he talked to me that night." She exhaled. She did not look satisfied with what she had shared.

"What is the *but*?"

"I know him. He only apologized because he wants me to come back home. It's clear that he doesn't understand why I was so upset. I don't know if I'm okay with that."

"What about you wanting to start working?"

"Oh yeah. He basically gave me a timeline. He is okay with that as long as we can start trying to expand our family in one year, at the very latest. And when we do, I'll have to stay home because he doesn't want to have a stranger raising our kids." Her features loosened, revealing uncertainty.

"I see. Do you know what you want to do?"

"I'm not sure." She sighed. "I mean, I eventually do want to expand our family. And one year is a decent amount of time. And I do love him. I don't want to lose him." She was quiet for a moment. Nova didn't speak. She knew that Kameela was not finished. "And it wasn't perfect, but he did apologize."

At that moment, Nova wished she was bold enough to say what she really thought: *How dared he?* He did not get to decide the course of both of their lives. She would be the one having to carry the baby; thus, they should both agree on the timeline based on what *she* was comfortable with. If he loved her as much as he said he did, he would be considerate enough to give her a genuine apology. He would not put her in a situation where she felt so uneasy. Unfortunately, her boldness was awaiting her on the magic side. She felt like she did not have the expertise or experience to give relationship advice to a married woman.

She inhaled quietly and took a moment to acknowledge what lied underneath her initial reaction. She wasn't transparent with herself. She was making excuses. This was not just a married woman. This was the person she considered to be her best friend. At the minimum, she owed her sincere feedback.

She thought carefully about her words before she spoke. "I do not want to cross any boundaries and I know that I'm not married, but I think that you should be able to make your own decisions and have the support of your spouse. He shouldn't give you a deadline as to when you guys should start trying to have kids. If you want to have a job, I feel like you guys can make that work as well. Your say is worth as much as his."

The moment of silence before Kameela's response felt so thick a knife might not have been heavy duty enough to cut it. A chainsaw, maybe.

"You are right," Kameela began. "You are not married, and you have no idea what it takes to make a marriage work. It takes compromise. I can't always have what I want, the way I want it, and when I want it. I have to consider my spouse as well. He is not perfect, but he loves me. I know he has both of our best interests in mind with everything he does. I appreciate your feedback, but I think I know what I need to do. I'm going home."

Nova was not sure what to reply. This was what she got for speaking her mind. She knew she should have kept her thoughts to herself like she always did...on this side at least.

Kameela's shoulders were stiff. Her mouth was tightly sealed. She was clearly upset. Nova hated to be the cause of her anger. She had to fix it.

"I'm sorry. I didn't mean to upset you. I was out of line. I apologize."

Kameela' shoulders dropped. The tightness that gripped her lips loosened. "I know you just want what's best for me. I appreciate you letting me stay here and being here for me the past few days."

"I love you."

"I love you too."

They hugged. A warm, reconciliatory hug. Arbitrarily, Nova thought to check the time. It was 9:01 PM. She had only five minutes to go back to the other side. Oh god, she had to go!

"I need to get in the bath! Much needed after today," she said brusquely.

"Hmm, okay. I'll start packing my stuff while you do that," Kameela said.

"Perfect!"

Nova shut the bedroom door behind her. She ran inside her bathroom and started the water. She could not find her music player. She did not have enough time to look for it. She ran back out toward her closet and swung her bathroom door on her way there. The door did not fully close, remaining slightly ajar. In her rush, she did not notice. She had to get to the mirror. She could not lose her paradise.

9:03 PM.

Lips against glass. Eyes closed. Warmth. Magic.

CHAPTER 9

Naveen listened to Michelle's voicemail for the second time. *"Hey, Nav. This is Michelle. I know you don't want to talk to me. I'm so sorry for hurting you. I love you. I miss you. Please give me a chance to talk to you. I'm not trying to justify anything. I just want to tell you what happened. Please forgive me. I love you. Call me."*

Her voice was hoarse. He knew she had cried before calling him. But Michelle cried liberally. Sometimes she cried to make things go her way. He was no longer fazed by those waters. It had been almost a year. Why did she want to talk to him now? Granted, she had tried to contact him the first few weeks after he had walked in on her cheating on him in her living room. He had blocked her number then. He had made sure she had no way of getting in contact with him. He had changed his lock and cut contact with her. A couple of months passed, and she was still on his mind. He thought about hearing her out. Perhaps there was an explanation as to why she did what she did. Perhaps he had been too harsh and abruptly final. Perhaps he should have given her a chance to explain.

He started to consider contacting her to ask what had happened. However, one evening when he was out grabbing drinks with Golibe and Ada, he saw her. She was with him: the living room guy. He could not forget the bastard's face.

They were both smiling, happy. She had moved on. That night he had walked out of the restaurant the same way he had walked out of her living room. Wordless. Only this time, he promised himself never to look back.

He deleted her message. He would keep the promise he made to himself to never open that book again. And he felt even more comfort and confidence knowing he had found someone with whom he had the potential to have something special.

"Hey Nova! I hope your day is going well. How is 9:30 PM at Blue Moon?" he texted her.

***

Nova smiled as she read Naveen's message. *Blue Moon* sounded magical. How fitting. Her workday was getting closer to its tail. She was expecting Lily to walk in sometime before she left, as she had on the real side. But she didn't. That was odd. Being on this side of the mirror did not interfere with whom she interacted with, just how it happened. It would have made sense if things had happened differently with someone she had a previous encounter with. Priorly being in contact with them could justify the different outcomes between both sides. But she had never interacted with Lily on this side, so it was strange that she had not walked in to inquire about the membership. Another question for Carole.

"You haven't had any appointments today. How come?" Paul said, pulling her out of her thoughts.

She had been working on the assistant manager's training. Per Jeff's request, she had not revealed the news to anyone yet. "I have to catch up on some of the sales trainings, so I'm only taking walk-ins."

100

ACROSS BOTH SIDES OF THE MIRROR

"I have been there before." He smirked. "But I was able to get caught up and still get a few consultations in at the same time."

In that instant, she wanted to break the news to him to see how quickly that smirk would fade away. She felt great satisfaction knowing he would find out soon. She could not wait to see the look on his face then. "Good for you. I wish I could do that."

Before Nova could get in her car to drive home when her shift ended, she heard someone yell out her name. She looked in the distance and recognized Hakeem. Even from afar, his Greek godlike stature was unmistakable. Yet, she had not thought about him much today; especially after she received the message from Naveen.

"Damn girl, not even a hello today? That's what we do now?"

He hugged her. His body was firm, and his arms were strong. She felt good inside of his embrace.

"Sorry, today was hectic. Hello." She grinned.

"Hello, Miss Nova. What are you doing this weekend?"

Was he about to ask her out? "Nothing set in stone yet."

"In that case, let's grab brunch on Saturday."

Her heart skipped a beat or two. Finally! She was able to get an outcome she had wanted for almost two years on the real side. It only took a few days for it to happen here. Every day it made more sense why Carole stated that the mirror could become addictive. Though, she did not feel addicted. She could get the same results on the real side in due time. Frankly, she was not doing anything spectacular on this side. She was simply carrying herself with more confidence. She was more vibrant, bold, and a little bit more candid. That was all. Those traits were merely lying dormant on the real side, waiting for her to activate them. And she would. It was just so much easier on this side. She did not have to do any work or put any effort. Things were already the way she wanted them to be. It was effortless. Why not enjoy it?

"Yes, let's do that."

"Awesome! I have your number." He winked at her and hugged her goodbye.

She had forgotten that he had her phone number. He had only messaged her a handful of times on the real side to ask some work-related questions. Here, he would use the same digits to arrange their first date. Life was looking good. She was excited to see how things would develop with him. Yet, the eagerness for her upcoming date with Naveen quickly overshadowed her excitement about her first date with Hakeem. A delightful quagmire.

When she got home, she prepared her outfit for her date with Naveen while humming Nina Simone's *Feeling Good*. She was happy. She had to travel back to the real side soon. She could not wait to return to this side to meet with him. She hoped she could discover something about Naveen that might justify why he had not contacted her in reality.

Before traveling back, she sent a message to Kameela. **"Hey! I just wanted to check on you. How are you?"**

The response will await her. Time will wait for her.

8:38 PM. Lips against glass. Eyes closed. Still motion.

***

Back to reality.

Kameela was packing her bag silently, wondering why Nova acted so strangely after their talk. Maybe she was still upset with her because of the situation with Ana. Or was

Nova upset because she told her she did not know what it took to make a marriage work? That was a true statement. She was not trying to be hurtful. However, her delivery had been harsh. Nova always meant well, and she knew it had taken a lot for her to speak up. She wanted her to be happy. Kameela needed to talk to her and let her know how much she valued her advice and friendship. Although she did not want to interrupt her bath, she also did not want to sit with that icky feeling any longer. She went to the kitchen and poured two glasses of sparkling rosé. Bubbles and a good-hearted chat would resolve any lingering tension between them.

She walked into her bedroom. She could hear the water running, but the bathroom door was ajar. She knocked carefully. "Hey, Nova. Sorry to disturb your peaceful bath, but can we talk? I got some rosé to accompany your bath!"

No answer. She must have fallen asleep in there. Kameela had taken a lot of naps during her baths. She did not want to wake her friend up, but she knew that Nova would enjoy the drink more than the water-filled sleep. She giggled as she opened the door slowly. To her surprise, Nova was not in the bathtub. Her phone was lying face down on the counter. The water was running aimlessly. She turned it off. She walked back out to look around her bedroom. Where was she? There were no other rooms for her to go into. Except for the closet. Nova would have heard her knock from there.

Kameela opened her closet door. Instead of Nova, she discovered a beautiful gold oval-shaped lotus flowers framed mirror. It was stunning. Regal, even. She wondered why Nova kept it hidden in there. It was unquestionably the most beautiful adornment in her apartment. The closer she got to the mirror, the more drawn she felt to it. It was an intense yet comforting feeling. She looked at her reflection. It was impossible to look away. She felt an incredible feeling of peace. That feeling was followed by an urge to wink at her reflection. So, she did. What a beautiful mirror, she thought to herself.

Kameela walked outside the closet. She was starting to worry. There was a window in the bedroom. Nova must have gone outside through it. But why would she leave that way? What was she hiding? She walked back into the living room. There was no sign of struggle in the bedroom, and she had heard nothing. It had only been a few minutes. It was impossible someone had come in. The only plausible explanation was that Nova had snuck out of her bedroom through her window. That would explain why she ran abruptly in the room. Kameela hoped she would tell her the truth on her own. She did not want to confront her and make her feel uncomfortable. She went back into her bathroom and turned the water back on. She put everything back the way it was. She sat on the couch and quietly waited for Nova to return.

CHAPTER 10

9:26 PM.

Nova opened the closet door slowly. She could distinctly hear the water she had left running the closer she got to her bathroom. She had not closed the door shut. Her heart raced in panic. She inspected her bedroom carefully. Everything looked the same. Her bed. The dresser. She checked her bathroom. It looked as she had left it. Thank goodness. Her secret was safe.

She walked out to the living room, relieved. "All packed?" she asked Kameela.

"Yes. How was your bath?"

"It was wonderful and relaxing, as always. I almost fell asleep."

"I see. And you were in the bath the whole time?"

Nova's heart resumed its race. She tried to mask her panic the best way she could, by maintaining a robotic smile. "Of course. Why do you ask?" She attempted a laugh which immediately reminded her of a politician trying to explain their way out of a scandal.

"I was just curious as to how long your baths were." Kameela squinted her left eye. Nova had learned that she did that when she was skeptical. When she wanted to say something but chose to hold her peace instead. Nova looked at the floor to hide her nervousness. She was probably overthinking because she felt guilty about lying.

She looked back up. "So, are you going back home now?"

"Yes, I think it's time."

"Well, it was fun having you here for a little while. And if you ever need to come back, the door is always open for you, of course."

"Thank you, but I don't think I'll need to," Kameela waved her off. "Nova, if you ever need my help or if you need to talk to me about anything, I hope you know that I'm here for you too."

Why was she saying that? It was not what she said, but the tone she used. It was accusatory. No, no. She probably wanted her to know that she should expect reciprocity from their friendship. "Of course, I know that." They hugged goodbye. "Text me when you make it home."

"I will. Thank you so much for helping me through this." Kameela blew a kiss and walked out.

Nova was happy she helped her friend, but most importantly, she was happy that she was leaving. The past few days had been so nerve-racking with her having to hide the mirror and mask her travels with a nightly bath. On one hand, she was thrilled she was gone, so her secret could be safe. On the other, she wondered if it was the right time for Kameela to go back home. She felt like her friend was settling for a setup she did not want in order to avoid a difficult conversation. To her credit, she tried to voice her concerns and give her opinion. That was all she could do. Perhaps that level of compromise was what it took to make a marriage work. What did she know, anyway? She was just now going on a couple of dates—with the assistance of a magic mirror—after years of spending her weekends telling Netflix that she was still watching. Kameela knew better than her when it came to relationships. She had made the right decision for herself and her marriage.

The next day, Nova walked into *Fit Gals and Pals* with an absent mind. Her body was present, but the rest of her was already in front of the mirror, ready to be transported to the better side.

"Hi, Jeff."

"Hey, Nova. Let's all meet in the common area at 10, okay?"

Her heart sank. The announcement was today. "Okay."

Paul's grin was making her skin crawl with irritation. "Hi, Nova! How are you this morning?" he said. He was more animated than a Pixar character. How was that humanly possible?

"I'm good. Yourself?" She struggled to get the question out.

"I'm freaking fantastic! It's an amazing day, ya know!"

She sat in silence. Waiting to hear the official announcement that what should have been hers was now someone else. Someone she could not stand. She felt defeated. For once, she wanted time to go slow on this side, so the announcement of Paul's promotion could remain in the treacherous future. But ten o'clock came fast. Too fast. She was not ready. The entire staff gathered around Jeff. Hakeem was standing next to Paul. She did not want to look his way. She was afraid her face would reveal all the anger and frustration she was trying to contain inside of her.

"Hello, everyone," Jeff greeted. A responding hello from

the crowd rose. "I have asked all of you guys to gather here today to make a quick announcement." Nova clenched her jaws to hide her emotions. "Paul has been promoted as our new assistant manager."

Everyone clapped, including Hakeem. "Congrats, man," he said, patting Paul's back.

Could he not see her? He knew how hard she had worked over the past years. He had been there for the last two. Why would he say that out loud, knowing she was the one deserving of this moment? Knowing she was standing there. Was she invisible to him?

"Would you like to say anything to the team?" Jeff turned to Paul.

"Yes. Jeff, first, I would like to thank you for trusting me to take over this position. I can promise all of you guys that I will do my best every single day to remain deserving of my new role. If any of you need anything, please do not hesitate to ask me. I'm honored to be a part of this amazing team. I am looking forward to help lead this gym to the next level!"

Everyone clapped in response. Congratulations rose above the sounds of dumbbells being dropped on the floor behind them. They all hugged him, shook his hand, or fist bumped him one by one. Nova observed silently. It should have been her. She looked down. It should have been her moment. She inhaled quietly. She remembered that this moment would be hers on the other side. She straightened her posture and looked back up. She did not want to appear envious, even though every part of her was. She reminded herself that she was a few hours away from being the one to be congratulated and hugged. That thought comforted her.

She walked toward Paul. "Congratulations." She gave

him a high five.

"Thanks, girl. I know it was between you and me, so I appreciate your sportsmanship," he replied, a smirk still angling the corner of his mouth.

She wondered how long it would take for a slap to erase it from his face. She put her hands behind her back as a preventative measure. She took another quiet breath. *A few hours away*, she repeated internally to stop herself from striking the left of his smug face with an open hand.

"Of course," she said out loud.

She immediately walked back to her desk when the meeting was adjourned. A familiar tap on her shoulder halted her steps.

"Are you okay?" Hakeem asked. His concerned look made her feel seen. He cared.

"Yes. Paul works hard, so he deserves it." *Not as much as me, though.*

"I know. But you have worked very hard as well. I'm sure it's disappointing."

"Yes, but it's okay."

"Alright, just wanted to check in on you." He punctuated the interaction with his sparkling and soothing smile.

"Thank you, I appreciate it." She cracked a timid grin.

"No problem." He walked away as quickly as he had walked toward her. A courtesy concern. Then, it meant the world to her. And that smile, that healing smile. She could not wait for their date on Saturday on the other side of the mirror.

Paul was up and down for the remainder of the day. She could overhear him tell all the members he was the new assistant manager and that they could go to him if they had any concerns. It was already unbearable.

"What a day!" he said to her when he finally sat back down.

"How does it feel to be the new assistant manager?" It took everything in her to ask him that question.

"I don't think it has fully registered yet. And my position does not actually take effect until Monday. But I'm feeling great," he said. "And I just want you to know nothing will change between the two of us. I know that you know what you are doing, so I will not need to be on your ass to get things done. But obviously, you can come to me if you have any questions."

That stupid smirk was permanently drawn on his face. The nerve of him to ask her to come to him for questions. She had basically trained him when he was getting started. But here he was, already asserting his new authority. She quickly nodded to end their exchange. This day could not end faster.

She got up to stroll around the gym. She could use this time to put misplaced pieces of equipment back to their rightful places. She never understood why people did not put dumbbells back where they belonged. At least close by. It was not that hard. Typically, she completed this task when she wanted to get close to Hakeem on the days when she did not have many consultations. But today, she was doing it solely to get away from Paul. She knew her frustration could be seen. She did not want Paul to know how bothered she was.

During her walk around the gym, she saw Lily in the distance. Their eyes met. Lily waved at her. She waved back and rapidly looked away. Something about her made Nova's insides knot. A gut feeling. She took a quick glance back at her. Lily was now walking toward her.

Christ! What could she possibly want?

"Hey, Nova. How are you?"

She was surprised that Lily remembered her name. "Hey, Lily. I'm great. How do you like the gym so far?"

"So far, so good. I'm glad I found *you*. I really think this will help me get back on track."

The way she said *you* sounded like she was talking about Nova and not the gym. "I don't think we got a chance to get into it yesterday, but what are your fitness goals?" she asked. This was one of the few times Nova cared to hear the answer to this question.

"Well, it's more so life goals than fitness goals."

Nova did not know what to make of Lily's strange demeanor. She did not have the time or energy to figure out random people's issues. She reckoned it would be best to dismiss it. As long as she did not direct her intense gaze toward Hakeem, Nova did not have any reason to be concerned by her peculiarity.

"Glad to hear. Have a good workout!" She put on her friendliest smile and walked back toward her desk. She could not dare to look back. She was certain Lily was standing there, staring at her walk away.

When she made it home, she called Kameela before traveling back to the other side. "Hey, I miss coming back home to you."

"Hey, Nova! I miss you too."

"Are you all settled back in?"

"Yes, ma'am. We had a good talk, and it's all good," she replied in one breath. "Bath time?"

"Yes. Paul got promoted to assistant manager today. I was hoping the position would be offered to me. Long story short, I need to melt my negative thoughts away."

"Nova, I'm sorry. That's such bullshit. You deserved it," she said, indignation dotting her i's and crossing her t's.

"I know, but apparently, I didn't make it known, so I guess it's my fault."

"I'm sorry."

"It's okay."

"If you need to talk about this or anything else, I'm here for you."

Again, with that suggestion and tone. It was not the fact that she offered a listening ear. It was the way she offered it. As if Kameela knew Nova was not telling her something, and she wanted Nova to know that she could do so. She was probably reading too much into it. Kameela was just being a good friend.

"I know, thank you."

They ended the conversation with the promise to catch up again soon. Nova secretly hoped Kameela was starting to feel closer to her than she did Ana. It was so pathetic. She was competing for friendship. She was looking to get her self-worth and validation by doing what exactly? Winning the Friendship Olympics when the other party was not even aware that it was a competition? It was not rock bottom yet, but she was getting close to the rock bottom exit. A U-turn was imperative.

8:05 PM.

Nova couldn't wait any longer. She slowly dragged the mirror outside of the closet. She could freely access her paradise again. She closed her eyes and allowed her lips to meet the magic glass. She felt her heartbeat stop for a few seconds and pick back up when she appeared on the other side.

CHAPTER 11

It was time to get ready for her date. Nova confirmed that red was definitely one of her colors when she noticed how well her scarlet dress complimented her complexion. She heard her phone vibrate on her bed and reluctantly walked away from her reflection. It was probably Naveen checking in.

"Hey! I'm fine. I'm still at Ana's. Josh called today and apologized. Long story short, I'm not satisfied with his apology. After talking to Ana, I think I need more time to figure out what I want to do. I'll keep you posted."

She had forgotten that she had texted Kameela before she left. She immediately recalled that on the real side, her talk with Kameela had not convinced her not to return home yet. Here, whatever Ana had said to her was enough to make her feel like she needed more time to consider her next step. Nova believed the reason Kameela did not take her feedback into consideration was that she was not married. She understood that. But Ana was not married either. In fact, her "relationships" rarely lasted more than a few months. Why would she value Ana's advice more than hers? It was becoming increasingly clear to Nova that Kameela and Ana thought less of her. They did not value her advice as much. She was the loser friend who was part of the group because of college nostalgia.

The sadness she felt was quickly washed away by that fluid energy that existed on this side. Its mist left her with confidence that their opinions of her would inevitably change in this reality. Kameela and Ana had yet to interact with her on this side of the mirror. They had no idea who she was here: the new *Fit Gals and Pals* assistant manager who was steadily getting all her life boxes checked. She could not wait for them to find out and see her in that new light. She was certain that whatever they thought of her would change the second they interacted with her *here*.

She texted Kameela back, "**Please do! Actually, why don't we all meet for drinks on Friday. I have something to share with you guys.**"

Her phone vibrated immediately. "**Am I about to become an auntie?**"

"**Unless it is a miracle, no,**" she replied with a laughing emoji. When she finished getting ready, she agreed with her reflection: beautiful. Naveen would be speechless.

"**Great. Ana is in. Our usual spot 8ish,**" Kameela wrote.

***

Everyone looked so elegant at *Blue Moon*, wearing their Sunday best and having conversations which stayed neatly between their respective parties. The dimmed lights, the blue velvet drapery, and the jazzy music selection created an ambiance that made you want to punctuate all your sentences with *darling*. Her red décolleté caused men and women to give her a double take when she walked in. It was more suggestive than revealing, but it was suggestive enough. Nova was fashionably late. Her attire called for such an entrance.

Naveen had let her know where he was seated. And there

he was, with his salmon dress shirt and his hair back in a bun. Even more handsome than she remembered. She walked slowly toward him, accentuating every step. Naomi Campbell would be proud. He turned around to watch her. She felt like no one else existed. The spotlight was on her. Only her.

"Wow. Ahem. Hello. Hi. You look stunning! Wow. Hmm…Yeah…How are you?" He got up to hug her and pulled her chair out for her.

She smiled. "Hi! You don't look too bad yourself."

"Every time we meet, you manage to look even more beautiful than the last."

"Well, thank you, Naveen." She continued to grin, looking directly into the brown of his eyes.

The waiter approached and took their drink orders in a formal tone. She felt adventurous, so she decided not to go with her usual strawberry margarita. The Manhattan sounded luxurious, so she went with that. Naveen ordered a Jack on the rocks.

"So, how is your week going so far?" he said the moment the server walked away.

"Wonderful, actually. I got promoted to assistant manager yesterday!"

"Congratulations!" He high fived her. "Beautiful and accomplished. I'm very happy for you. I know it's well deserved."

"Thank you! I'm happy for me too."

The drinks arrived promptly. The server took their food orders in an even more ceremonial manner than he had taken the drinks. His mannerisms could blend perfectly in Shakespeare's play. Nova went with the prime ribeye, medium rare, with a side of grilled asparagus. Naveen ordered the

Lobster tail with green beans. She would omit the foregoing meaty details when recounting the date to Kameela.

"Well, let's cheer to your promotion!"

After they raised their glasses, Nova spoke first, "Naveen, tell me more about yourself. What made you get into your field of work?"

He took a moment to think. She appreciated the consideration that went into all his responses. "To be honest, growing up lower caste in India, my parents strongly advised that I should pursue a stable career path, like a doctor or an engineer. They saw these options as the top two that would guarantee that I will live a better life and make a good living. I did not want to be around blood, so engineering was the better choice."

She had not expected such an honest, simple, and straightforward answer. Her parents had not suggested any professional careers for her. It was for the best. "If it wasn't for them, would you have preferred another route?"

"Honestly, I prefer not to think about it too much. Logically, I understand why they thought that. And they were right. I'm doing well. I do enjoy what I do for the most part."

He was answering her questions with a soft tone, but she sensed a stiffness buried behind his words. She did not want to push it. Not yet. She took a sip of her Manhattan without breaking eye contact.

"What about you, Nova? Last time, I shared my dating stories, and you did not tell me much about your romantic history."

She took another sip to give herself some time to think about her answer. There was not much to tell. Her longest relationship occurred her sophomore year of college. He was

116

a senior. It lasted a little over nine months. He was her first. The sex was okay. She cared for him, but she was not in love with him. They broke up soon after he graduated. Aside from that, she had no other non-platonic relationships worth the mention.

She had dated one guy she had met during her hiking phase: Bryan. It lasted close to five months. The sex was better. They ended things because they were on *two different wavelengths*, according to him. Whatever the hell that meant. She did not care. In addition to the summer heat, it was a good reason to stop hiking. Then she had a one-night stand, one soirée when she felt frisky. She had gone to the club with Ana.

Her audacious friend was all about it, of course. "Yes, girl, get you some! It has been months since what's his face," Ana had yelled over the loud music, right after chugging a shot.

She regretted her decision the next morning. The guy was not as cute as she remembered. At dawn, his jokes did not make her laugh. And for the life of her, she could not remember his name. The sex was horrible too. Never again. That was it. That was her dating history, if she could even call it that.

"My longest relationship was less than a year back in college. Since then, there hasn't honestly been anything worth mentioning," she said at last.

"I understand." He nodded.

"You did tell me about your online dating horror stories." She chuckled at the memory of his expression when he had recounted his catfish encounter. "But when was your last serious relationship?"

117

She immediately noticed the shift in his demeanor. He sat up straighter. His jaws tightened slightly. He took a sip. "It was about a year ago," he said. "We were together for two years." He looked down at something that wasn't there.

"We don't have to talk about it if you don't want to."

"No, it's okay. It didn't end well. I walked in on her sleeping with another guy."

He looked at the horizon for a moment. She let him get through the moment. "I'm sorry you went through that," she said.

She rested the palm of her left hand on top of the back of his right hand. The warmth was comforting.

"It's okay. She just wasn't my person. And if it didn't happen, I wouldn't be sitting here with you today."

He rested the palm of his left hand on top of the back of her right hand. The warmth was promising.

The meals arrived. She took a bite and instantly understood why no one could walk out of this place spending less than three figures. The food was outstanding.

"Oh, what is your astrological sign?" she remembered to ask after a couple of bites. She had forgotten to ask him on their first date. Kameela would want to know when they met on Friday.

He sighed. "The date was going so well." He shook his head in an exaggerated manner.

She laughed. "It's not for me! One of my friends is really into that, and this is part of her vetting process. I have to give her an update. Apparently, I'm mostly compatible with four signs. The odds are not in your favor, my friend."

"Oh boy. I'm a Taurus."

She gasped. "We are just off to a great start, aren't we?

You are one of the four!"

She was excited that they were astrologically compatible. She did not care for astrology, but an endorsement from the stars could not hurt.

"Phew." He wiped his forehead with the back of his hand in one dramatic motion. Nova watched him, amused.

The rest of the night went smoothly. Things with him were breezy. Simple. Easy. He shared that he had one younger brother in a medical school in London. He shared some fun travel stories. She shared that she was an only child. She did not tell him about her strict upbringing. Not yet. She shared the funniest thing she had heard during one of her many consultations at *Fit Gals and Pals*. One lady had told her that the main reason she was trying to lose weight was to get drunk faster. Nova emphasized that the lady was not joking.

"That is so funny! I feel motivated to shed a few pounds now." Naveen laughed loudly.

The restaurant was emptying as they continued to talk and laugh the night away. The server came to politely announce that they were closing soon. Nova thought that all his appearances needed to be preceded by trumpets. She looked at Naveen. They both were visibly disappointed that time had gone by so fast.

They got up and left after the bill was covered. Naveen slowly walked Nova to her car. They stood silently in front of the driver's side door. No word needed to be spoken. His lips looked like the dessert she was too full to order. He was staring directly at hers. He brought her closer, wrapped his arms around her waist tightly, and leaned in for a kiss. She yielded and closed her eyes. She had not felt this way in so long, maybe ever. She could hear her heart pounding inside her chest. Or was it his? She opened her eyes. He held her tight for another moment. She belonged inside his embrace.

"I had an amazing time," he finally said.

"Me too."

"Let's do it again very soon?"

"Absolutely!"

He opened her door. She gave him a final kiss on the cheek and drove off under the star-filled night.

The next morning, she woke up with Naveen occupying her entire brain's real estate. She walked into work with last night playing in her mind, on a loop.

She almost did not hear Jeff. "Nova," he said louder, motioning for her to come his way. She walked toward him, knowing what he would say.

"Hey, Jeff!"

"Hi. So, I will be announcing to the rest of the team that you are our new assistant manager today. We will all meet in the common area in the next couple of hours. You are welcome to say something, but do not feel obligated. This is just a quick FYI."

"Got it." She wondered if her feet were meeting the ground on her walk to her desk. She had to be levitating with excitement.

"Hey, Nova."

"Hey, Paul!" She could not contain her grin.

"Someone is in a great mood, I see."

"It's an amazing day, ya know," she said enthusiastically, mimicking his energy on the real side of the mirror.

He looked, furrowed brow. She knew she was not the Nova he had gotten used to. She could tell he was bemused. She had been waiting for this moment since his little speech in reality. It was her turn to look at the disappointment in his eyes while people were clapping for her and congratulating her.

"Apparently, the entire staff is meeting in the common area at 11. I wonder what it's about," he said.

She shrugged. Time needed to speed up. It did. A couple of hours flew by like minutes. They all gathered in the back room. Hakeem was standing on the opposite side of her, next to Paul. She glanced his way when Jeff spoke.

"Hello, everyone," he said to a responding hello from the crowd. "I have asked all of you guys to gather here today to make a quick announcement." She could hardly contain her elation. "Nova has been promoted as our new assistant manager!"

Applause erupted. "Congratulations, Nova," Hakeem said, smiling and clapping. Other people were congratulating her too, but she could only hear his voice.

"Would you like to say anything to the team?" Jeff asked her.

It felt like a dream. In a sense, it was. No, this was different. She was in her physical body. These emotions were real. This experience was real. This moment was real. This was real.

"Wow," she began. "I'm so thankful. Thank you, Jeff, for entrusting me to become *Fit Gals and Pals* new assistant manager." She paused. Tears came up. She was a lot more emotional than she had anticipated. "And to you guys, I'm so thankful to be part of such a wonderful team. I promise you all to do my best every day. Thank you," she ended before her voice went hoarse.

More applause. More congratulations. Hugs, fist bumps,

and high fives.

"Congratulations, Nova," Paul high fived her quickly and walked back to his desk. She took a mental screenshot of his discontented expression, knowing she would need to visualize it on the other side when he would inevitably get on her nerves. Here, she needed the image frame to savor the moment.

Hakeem was standing still behind the crowd. He walked toward her with the widest grin when everyone dispersed. "Nova, I'm so happy for you. Congratulations!" His hug almost lifted her off the ground.

"Thank you!" She wished no one else was around, so the moment could last longer.

"We are definitely celebrating on Saturday," he whispered in her ear.

She felt goosebumps rising on top of her skin. "Can't wait," she murmured as they parted ways.

The rest of the day felt like a movie she was both starring in and watching from afar. Paul was remarkably quiet. He made a noticeable effort to look very busy. She chuckled the few times she looked his way and caught him staring at his screen intensely, typing vigorously, or turning the pages of his notebook very seriously. A few members who heard the news came to her desk to congratulate her. Alicia, who she had signed up a couple of weeks ago, was one of them. She looked like she had lost a few pounds. She mentioned how happy she was to have such an eye candy as her personal trainer.

"My husband doesn't understand how I'm so motivated to come to the gym almost every day," she said. "I think if he saw Hakeem, he would sign up too." She cackled.

Nova was happy to see the change in Alicia's energy. She

remembered the day she had come in for her first consultation. She was timid and hesitant. And here she was just a couple of weeks in, cheerful and lively. Nova felt proud of her job. She was proud of herself for the positive impact she had on someone's life.

When she got home, she took a moment to reflect before traveling back. What if she used the mirror forever? Okay, maybe not forever, but at least for a very long time. Carole did not mention there was an expiration date. She would not stay on this side for twenty hours, but what if she kept the mirror for a while, a long while. Things were just so easy here. The effort it would take to replicate what was already happening here on the other side made her feel anxious. Why did she have to stop using the mirror when everything was effortlessly happening the way she wanted to on this side? Perhaps the mirror was meant to be a part of her life forever. Upon further reflection, she came to a simple conclusion. She would go see Carole on the real side the following Saturday to get some clarity. She would get more tools to make a sound decision then.

7:38 PM.

Eyes closed. Sigh. Pause. Eyes opened. Inhale. Eyes closed again. Lips against glass. Dread.

CHAPTER 12

Reality.

Naveen asked Golibe to meet him for drinks when they got off work. He needed his advice. He had decided not to tell him about his date with Nova because it had not gone as well as he had expected. It was not a bad date, but he had hoped to feel a spark. However, that initial fire never got lit during their conversation. Yet, he had been thinking about her since. The conversation was okay. There was some potential. She just seemed absent. Something was obviously preoccupying her. Perhaps it was the situation with her friend which had caused her to be late. But she looked unbothered when he brought it up. Her response when he asked if her friend was fine had given the impression that the situation was trivial.

For a moment, he thought Nova had another guy on her mind. The date with him was a way for her to occupy her thoughts and time when she was thinking about and wishing to be with someone else. After a few days of reflection, he had realized it was quite a leap he had made. First dates could be awkward, even with someone that one was into. And he was very much into her. He still remembered how beautiful she looked when she walked in. Behind her awkwardness, he recognized there was a person worth getting to know. He had jumped to conclusions prematurely. The situation with Michelle had done a number on him. His alarm bells were always on, and sometimes they untimely rang as a defense mechanism. He now realized this was one of those instances.

He was thinking about messaging Nova yesterday, but then he received a message from Michelle, *"Hey, Nav. This is Michelle. I know you don't want to talk to me. I'm so sorry for hurting you. I love you. I miss you. Please give me a chance to talk to you. I'm not trying to justify anything. I just want to tell you what happened. Please forgive me. I love you. Call me."*

He had promised himself never to even glance at that chapter of his life again. However, he would have been lying to himself if he did not admit that he wanted to know the "why" behind her actions. Maybe if he had something else going on with someone else, even if it were still in the infancy stage, maybe in that instance, he would have shrugged it off and ignored her. Maybe. But in the situation he was in, the need for answers felt necessary. If he wanted to move on completely and potentially give it a shot with Nova or anyone else, he needed to get clarity from Michelle. But he was not sure how to go about things. Entered Golibe.

"Hey, Go!"

"Hey, bro, you got off early today," Golibe said when he sat down.

"Yeah, I just had to get some testing done today."

"Got you." He nodded. "So, to what do I owe the pleasure of you asking me out for drinks, mate?" he asked with an attempted British accent.

"Michelle called me and left a message saying that she wants to talk and tell me what happened."

Golibe opened his eyes wide in disbelief. "Now? After a

year? What else did she say?"

"Basically, she is sorry for hurting me. She misses me. Apparently, her goal is not to justify anything but just to tell me what happened. Oh, and apparently, she still loves me."

His mouth was now as wide open as his eyes. "I'm actually at a loss for words."

"A rare sight." Naveen laughed.

He ignored the teasing remark. "So, what do you want to do?'

"To answer that, I have to tell you that I went on a date with this girl that I met at the grocery store about a week ago."

"Okay?"

"It was just an okay date, so I didn't think I needed to mention it. But she has been on my mind since. I was thinking about reaching out to her yesterday, but then I got that voicemail from Michelle."

"Do you still have feelings for her?"

"No, I don't. But I would be lying if I said that I have not been wondering why she did what she did. I was completely blindsided. I thought we were good. I was going to propose, man."

"I know, bro. So, you are looking to get closure?"

"I think so, yes. Well, not really. I just need some answers. Like why, you know? I thought she was it."

"Damn. I get it. Do you think there is any way you would get back with her if the reason she did what she did," he paused, then continued, "and I can't possibly see how, but what if the reason she cheated…made sense? Would you entertain the thought of giving her another chance?"

"I can't think of a single scenario where cheating would be justifiable, so no. The trust has been broken and cannot be repaired. But I still would like to know why so we could potentially be cordial at the very least, since she meant a lot to me for a long time."

Golibe nodded vigorously. "I agree. If Ada did that I would have been done with her completely, so I understand."

"How are things going with you two, anyway? It seems like you guys have been smooth sailing lately."

He pursed his lips. "I thought so too, but she basically gave me a deadline to propose yesterday."

"Wow. Did she give you an actual date?"

"She said, and I quote, *I need my title to be upgraded from girlfriend to fiancée within the next six months; otherwise, I'll have to move on to someone who is ready for what I'm looking for,*" he recounted with a higher pitch, his best Ada's impression.

"Damn. At least she was honest and upfront. So, what is your next move?"

"I guess I have six months to figure out if she is the person that I want to spend the rest of my life with."

"You don't know yet?"

"I think she might be, but I still have doubts. And I just don't know if I'm ready for a lifetime commitment. Divorce is not an option for me, so I really need to be one hundred percent sure and ready before I jump the broom. And at this very moment, I'm not."

"Do you think you'll be able to figure it out within the next six months?"

"I hope so, oh." He sighed. "Anyways, meet up with Michelle and get the closure and answers you need. Once that is done, contact the grocery store girl and ask her out on a second date to see if there is something worth pursuing there." He took a sip of his drink. "What's her name, by the

128

way?"

"Nova."

***

This day felt like a chore. Workdays were never that exciting for her on the real side. However, today felt especially excruciating with Paul being formally announced as the new assistant manager. She could almost hear every single breath he took. It seemed like he was actively trying to get under her skin. Every movement that he made looked theatrical and exaggerated. He had probably spoken to every single member who had walked in today to let them know that he was promoted, and that he was the one they needed to go to if they had any urgent matters.

It did not help that when she looked over the free weights area, she saw Hakeem interacting with Lily. She had not seen who had approached the other, although she had a feeling he did. She could not blame him; the girl was stunning. Although, she still was assured something was off about her. Hakeem was probably too distracted by her looks to notice. Thankfully, Ana had confirmed that she could meet her at 6:00 PM for drinks. At least she had something to look forward to.

She rushed home as soon as the clock displayed that it was an hour till her meeting with Ana. According to her travel notes, the last time she got back, it was 8:28 PM. So, her plan was to be back in front of the mirror by 8:00 PM. Their meet-up spot was less than ten minutes from her place. She would make sure her rendezvous with Ana didn't go over an hour and a half. That way, she would have plenty of time to get ready to travel back there. She could not wait to be back *there*.

Nova had considered rescheduling their meetup for later

in the evening after she had gotten back from the other side. However, she wanted to meet with Ana here before she met with Kameela and Ana on the other side. She wanted to make sure things were fine with Ana on this side before she saw her on the magic side. She was confident things would go well on the other side, but she needed them to go well on the real side first. She did not want to consciously or even unconsciously leverage any information she would have gathered on the other side during her conversation with Ana on this side. She wanted an organic win here. Something that would excite her when it was time for her lips to meet the glass and get back to reality.

Nova walked inside the restaurant at 6:02 PM. Her friend was already there.

"Hey, gorgeous," Ana greeted her.

"Hello, Miss Tadhana!" Nova leaned in for a hug. "I hope you haven't been waiting for too long."

"Please don't call me that." She half-smiled. "And not at all, I just got here."

Nova never understood why Ana did not like to be called by her full name. She had always thought it was so beautiful. She sat down, and the server immediately came by to take their orders. Ana ordered a long island iced tea, and Nova went with her usual strawberry margarita. She was not feeling very adventurous. Perhaps it was the familiarity of the place. The brightness of the lights. The noisiness of the crowd. Or perhaps it was the absence of the magic boost of the mirror.

"How have you been? How is everything going with your new role at work?"

"I love it!" Ana said. "It's a lot of work, though. I'm in charge of developing new marketing and advertising strategies. I'm also managing the budget for our new campaigns. I've been putting in a lot of hours to pay my dues, so I had to end things with Luke. He felt like I did not have any time left for our relationship, and I agreed."

Who the hell was Luke? Oh, the guy from accounting. The latest casualty in her corporate ladder climb. Nova felt a sense of relief at Ana casually sharing the news with her. She had been so hurt hearing about Ana's life updates from Kameela. She felt even more distanced from her then. But here Ana was, catching up her with no hesitation. Pulling her back closer. Nova realized she had overreacted. They were fine.

"I'm sorry it didn't work out with Luke," she said his name as if she had known it all along. "But I'm glad things are going well at work. At this pace, you'll be running that place in no time."

"That's the plan." Ana took a sip. "What's going on with you?"

Nova desperately wished she had some exciting news to share. "Hmm, not much. Paul got promoted to assistant manager yesterday, so I'm kind of bummed about that. I was hoping they would have offered me the position instead." *Like they did on the other side.*

"Did you make your interest in the position known?"

"Not really, but I have been working there longer than him, and I've been very consistent. I was hoping they'd recognize that."

"You can't expect to be offered something if people don't even know you want it," Ana countered firmly.

Nova was used to her frankness, but the sharpness of her delivery cut deeper than she was prepared for. "I know, but I feel like it's not fair. It seems like things never go my way. I can't win." She sighed.

"Fucking Christ, Nova. I love you, but you have got to stop this pity party. Every time we meet, you complain about something. We give you some encouragement and advice, but you do very little to nothing to change your circumstances. If you hate your job, quit and find something else. If you want to be promoted, let your manager know that you are interested in a promotion. If you want a man, put yourself out there. You cannot complain your way into betterment. It's starting to look like you enjoy feeling sorry for yourself."

Silence.

Nova did not know how to react. She could feel tears hinting at their arrival. What emotion was she even feeling? It was not quite anger; it was an emotion neighboring indignation. Those words were unfair, and the delivery was uncalled for. She was merely confiding to her friend about how she felt regarding something she had deemed unjust. She needed a listening ear. She wanted her friend to be supportive, to be on her side and let her know that it was all going to be okay. Instead, she got a condescending lecture. It did not feel like it was coming from a loving place, either. She had been right all along. They had drifted apart over the years. Someone who cared about her wouldn't have spoken to her in that manner.

She cleared her throat before speaking. "Thank you for letting me know how you feel about me. I'm sorry I don't have my shit together like you. I'm sorry I'm such a fucking loser and that I've been a burden in your life over the last few years. Don't worry, you won't have to deal with my self-pitying ass anymore."

Tears rushed down her cheeks. She stood up in one brusque motion, slammed some cash on the table, and stormed out.

"Nova, wait!" She heard as she got in her car. She drove away without looking back.

7:56 PM.

She had gotten a few calls from Ana since she had made it back home. She did not answer. Then a text. **"We need to talk. I'm sorry if what I said came out as hurtful. Call me."** *I'm sorry if what I said came out as hurtful?* She was not sorry that she had said those words to her. She was sorry that Nova was too weak to handle what she considered the truth. She had hoped that her meeting with Ana would have helped them rekindle their friendship. Instead, she discovered that one of her closest friends thought of her as a person who wallowed in her own misery.

The most hurtful part was that if she was being brutally honest with herself, she did. At the core, she had felt hurt because someone else had told her an uncomfortable truth she had not been courageous enough to tell herself. She was upset that Ana had vocalized what she had kept quiet, hidden inside of her deepest parts. Now that Ana had said those words out loud, Nova did not have a hiding place anymore. Not on this side, at least.

8:01 PM. Lips against glass. Eyes closed. Refuge.

CHAPTER 13

7:38 PM.
The moment Nova was transported to the magic side, she immediately felt all her anguish evaporate. The situation with Ana was still alive in her memory. However, all the feelings that she had toward it dissipated the second her lips met the glass. All her negative emotions disappeared the instant she was shaken by the motion of the transport to the other side. She now saw the encounter in her mind as if she were an objective bystander, merely a spectator. She still recognized that it was her, but she felt very detached from those circumstances.

Here, she felt the joy from the announcement of her promotion. She felt excited about the potential of a relationship with Naveen. She also felt the cheerful anticipation for her first date with Hakeem and what that could lead to. She even felt more excited about meeting her two best friends in the evening for the first time on this side. She recognized she had not liked how Ana had delivered her opinion on the real side. But that had happened *there*, not *here*. Nova was convinced that the second her friends would interact with her on this side, whatever opinion Ana (and even Kameela) had formed of her over the last few years would change. She would not hold what happened in reality against

Ana. Here, she chose peace, love, and happiness. Oh god, was she about to hang framed clichés on her wall? The thought made her smile. She was happy *here*.

Her last day as a mere sales rep was coming to an end. The same effort that Paul had put into the theatrics of making everyone—and especially her, she was convinced—know that he was the new assistant manager on the real side, he had put into avoiding making eye contact with her on this side.

The day was uneventful otherwise. Jeff had let her know that she would be in charge of training the new hire. She had conducted most of Paul's training, so it would not be a challenging task. It seemed that most of her tasks were the same: meeting with prospective clients via sales walk-throughs, contacting leads, and making sure existing members were satisfied with their services. Her added responsibilities would be to conduct some of the inventory counts, train new hires, and make sure offers were up to date against competitors. She had previously helped with those tasks. They were not that much of an additional workload. She was essentially doing the same amount of work for a higher pay and a better job title on her resume. Life was looking sweet 'round these parts.

"**Can't wait for tomorrow**," Hakeem texted her.

She scanned the floor to find him. Their eyes met. He smiled. She smiled back. "Life is good," she whispered for her own sake.

When she got home, she immediately checked her travel entries. Per her twenty-three-hour rule, she had to leave the good side at 6:38 PM. Travel times would become tricky soon. She would have to figure out a plan to travel during work hours. She was planning on going to see Carole tomorrow, on the real side. Nova hoped she would give her some advice on how to navigate her travels across both sides. She had already written down a few questions to ask her. She could add that one to the list. Carole told her it was her responsibility to make sure things went smoothly for her while she had the mirror. Thus, Nova felt no shame knowing she would show up there unannounced with a laundry list of questions for her to answer. She was hoping to get enough clarity to decide what her next course of action should be.

6:38 PM. Eyes closed. Blurriness. Reality.

***

Carole gave her a smile that read, *I knew you would be back* when Nova appeared at the entrance. She directed her to sit on the same couch she was seated on when she learned that alternative realities existed. Like she had done the first time, Carole went to the front door and turned the open/closed sign around.

"How have you been, darling? It's good to see you again," she said, sitting down.

"I've been fine. A lot has happened since I last saw you. I was hoping you could answer some questions for me."

"Of course."

"Thank you," she said. "Can two people use the mirror at once?" she immediately asked.

Nova could see that Carole was both surprised at her query and amused by the abruptness of her delivery. "No. Whoever initially kissed or winked at their reflection after the previous owner has chosen to stay on the other side or stop using the mirror is the person who can travel across both sides," she answered in one poised breath. "Have you told anyone?"

"No, but I had a friend who stayed with me for a few days. I hid the mirror because I was worried that she would kiss or wink at it and be transported to the other side."

Carole nodded. "Unless you make the conscious decision to stay on the other side for twenty-four hours or to stop using the mirror altogether to stay in reality, no one else can use it while you do."

Nova felt relieved. She looked at her notes for the next question. "When I hid it, I had to drag it in my closet, and I was actually wondering what would happen if the mirror broke."

"It wouldn't, dear."

"Wait. Are you saying that this mirror is unbreakable?"

"Precisely."

Nova was shocked at that revelation until she realized she had been traveling in an alternate reality via said mirror. So, it being unbreakable was barely worth mentioning in comparison. She looked at her next question under Carole's amused grin.

The main question she had come to get an answer to was next. "How long do people typically keep the mirror? I'm thinking of keeping it for a long time."

"A few more days?" Carole furrowed her brow.

"A very long time," she replied, emphasizing *very*.

"Weeks?"

"Longer."

"Months?" Carole said, her pitch higher than normal.

"Years."

"Oh, dear." She gasped. "I warned you that this would get very addicti—"

"I'm not addicted," Nova cut her off. "It's just so much

easier on the other side. Everything is happening the way I want with minimum to no effort from me. I just want to enjoy that for a while. I don't want to stay on that side forever. I just need things to be easy...to go my way, right now. I will try to translate things on this side as you advised. I just think it's going to require a lot more time and effort than I expected. But I need things to be good right now, and they already are there."

At first glance, Carole's demeanor seemed unaffected by what Nova had shared. However, her deep blue ocean eyes whispered the unspoken. They seemed to say, *we have heard that speech many times, and we know how this story ends.*

"Darling, you are on a risky path," Carole said. "This is how it begins. First, you tell yourself that you will just keep the mirror for a little while longer. What's the harm? To answer your question, you can keep the mirror for as long as you want to. However, most people only have it for two to three weeks at the very most. Within the first week, most of them have made up their mind and have decided to stop using it or stay on the other side. If you allow it, the other side will look more and more like heaven, while reality will begin to look like a prison you need to escape from. I cannot emphasize this enough: no matter how great things seem *there*, the other side is not real."

Nova looked at her quietly. Carole was wrong. She remembered how she felt when the assistant manager's position was offered to her. She remembered how she felt inside of Hakeem's arms. Inside Naveen's embrace. And the softness of his lips. She couldn't feel it here, but she remembered. Those things happened. She had experienced them. It was an alternative reality. A parallel universe. Her unconscious mind. Whatever. Sure. But she was physically there. That is why she was gone in the real world. It was unclear how the time change worked. How the mirror worked. But what was clear was that it was her. A better her. The her she should be. The her that lived the life she deserved to live. She would not stay there forever. Just for a while, until she could figure out how to be that person in this reality. Carole did not understand. Perhaps she even wanted the mirror back for herself.

Nova ignored her plea. "So, there is no deadline. I can use it as long as I want, and no one can interfere until I choose to stop using it."

Carole sighed. She opened her mouth to say something but didn't. Nova could tell she wanted to talk her out of her decision, but in the midst, she understood it was pointless.

"Yes," was the only word she let out.

So far, Nova was satisfied with all the answers. She read the question at the bottom regarding Lily. "This is probably nothing. This girl came to the gym where I work to sign up for a membership on this side, but she never came on the other side. Is it possible to not meet someone that I have met on this side on the other one?"

Carole's body immediately stiffened. It looked like she was holding her breath. "Have you had any prior encounter with her in reality before you began using the mirror?"

"No, never," she said rapidly, concerned by Carole's uncharacteristic tense posture.

"As I told you last time, people on both sides are the same. The only person who is different is you. Outcomes with people only change when you have previously interacted with them. Are you sure you have never interacted with that person prior?"

"No." She was now anxious. Carole obviously knew what the non-appearance of Lily on the magic side signified. And it didn't seem like an inconsequential matter. "What does it mean?"

Carole took a breath in. "The only explanation would be that whoever that person is has previously owned the mirror. The only instance when someone that you have interacted with in reality would not be on the other side of the mirror is when they have previously owned the mirror. This person must have made the decision to stop using the mirror."

Nova's heart dropped somewhere around her belly button—or her solar plexus chakra, compliments to Kameela. Lily's odd behavior now made sense. *I'm so glad I found you,* she had said. She had specifically meant her and not *Fit Gals and Pals,* as Nova had suspected. Two people could not use the mirror at once, so what did she want from her? The only explanation was that she wanted to take the mirror from her. She wanted to steal her paradise.

"She wants the mirror back, doesn't she? She is going to try to steal it so that I would not use it for twenty-four hours. That way, she could kiss it or wink at it and become the owner again." Nova gasped. "God, I knew something was off about her. How did she even find me?"

"I have no idea, dear. What is her name?"

"Lily."

Carole shook her head slowly. She evidently knew who Lily was. "She is very troubled. I was surprised when she chose to stop using the mirror. I'm not surprised she changed her mind."

"So, I'm right, right? She wants to steal the mirror from

me?" Nova heart raced. She was not ready to give up her doorway to paradise. Whatever Lily had planned, she would not let it happen. No one would get in her way to happiness.

"The mirror cannot be stolen from the owner. If she attempts to take it, it will just come back to you. And it wouldn't allow her to get back to the other side anyway. Once a person stops using the mirror, they cannot go back to the other side on their own."

Nova frowned in confusion. "So, what does she want?"

"I'm not sure how she knows about this. Over the years that the mirror has been part of my life, it has only happened a couple of times." She stopped her speech.

"What has happened?"

"If a current owner and a previous owner kiss or wink at their reflection at the same time, they can essentially do a transfer of ownership. The person who gives up the mirror can never go back, under any circumstances. The former owner who gets the mirror back can return to the other side, but the rules might be different. It is not exactly clear how from the two instances that I know of. It seems like the time that they can spend on the other side is different, as well as some of the personality traits of the other people there." She paused for a moment. "For someone to want to get back there after they have stopped using the mirror, it would mean that they are truly desperate. They essentially are thrown in this other alternative reality where the rules are mostly unknown."

Nova covered her face with her palm to hide her frustration. "Why didn't you tell me all this when I came here the first time?"

"I could have never imagined that a previous owner

would track you down, dear. This almost never happens. Again, it has only happened twice in the forty-one years that the mirror has been a part of my life. I'm assuming she has been watching, waiting for someone to come in and purchase the mirror."

"If she knows where I work, she definitely knows where I live." Nova's eyes widened at the realization.

"Yes."

"Oh my god!"

"Darling, I want to reassure you. Everything requires volition when it comes to the mirror. Just like you cannot get accidentally stuck there and have to choose to stay, you would have to voluntarily choose to give up ownership if that is what she is after. She cannot threaten you or force you to do so, the magic will not happen, and I'm sure she knows it."

Nova chuckled, relieved. "So, she is hoping to convince me to willingly transfer the ownership of the mirror over to her?"

"I would assume so, yes."

Nova immediately felt at ease. She relaxed her shoulders. Her paradise was safe, and she had no intention of giving it up. Lily had her a chance. It was her turn. She was ready to get up and thank Carole for answering all her questions. The clock by the main entrance was in her line of sight. Time. She almost forgot to ask her final question.

"One final question, Carole. More so advice or a tip, if you don't mind?"

"I don't mind, darling. Ask away."

"So far, my travels have been in the evening, so it has not been an issue. But soon, the time that I would need to travel will conflict with my work schedule on the other side.

I'm not sure how to navigate that. Any advice?"

"This is one of the reasons people only keep the mirror for a couple of weeks. Some people take a few days off work. Some people take their lunch at different times. Some people find a way to sneak out. I recall one gentleman who drove a van and kept the mirror in there during those conflicting times. He told me that he would just pretend to step out to get on some air. You will have to get creative, darling."

Nova nodded in agreement. "I can definitely figure something out."

"Sure. But this will happen again the following week, then a couple of weeks after that. This can start affecting your life on the other side. You will have to make a decision soon, dear. Which side of the mirror do you want to stay on…forever?"

In this very moment, the answer to that question was ridiculously easy, at first glance at least: the other side. It was not even close. But no matter how much she was trying to convince herself the other side was real, deep down, she knew that it was not…not completely. Yes, she felt those emotions, and she was even physically there. However, if she stayed there, her physical body would return to reality in a state of coma. Only a piece of her being would stay on the other side to essentially live in her mind or some alternate reality. But was that so bad? What if she lived the life she wanted to live solely in her mind?

She had essentially been reliving scenarios the way she would have wanted them to have gone in the flesh in her mind for years. She recalled the time during the meeting with the elders when they asked her if she was still a virgin. She had nodded yes but had wanted to answer, "Fuck off, it's none of your business." And the fact that her parents had allowed that to happen. She should have told them how hurt, unprotected, and rejected she felt. Instead, she quietly accepted her role as the black sheep.

Oh, and when Bryan, her hiking ex, sent her that message out of nowhere, saying he wanted to end things because they were on two different wavelengths. She had simply answered by thanking him for the times spent together and by wishing him the best in his future endeavors; like it was a freaking job interview that did not go well. She had really wanted to say, "You could have at least called me, but I guess I shouldn't expect much from a guy who doesn't know the difference between your and you're. Have a nice life."

Or when Jeff let her know that the promotion had been offered to Paul and not her. Yes, she had not made her interest clearly known, but so what? He knew that she deserved it. He could have offered it to her regardless. She should have spoken up or walked out then. Something. She could have done more than simply accept what was positioned in front of her.

And she thought about when Ana told her the truth about her self-pitying behavior. Instead of going off and walking out, she could have handled things more maturely and talked it out. She could have also had a deeper conversation with Kameela before she left to go back to Josh. The point of the conversation would not have been to force her to do what she thought was best but to make sure Kameela felt heard. To make sure that her friend knew she would be there for her no matter what.

Then, Hakeem. How many times had their eyes met? What if she held a smile a little longer? What if she had hugged him a little tighter? And Naveen? They had not had an amazing first date, but she did like him. She could have contacted him. But she was too afraid. Afraid of what exactly? Taking a chance? At life? If she were so afraid to live fearlessly in reality, living happily in her mind could not be such a bad alternative.

Carole was right. She realistically could not keep the mirror forever. It would get too overwhelming and interfere with her paradisiacal experience. She would need to decide soon.

"I understand," she said to Carole. "To summarize, if I choose to stay on the other side, my body will return to reality in a state of coma, and I'll essentially live as the best version of myself on the other side."

"Yes."

"And what happens to the mirror?"

"It will find its way back to me."

"And if I choose to stop using the mirror?"

"The mirror will find its way back to me as well. You might or might not remember its existence. However, even if you do, you might not have specific memories of events or interactions with people. You might just generally remember how you felt there. Some people have more vivid and specific recollections, especially if they regret their decision to stay on the real side. Some people go on with their lives as if the mirror was just a dream."

Not only would she lose paradise, but she might also not remember most of it? A decision started to take form. Nova wanted to ask Carole about her story, but she was exhausted and overwhelmed by everything she had just learned. She could also hear the awaiting crowd's complaints growing louder outside. It was close to 8:30 AM now.

Carole did not look concerned. "Do you have any other questions, dear?"

"No, that is all. I think I'll try to make a decision soon. Thank you so much for answering all my questions and keeping your shop closed for me."

"You are welcome, darling. I could have used someone to guide me when I was in your shoes," she said, slowly getting up. "I think my customers are getting upset, so I should probably let them in now." She smiled. "I wish you the best of luck, and I hope you make the right decision for you."

"Thanks again, Carole. Goodbye."

***

Carole watched Nova walk out while she opened the front door to let her irritated customers in. She was transported back in time to when she was the owner of the mirror. She could see so much of herself in Nova. A twenty-something-year-old: insecure, timid, and fearful. Being on the other side had felt so liberating and empowering. She could finally be who she knew she was deep down. Live the life she deserved. Everything fell into place so quickly on the other side. Everything worked in her favor effortlessly. The man who had the mirror before her was not very helpful. He told her the basic rules: no more than twenty-four hours and staying on the other side would result in returning to the real side in a state of coma. If she stayed on the other side, she could live there as the best version of herself forever. A seductive offer.

There, her relationship with her then-husband improved miraculously whilst they were considering getting a divorce in reality. There, she had the courage to quit her bank teller job she hated and go back to school to begin her higher education. In reality, she kept her job and dreaded waking up every morning. It soon became clear that living on the other side, even if it meant living in her mind, was better than her reality.

That day, she had made her mind up the moment she winked at her reflection to be transported to the happy side. Twenty-three hours passed, and she stayed: assured. Another thirty minutes: doubts. Another fifteen: uncertainty grew. Another ten: the magic side, although paradisiacal, was not real. Deep down, she knew it. Another three minutes: was an ideal life in her mind better than a mediocre reality? Another minute: yes. Five seconds: Of course not! What the hell had she been thinking? She ran to get in front of the mirror and winked at her reflection.

One second. Eyes closed. Tentative static motion. Stillness. Darkness. Neither warmth nor coldness. Hesitant motion. Nothingness. Lingering nothingness. Eyes closed still. A hiss? Somethingness. Waters. Light shining through darkness. A familiar smell. Eyes opened.

Thank goodness, reality?

Carole walked to her cash register with an ambiguous air. She had never gotten an official explanation since there was not exactly a manual on how the mirror worked. However, she knew the reason the mirror had stayed with her after she had stopped using it. She had been so microscopely close to the twenty-four-hour mark when she attempted to return to reality that instead of getting stuck on the other side of the mirror, she got "stuck" with the mirror—at least that was how she felt initially. Somewhere between both sides. A sort of gatekeeper. She eventually came to terms with her fate. She accepted her role, honored. She was the guide who facilitated the exchange from the land to the waters...for *her*. It had been forty-one years now. She had witnessed hundreds of people decide, with her guidance, which side of the mirror they wanted to stay on. With her experience, she could easily tell whether someone would stop using the mirror or stay on the other side. The moment Nova put her eyes on the mirror and saw her reflection, Carole immediately knew which side she would choose.

CHAPTER 14

Michelle walked toward Naveen, her tread apprehensive and timid. She looked as beautiful as he remembered. She had let her silky dark hair grow past her tailbone. She had gained a few pounds, and it suited her. He was undeniably attracted to her still. However, the pounding that used to resonate inside of his chest every time he saw her was loudly absent.

"Hi, Nav, it's so good to see you," she said. Her voice was low, quieter than the vivacious woman he had dated for two years.

She seemed to want to get closer, hoping for a greeting hug, perhaps. But Naveen answered, immobile. "Hi." He had already ordered an Americano. "Would you like to order anything at the front before we start talking?"

"No, I'm fine. Thank you."

He gazed at her. He had almost forgotten the hazel of her gaze, the beauty mark on her right cheek, and the way she pinched her lips when she was nervous. "Why did you do it?" he finally asked.

She inhaled deeply and exhaled silently. "First, I sincerely would like to apologize for what I did. You did not deserve that." She paused, perhaps expecting an acknowledgment, but Naveen was wordless. "I wish I had some grandiose explanation, but I don't." She took a deep breath in. She sighed. "Nav, I was bored. I felt like we had fallen into a routine and became this old married couple before we even got married. I saw our future life together flashing in front of me, and it scared me. We did the same things every day. Every week. Movie night at your place on Mondays. Dinner at your place on Wednesdays. You would bring take-out to my place on Thursdays. We went out for drinks on Saturdays. We slept in on Sundays. We did the same exact things every single week for almost a year. When I tried to tell you that I wanted to try new things, explore new places, do something else, you just shrugged it off. You were happy with our routine, with things being the same...forever. I'm not blaming you. I was so wrong. But I was bored. I felt like I saw our entire lives already written, with no surprises. I wanted to try something new. I wanted to feel some excitement." She finally caught another breath. "I wanted some adventure."

Naveen was speechless. Until now, his silence had been a choice. However, at this moment, he did not speak because he did not know what to say. He was not sure what he had expected to hear, but "I was bored"? From his perspective, they had a terrific two years. Movie night at his place on Mondays! Dinner at his place on Wednesdays! He would bring takeout to her place on Thursdays! They went out to eat on Saturdays! They slept in on Sundays! To him, the routine they had established was comforting and reassuring. He thought he had found his forever. The person he had loved watching all the Godfather movies with. The person he had enjoyed Chinese takeout and cabernet with. The person he had loved waking up to on Sundays when the sun was close to its zenith. While he thought she had equally enjoyed those moments, she had been bored all along. He felt deep sadness and grief for what he thought they had at that time. Coming in today, he had expected to feel upset. However, he just felt sad.

"That day I came in was a Thursday. So, you wanted me to find out, right? That way, I would end things."

"Yes," she replied, choking on the one-syllable word. "And I have been regretting it ever since. That was a mistake. I just wanted to get a reaction out of you. I regret it so much. I know you loved me. And I loved you. I love you. You have no idea how much I regret doing what I did. I'm so sorry."

"You know, a couple of months after it happened, I was thinking about reaching out to you to ask what happened. To have a candid conversation with you. Then, I saw you with him. You looked happy, not regretful whatsoever."

She put her hands on her temples. "Nav, you completely cut me off, blocked me on everything. I tried for weeks to find a way to speak to you, but I had no way to reach you. I thought you wanted nothing to do with me. I felt alone, so I accepted to go on a couple of dates with the guy. It meant absolutely nothing! I do not have any feelings for him. I never did. It has always been you."

He furrowed his brow; something was not quite adding up. "But you found a way to reach out to me a few days ago. So, you could have done it then if you really wanted to. Why did you reach out now, after a year has passed?"

She sighed. "I saw you at *The Route* about a week ago with someone. You looked so handsome. So happy. I realized how much I had missed you and that I still love you. I never stopped loving you. You are the one, Nav. Please forgive me. Tell me what I need to do to make it right."

And there was the missing piece. Coming in, he had hoped she had been reflecting on what she did. He had hoped that after a year, she had found a way to verbalize the thoughts that had led her to carelessly break what they had built. He wanted an explanation that justified her actions, not because he wanted to get back with her, but because he wanted the relationship they had to remain in a special place in his heart. He wanted the memories of its first real relationship to remain sacred. He could never forget what she had done and get back with her. That was not an option. However, if her motive for cheating had been more meaningful, he could have forgiven her, thus, salvaging the integrity of his first love. But, she did not contact him because she had been thinking about him, regretful. She contacted him because she saw him with someone else and felt a sense of ownership. In her mind, his happiness only belonged to her.

"There is nothing you can do to make it right, Michelle."

"Nav, please! I fucked up, but you know that we are made for each other. Please give me another chance. Do not throw what we have away," she cried out.

"You threw it away." He got up quietly. "Take care," he said as he walked away from a teary Michelle.

There was so much on his mind he needed to sort through.

***

There was so much on her mind she needed to sort through.

The conversation with Carole had given her all the answers she thought she needed. But as she lay motionless on her bed, the real question remained unanswered: *To be or not to be?* Essentially, that was what it came down to, wasn't it?

Staying on the other side, *not to be*, essentially meant that she would be gone in reality forever. A sort of death. However, unlike Hamlet, she knew what would happen if she stopped existing in this reality: she would continue to live on the other side, paradise. And not the one her parents believed in. The one she had been in with her actual mind and her physical body. The one where she was the best version of herself, and everything worked in her favor. Yet, Carole's warning was still echoing within her: *it is not real, it is not real, it is not real…*

She needed more time to make her decision. Per Carole's advice, she would need to figure a way to get to the mirror on time when the travel times would begin to conflict with her work schedule. It would only last for a few days. For a couple of days, she could simply use her lunchtime. If she got on the toll road, her back-and-forth travel would be right around thirty minutes. She could get back to work just on time. The days when it was too early or too late for lunch, she could call in sick. Being recently promoted, she realized it would not be a good look. She had to preserve paradise. She sat up, hoping that a better idea would run through her mind.

Whilst her back was against her headboard, a thought rose. Promising. She could tell Jeff she would go business to business to drop some of their flyers to attract new prospects. She had done that a few times when she was initially hired. She had not enjoyed it, but that was her best option. She knew that Jeff would encourage her initiative. He would probably agree to give her an hour to do it; that way, she could get back to the gym and work with the new hire. An hour was enough. She could probably do it in about thirty minutes and use the rest of the time for her travels. Booyah!

She got up slowly. Now that she had figured out a plan

of action, she had nothing left to do on this side. Typically, when she was bored, she would message Kameela and sometimes Ana to strike up a conversation so she would not feel the melancholy behind her boredom. She still did not want to speak to Ana. Some of the anger she had for Ana had rubbed off on her sentiments toward Kameela. Nova was sure Kameela knew how Ana felt about her. Yet she did not warn her. She probably felt the same way, which would explain why Ana was able to convince her to take more time to reflect on her decision to go back home to Josh on the magic side. Kameela valued Ana's advice more simply because she respected her more. It was evident.

Now that Nova was here in reality, with the lack of option to band-aid her feeling of inadequacy by contacting her friends, dejection hit her like a bullet to the chest. She sat on her living room couch and cried uncontrollably. She cried because of who she was and who she was not. The tears cascaded to water her soul, her essence, which she had left to dry for years. Why did she let things get to this point? Why did she let the mundaneness of her day-to-day life take over her individuality? Why did she let life happen to her? She never took the time to figure out what kind of existence she wanted to live. She had no idea what things she genuinely enjoyed. What was she passionate about? Hell, she did not even have any hobbies. She simply existed, aimlessly.

She wiped her face and kept her hands over it. The tears lost their steam. However, the mist of her moroseness lingered. She knew how to make it go away.

7:43 PM. Lips against glass. *Not to be.* Paradise.

***

7:39 PM.

"We are on our way there. See you soon!" Kameela texted her.

Nova smiled when she read the text. It was amazing how light she felt on this side. If she smoked some marijuana here, she was certain that she would be convinced she could fly. She still remembered the first time she had smoked weed. Unsurprisingly, Ana had been the culprit. God only knew where she bought it. They met in Ana's dorm room. She and Kameela stood side by side, next to Ana, to "pass the blunt." Nova vividly recalled how she felt. The instant she inhaled the herb's fumes, it felt like someone had lit a match inside of her chest. She coughed uncontrollably for what felt like an eternity. Kameela and Ana laughed frantically in response. Eventually, the fire inside of her chest was replaced by an enveloping warmth and the cough lessened.

And then, she left earth.

It had to be heaven; she was sure of it. She could see every color in its purest form. Every word had a deeper meaning. Jokes were so much funnier because she understood them at their core. Although she could not see clearly, it was the clearest she had ever experienced everything. For an instant, she understood the meaning of life. Unfortunately, the morning after, when she woke up, she could not recall life's meaning and colors had regained their dullness. On this side of the mirror, it seemed that colors had retrieved the brightness and sheen she had only witnessed the first time she had gotten high. Life was making sense again on this side. She had found the sober access to heaven.

She got to *Lulu's*, their habitual meetup spot first. She had never noticed how eclectic and vibrant the décor was. There were funny signages all over the wall: *I drink to make other people more interesting. You're neat. There is nothing wrong with sobriety in moderation.* The last one she read made her give up a chuckle: *Liquor might not solve all your problems, but it's worth a shot.* The contrast between the beaded chandeliers and the silly alcohol puns worked somehow.

Suddenly, everything went dark. She instantly recognized Kameela's eucalyptus-scented perfume. She gently removed the hands covering her eyes.

"Hey, girl!" Kameela hugged her.

"Hey!" She beamed.

"Someone is glowing." Ana noticed and then embraced her.

"Thank you." Nova continued to grin.

She wished she could share the source of her glow with them. Actually, she did not. She enjoyed the fact that everyone believed this was just who she was, unassisted by magic.

"Nova, you look amazing! What have you been up to?" Kameela asked with a smirk and a raised eyebrow. Ana nodded in agreement, with a similar look on her face.

"Well, a few things," she began. "Drumroll, please," she demanded, giggling. Ana and Kameela immediately pounded on the table in rapid successive motions. "You are looking at *Fit Gals and Pals'* new assistant manager!"

"Yes! Congratulations, Nova. I'm so proud of you!" Ana instantly jumped to hug her.

Nova couldn't help but to think about how her rendezvous with Ana had gone on the real side. She now realized that Ana was not so much annoyed as she was disappointed. She could see through Nova's endless complaints, the fear to take a chance to figure out and pursue what she truly wanted. The hug Ana gave her was more telling than any other words she could have uttered. In the embrace, she heard what Ana had wanted to tell her over the years: *If you have the courage to go after what you want, you might just get it.*

"Oh my god, Nova! I'm so happy for you." Kameela embraced her.

Ana motioned to their server and ordered three shots. "To the new *Fit Gals and Pals* assistant manager," she chanted. They all raised their tiny glasses, struck them on the tables, and drank the liquor in one gulp.

Kameela was the first one to finish. She immediately stared at Nova. "You said that you have been up to a few things. So, in addition to the promotion, what else is new?" Before Nova could answer, she added with a smirk, "Although I'm sure that being promoted brightened your aura, I think that the source of your glow-up might also be non-work relat—"

"Who is he?" Ana cut Kameela off. She looked at Nova, moving her eyebrows up and down repeatedly.

"Naveen." Her heartbeat accelerated when she said his name.

"The guy who took you to *The Route*?" Ana said.

"Yes. We went on a second date on Wednesday to *Blue Moon*," she replied, looking up and to the side, with a wide tight-lipped smile, as if she was holding a juicy secret inside of her mouth.

Ana gasped. "You fucked him?"

She laughed. "Something a lot milder and north of that"

"She kissed him," Kameela sang.

"Deets!" Ana demanded.

"It was perfect! His lips were so soft. His grip was firm.

Our hearts were beating in unison. It felt like time stopped for a moment. It was...magical." She took a long deep breath in.

"Damn," Ana and Kameela said almost simultaneously.

"That's hot." Ana fanned herself.

"What's his sign?" Kameela inquired in a more serious tone.

Nova had expected that question and was proud to have the answer. "He is a Taurus."

Ana shook her head and giggled. Nova and she knew that the compatibility breakdown was loading. Kameela put her hands in front of her mouth before she spoke. Ana and Nova looked at each other, not sure whether it meant that the stars approved or disapproved.

"Water and earth, it is almost a perfect match," Kameela finally said. "You two will balance each other so well. You will water him, and he will ground you," she finished almost emotional.

"Sounds kind of dirty, can I join?" Ana giggled.

"Hell no! Your non-committal air sign behind would ruin it." Kameela rolled her eyes.

"C'mon, it's the perfect throuple! She will water him, he will ground her, and I can blow them." Ana laughed out loud.

Nova cackled uncontrollably. Kameela gave in and broke into laughter. The server came by to check in on them with a huge smile, seemingly hoping to glimpse their conversation. They ordered more drinks; the night was young and carefree.

"Enough about me," Nova said, still recovering from her laughter. "What is new with you two?"

"I guess I'll go," Kameela began. "As you know, I had an argument with Josh. The gist of the issue is that he believes when we got married, the understanding was that I would become a stay-at-home wife to easily transition into becoming a stay-at-home mom. I told him that I wanted to start working again, even if it was only part-time. He initially was opposed to it because, and I quote, *I'm thirty years old, and it is about damn time we start having kids.*" She said nothing else for a few seconds; those words had clearly hurt her deeply. "I guess I only have a few eggs left, and he wants a big family, so we need to start working on it like yesterday." Nova nodded empathically. She knew the story fairly well until that point. Ana, already in the know, was listening quietly, sipping her cocktail.

"He called a few days ago to apologize," she continued, gesturing air quotes while saying *apologize.* "It was obvious he was not really sorry and thought I overreacted. He said he could meet me halfway by giving me a year to work and get it out of my system. And after the year was up, preferably before, we would absolutely need to start growing our family. Of course, I will need to stay home until one of the kids is old enough to babysit the others because he doesn't want strangers to raise our kids." Ana continued to listen silently, shaking her head disapprovingly.

"Wow," was the only word that Nova uttered.

"Wow is right." Kameela half-smiled. "Thankfully Ana gave me some sound advice and I declined to return home under said obligations."

This was the part that Nova had been waiting on. What had Ana said to Kameela that Nova had failed to suggest on the real side. What advice was so profound that on this side, she took further time to reflect, whereas in reality, she concluded that going back home was the right decision.

Before Nova asked, as if she read her mind, Ana explained, "I told her that I did not want to speak out of turn, and obviously, I'm not married, but I do think that even in the confines of a marriage she should be able to do what makes her happy as an individual; and Josh should support her. I understand compromising, but he shouldn't give her a deadline as to when they should start having kids. She has the uterus, for fuck's sake. At the very least, her say is worth as much as his. They should equally come together on those big decisions."

A lot had happened since her conversation with Kameela about this very topic on the real side. However, she could have sworn she had given her almost the same exact advice. Ana's take was more elaborate and colorful. Sure. But essentially, the points made were identical. Once again, she was proven right. Kameela took Ana's advice and rejected Nova's because she respected Ana's opinion more than hers. It was undeniable. She felt a quick pinch to the gut, which lasted only a millisecond. It is almost as if all the negative feelings that she had toward the situation were washed away, awaiting her on the real side of the mirror.

Here she did not feel any animosity toward her two friends. In fact, she was proud of the support system they had built over the years. She could also tell they had immediately noticed that she was different on this side. Her aura had brightened, as Kameela had beautifully put it. She knew that on this side, Kameela would have valued her advice as much as she had valued Ana's. She knew that here, neither one of her friends saw her as a self-loathing loser. She was certain that soon, they would even come to admire her like she had admired them over the years.

"I couldn't agree more," Nova said.

"Me too," Kameela concurred. "I told him that I needed more time to reflect and decide how I wanted to move forward."

"What did he say?"

"I could hear the shock in his voice. He probably thought I would jump at the opportunity to go back home after his subpar apology. I think something clicked in his mind, and he realized that he could lose me. He told me to take the time that I needed."

After hearing that, Nova wished that she had commanded the respect needed for Kameela to follow her advice in reality. Had she been someone worth listening to there, Kameela would have stood her ground and the lightbulb would have clicked in Josh's mind on the real side too. The version of herself she was in reality had caused her friend to prematurely go back to an inadequate situation.

"What's your plan?" she asked Kameela.

"I'll give it a few more days, so he can feel the weight of my absence. Then, I'll have a serious conversation with him to establish that this is a partnership and not a dictatorship. At the end of the day, I love this man, and I know that he loves me. But this conversation is well overdue if we want to have a healthy marriage moving forward."

Ana snapped her fingers in agreement. "I'm proud of you for standing your ground."

"Me too." Nova beamed.

"Thank you so much, guys." Kameela wiped her face.

"Your turn." She pointed at Ana while a tear promenaded down her cheek.

Ana took a sip, then answered. "Not much has changed

on my end. I love my new role, but I have to put in a lot of hours to pay my dues. Kameela, you already know what I'm about to share." She paused, took another sip and directed her gaze toward Nova.

Nova also knew what she would say next since Ana had already shared the news with her on the real side. She felt a pull to display her "intuitive" skills. "You ended things with Luke," she said.

At first, Ana had a surprised look. Then she smiled quietly and took another sip of her drink. "Wow. I guess I've become very predictable."

Ana looked down for a moment. Nova regretted that she had said those words like they were a genuine guess and not the product of her travels across both sides of the mirror. However, if she were honest, Ana had become predictable; at least, with romantic relationships. Her number one priority was her career advancement, and she mindlessly discarded anything that dared to believe it could rival with it. Especially love.

"Guys, is something wrong with me?" Ana said, her eyes shining with concern.

It was the first time, in their years of friendship, that Nova had seen that look on her face. Ana was not afraid to express an extensive range of emotions: happiness, anger, frustration, amusement, determination, annoyance, etc. But the one she currently displayed was an emotion Nova did not think she had in her arsenal: vulnerability.

"Absolutely not," Kameela shouted. "You are the most badass boss bitch I know!"

Nova instantly shook her head in agreement. "I second that!"

"I know. But sometimes, I want to be a wimpy bitch. It just gets so exhausting being a badass all of the damn time." Ana drank the remaining of her watered-down cocktail.

In a weird way, Nova related to what she said. She considered herself to be that "wimpy bitch" on the real side of the mirror. She was on the opposite side of the effectiveness' spectrum, and it was exhausting being *that* all the time. It was a sort of revelation to witness someone who she believed had their life together admit that they were not entirely satisfied.

"Then don't be," Nova said. "It's okay to not be strong all of the time."

Kameela looked at her, her gaze widened with delight. "You took the words right out of my mouth, Nova." She turned toward Ana and her disposition intensified with the squaring of her shoulders. "Can I ask you something?" she said. Ana nodded, apprehensive. Kameela asked, "When it comes to your professional life, why do you feel like you cannot make any mistakes? Why do you put so much pressure on yourself to never fail at anything?"

This is something Nova and Kameela had discussed a few times over the years. They both appreciated and very much respected Ana's drive to win, to reach the top. But it seemed that it was deeper than the want to succeed. She was consumed by her work and seemed to care less and less about everything else, even their friendships. They had asked what it was about a few times, and she always waved it off as the desire to be as successful as she could be. Eventually, they believed that was all it was about, and they stopped asking. However today, she finally acknowledged this pursuit had become somewhat tiring for her.

165

Ana inhaled and exhaled deeply. She looked around. The crowd was growing progressively louder, occupying most of the colorful chairs, stools, and booths. "I have never shared this with you guys because I don't even think I quite understood what it was until more recently." Kameela looked like she was holding her breath and Nova stopped blinking, bracing for impact. "I don't know how to say it...," she paused and looked away.

Kameela got closer to her, and grabbed her hand, "It's okay, whatever it is, we are here for you."

"We will support you with whatever you need," Nova added.

Ana grabbed both of their hands and held them tightly, "I guess what I'm trying to say is..." Her sad expression suddenly transformed into a mischievous grin. "I just don't like to lose, bitches. I'm a fucking perfectionist! Yes, it gets tiring sometimes, but I want to be the best at everything that I do. I want to be the most successful person that I can be." She laughed loudly, the sound covering the rowdy crowd. "Guys, I keep telling you this. There is no deeper meaning, I just want to win at life!"

Kameela snatched her hand away. "You bitch! I was thinking about how much I had in my savings for whatever trouble you had gotten yourself into."

"I almost dropped a freaking tear too," Nova said, shaking her head.

"I'm so sorry guys," Ana continued to laugh. "I had to." Her laughter took a slower pace. "I do think I need to slow down a bit, though. I was serious about that part. I think I need more balance. Also, I do want to eventually find my person and be in a committed relationship, have the white picket fence and whatever else is included in that package. At least my own version of it."

"Yeah, right." Kameela rolled her eyes.

"I'm serious," Ana said.

"She does look genuine this time." Nova smiled, amused by Ana's antics. "So, now that things ended with Luke; do you have anyone else in your line of sight?"

"Well, Nova, as a matter of fact, I do. My offer to blow both you and Naveen is still on the table."

They all roared with laughter. They continued to talk the length of the night, until the noisy crowd thinned out. The drinks were pouring, the laughter was incessant, and the sisterhood was invigorating. In a sober moment, Nova remembered that she was experiencing it all on the magic side of the mirror.

CHAPTER 15

Nova stumbled into her apartment, still laughing from her evening with the girls. God, she loved them so much. She face-planted on her bed, amused by her own clumsiness. She suddenly realized that she had not checked her phone since she had gotten to *Lulu's*. She turned around and opened her messages.

"**Hello there, Miss Nova! I hope you had a wonderful day. Mine was a bit hectic but good. When would you be available for us to meet?**" Naveen had texted her at 8:28 PM.

"**I'm excited for tomorrow. See you at 12:30!**" Hakeem followed about half an hour later.

After reading both messages, she motioned as if she was making a snow angel on top of her comforter. Her heartbeat was accelerating with the speed of the ups and downs of her arms and legs. She could not think of a time when she had been this excited about life.

"**Hello there, Prince Naveen. I did! And I'm glad that, though hectic, your day went well. I'm free on Tuesday.**" She added a smiley face and sent her response.

"**Can't wait!**" She messaged back to Hakeem.

***

He was sitting by the entrance, hardly able to sit still while waiting for Nova to walk in. Over the past few days, he had begun to see her in a different light. That day he had run into her at the bar, he still remembered how taken aback he was. Her toned back paired with that yellow dress initially seemed to be the culprit. However, something was different about her. Something below skin-deep. Emily was right, Nova was not who he would have typically gone for. If she was his type, he would have made a move two years ago when he started working at *Fit Gals and Pals*. It was obvious she had a huge crush on him. She always found an excuse to get close to him and connect with him any way she could during her shift. He had heard her sales pitch and knew she did not need his help to close any prospect. She brought them his way, so she could interact with him. It was a mixture of sweet and, honestly, a tad pathetic. But she was a nice girl, so he was happy to oblige.

However, something had changed over the past week. She was not the same Nova who would look away and trip over her words any time he looked at her and spoke to her. She had this new confidence, charm, and je ne sais quoi, which made her incredibly attractive. He had always found her cute, in a non-arousing type of way. But now, he was sexually attracted to her. He had even found himself a little jealous when she was obviously flirting with the long-haired guy at *Fit Gals and Pals* a few days ago. And lately, when he looked her way, he rarely caught her already looking at him, then suddenly looking away in a panic the moment their eyes met. Her new vibrance seemed to be paired with a growing aloofness toward him. Hakeem had to change that.

***

Nova walked in the restaurant with her auburn romper, as bright as the sunny Orlando weather. She had combed her hair out, so her big afro would frame her face. Hakeem was already there, facing the entrance decorated with seashells. His face lit up when he saw her. *What a gorgeous man.*

"You look amazing. I love your hair," he said. He hugged her tightly.

Had his arms gotten bigger? His hug felt like a shelter she wanted to dwell in. "Thank you." She grinned. "You look great too."

"Thank you," he said, matching her smile. The waitress took their order while chewing gum. She was wearing a shirt that read, *Beach, please.* "So, how's your weekend been so far?" Hakeem asked.

"Wonderful! I met with my two best friends yesterday for drinks. It was a great time! What about you?"

"Not as fun as yours," he said with a mild grin. "I got some cleaning done, ran some errands, and caught up with a friend for a bit."

"Sounds like a productive day." The server came back with their drinks. She absently laid them on the table and walked away without asking if they needed anything else. Nova took a sip of her drink. "Tell me, what does Hakeem enjoy doing when he is not training our beloved *Fit Gals and Pals'* members?"

He let out a single chuckle. "Well, as cliché as it might sound, I do enjoy working out a lot."

"I figured." She explicitly eyed his bulging biceps.

He laughed a lot harder than she had expected. "I also enjoy riding my motorcycle when I get a chance."

"I didn't know that you had a motorcycle. How fun!"

He perked up. "I can take you for a ride sometimes if you'd like."

"I would love to."

Their food came in. Hakeem took a bite of his waffle before he spoke. "What about you, Nova? What do you enjoy doing for fun?"

This was her most dreaded question. The one she had avoided asking herself for years. The true answer was that she was not sure. After work, she usually watched television, mostly reality shows, while she ate her dinner. She had enjoyed hiking for a few months, but that ended when she and Bryan parted ways. She worked out fairly often. However, it was not in a *I love working out* kind of way, more so in a *I need to maintain my health and wellness* type of way. She enjoyed picking up a book here and there, but not so frequently that it deserved to be mentioned, in her opinion. She used to love dancing and running when she was younger. Did that still count?

Thankfully, she had the zest needed on this side to give a satisfying answer. "Well, I enjoy going out with my friends for drinks. I enjoy watching some trash reality TV—don't judge me. Reading, hiking when I can, and working out as well." Although she had fluffed up her answer, those were the things she had tried, did somewhat often or pretty frequently, and that she actually enjoyed. As the words came out, she realized that even though her interests were not as thrilling and numerous as she had wished, she did have some interests.

"Wow, alright," he said. "And how the hell are you single?"

"Who said I was single?" She smirked and raised her glass.

He laughed vehemently. He focused his gaze on her face. "Nova, I'm very intrigued by you."

172

She leaned in, maintaining his deep stare. "Tell me more about that."

He bit his bottom lip. "I want to say a lot more, but I think I need to pace myself. I'm very attracted to you and hope that we can continue to get to know each other better."

She rested her hand on top of his vascular forearm. "I hope so too."

They continued to chat for a little while. Nova wasn't sure what she needed more of, but something was missing. He congratulated her again on her recent promotion. They talked about *Fit Gals and Pals* and joked about some of the odd members who frequented the establishment.

"There is no doubt in my mind he is a serial killer," Hakeem began. "There are fingers in Mark's freezer, I just know it. I can already hear the news headline: *Florida Man who attended 'Fit Gals and Pals' was determined to be the Southeast killer.*" He cackled nervously.

Nova giggled at the hint of seriousness in his tone. "What is the funniest headline you have seen about Florida Man?"

He shrugged. "I don't know. I don't really pay attention to that stuff. I just know Mark is very suspect."

She nodded with a tight-lip smile. The server came by to announce that it was the last call for the bottomless mimosas. "I think I'm all set, thank you."

"Could I have the check, please?" Hakeem politely motioned to the waitress.

"Thank you for brunch."

"Of course. Thank you for spending some time with me."

They walked slowly to her car, raving about the beautiful

weather like they had just met at the dentist's waiting room. Nova was not interested in that conversation. She was too busy listening to the accelerated pounding behind her breastbone as they were getting closer to her vehicle. Did she want to kiss him? Absolutely. Was it too soon? Perhaps. She had known him for two years and had wanted to taste his full lips since the very first day she saw him. However, this was their first date. What was the rule for this instance? Fuck the rules, she decided.

They stood in front of her car. "Well, thanks again. I had a wonderful time," she said while searching for her car keys inside her purse as slowly as she could, without making it obvious she had already found them.

"So did I." He opened his arms for a hug. She melted into it, eyes closed and heart throbbing.

When she finally became solid again and opened her eyes, Hakeem gently tilted her chin up and leaned in for a kiss. His lips felt as soft as they looked. Everything disappeared, even her own body. The only thing left in the universe was the point where her lips met his. This moment she had dreamed of turned out to be as amazing as she had imagined. When she eventually reopened her eyes, the sunlight warmed her back to reality.

"Wow," he said. "Nova Wright, I'm just...wow."

"Get in line." She kissed him on the cheek and got in her car. "See you on Monday." She waved goodbye to a speechless and smiling Hakeem.

When she made it back home, Nova couldn't stop thinking about how her date with Hakeem had gone. She had been dreaming about the moment she had just experienced for the past two years. He had looked at her the way she had wished for. He had kissed her the way she had wanted to be kissed by him. He had suggested a potential future she had been silently hoping for. However, even in the midst of their flirtatious banter and his suggestive stare, Naveen had crossed her mind. She couldn't help but compare the two.

She felt the bulk of her laughter with Hakeem in her cheeks, whereas with Naveen, she felt it in her belly. When Hakeem touched her, she sensed interest, yes, but mostly lust. She did not mind it. In fact, her crush toward him had not been devoid of it. However, when Naveen's touch met her skin, she felt a balanced mixture of passion and affection. To be fair to Hakeem, she had only been on one date with him. Perhaps she was also grading him on a more rigorous curve because she had wanted him before he had wanted her. Before the mirror. She approached it quietly.

The mirror. The magic mirror. Paradise. 6:38 PM. Brightness. Eyes closed.

***

The reality. The dreadful reality. Misery. 8:06 PM. Somberness. Eyes opened.

Nova had not heard from Ana since Friday evening. Yet, her words were still resonating in her mind, *It's starting to look like you enjoy feeling sorry for yourself.* It was so difficult to admit it, but she had overly indulged in self-pity over the last few years. Hell, she had the right to! Life had not been kind to her. Yes, everyone experienced hardships; however, she felt like her circumstances had been especially extreme.

Her thoughts transported her back to the last time she went back to Miami to visit her parents after she graduated college. The last time she saw them. The last time she spoke to them, before she was officially disfellowshipped. She could

175

never forget the look in their eyes as she drove away. It's not the quiet sadness in their gaze that had hurt. It was the sheer disappointment in their disposition. In their eyes, she was a failure. In their eyes, her worldly existence was worthless. God, how had that affected her. Her parents were her family, her foundation. They were her world. And if her world thought she was a failure and that her existence was worthless, perhaps it was true.

Kameela and Ana had been her rock then.

She had not shared her upbringing with them until she was disfellowshipped, completely shunned by her own family. She knew that she shouldn't, but she felt some shame because of it. She was hesitant to tell them, but she knew she had to. They were all she had. They were now the closest thing she had to a family. They had immediately been supportive and encouraging. They had checked in on her every day until she had begun to regain some sense of self. A few months later, she felt better. She began to somewhat come to terms with her circumstances. She established a comforting routine.

Then, that handsome personal trainer was hired. And every time she got close to him and he smiled at her, she felt a little better. She hung on to that.

Gym walk-throughs, smiles from Hakeem, TV binges, and occasional drinks with her girls. Her life slowly became very monotonous. At first, it felt comforting. She had constants, which made her feel safe. But before she realized it, the monotony became a hindrance. The safety that her routine provided shielded her from figuring out her life's purpose. Why was she here? The more time went by, the less she could figure it out, and the more she gave up trying to. Her parents' eyes had been right all along: her existence was worthless…on this side at least.

She had spent the entirety of her Sunday at home, lying on her living room couch with the television on. Though, she had no idea what Netflix had been showing her after she had let them know that she was still watching and to not ask her that question again. Her thoughts were overwhelming her. She was not sure how much longer she could handle feeling this way. She wanted to turn things around. The mirror had also shown her what life could be like if she made behavioral changes. She had been telling herself that those changes were minor: a little more enthusiasm, confidence, candor, and boldness. That was all. But boy, was it easier said than done.

Every single instance she had tried to apply those changes in reality, she was met with resistance, pushback, and rejection. When she gave her honest feedback to Kameela about the situation with Josh, she was reminded that she was not fit to give such advice. That she had essentially spoken out of turn. When she gathered the courage to make her interest in being promoted to Jeff known, she was informed that it was too little too late. When she attempted to be flirtatious with Naveen and replicate the banter they had on the other side, he ended the night early and never contacted her again. And when she tried to be vulnerable with Ana and let her know how she felt about not being promoted, she was told that her constant complaining was getting old. What was even the point of trying? She was obviously inadequate.

She could so clearly recall the way her parents had looked at her when she got in her car and left Miami for the last time. She had desperately hoped they had said a final word. An acknowledgment. Anything. She needed some reassurance that they loved her still. That her existence was meaningful to them still. But they had not uttered a single word. She did not even deserve a goodbye from her own flesh and blood. She no longer meant anything to them. And it was becoming increasingly clear she meant very little to everyone else…on this side at least.

Although she wanted to make the final decision to travel to the other side and stay there past the twenty-four-hour mark, she knew the implications were irreversible. But the more time went by, the harder it was getting to press her lips against the glass to get back to *this*. The moroseness she felt the moment she was transported back to reality was growing to become unbearable. Before the mirror, she had nothing to compare her actual lived reality to. Comparing it to her friends did not make her feel utterly inefficient. She was who she was, and they were who they were.

She felt some envy because she believed they navigated their lives so much better than she ever could. But she had made peace with her subpar existence. However, comparing herself to the better *her* was on a different sphere. She could actually witness a play-by-play on how much better her life could be if she was the person she wanted to be. Admittedly, in reality, it would take a lot more work and effort to become that person than she had anticipated. She was now questioning whether it was even possible. Yet, she felt like she owed it to *her* on the magicless side of the mirror to keep trying for a little longer. She just was not sure how much longer that was.

7:34 PM. Eyes closed. Lips against glass. Solace.

CHAPTER 16

Nova was certain that the sun was objectively brighter on this side of the mirror. It was a beautiful day outside, so she went to the outlet mall. She couldn't remember the last time she went shopping. She worked hard and was recently promoted: she deserved to treat herself. She checked her travel entries before she stepped outside. She had to leave this side at 5:38 PM. Perfect. She had a few hours to have some fun before she had to go back *there*.

As she was going from store to store at the mall, she was amused by the tenacity of her frugality. Not even magic could deter her from immediately looking for the clearance section in every single shop she walked into. She just could not justify paying full price when discounts existed, waiting in the back corner of the store for her. She grabbed a couple of dresses, some leggings, a pair of sandals, and her favorite foundation. Once her total passed the triple-digit mark, she readily accepted that it was time to close up shop. She looked at her watch: 3:14 PM. She still had a couple of hours to enjoy being on this side. She was less than fifteen minutes away from her apartment. She went inside the food court and ordered a smoothie. She sat in one of the chairs which at a moderate distance from the entrance.

Nova enjoyed people-watching. In fact, it was one of the

only things that made going to the Kingdom Hall tolerable toward the end. She put her sunglasses on and sipped her fruity beverage while she observed the nearby mall attendees. On her left was a family of four. The mom was watching the little girl and little boy closely. They looked like they were both in their preschool years, probably a year or two apart. The dad was watching too, but not as closely. Some of his focus was directed toward his phone, which sounded like it was playing some of the weekend games' highlights. The mom gestured at the dad to pay attention to the little boy, who was excited to showcase that all the vegetables previously on his plate were now in his tummy. The dad smiled faintly and directed his focus back to his phone under the mom's irritated gaze. Nova swallowed a giggle.

On her right, two teenage girls were taking selfies. The brunette one was directing the blonde. They snapped one picture and then looked at it with surgical scrutiny. The brunette shook her head and seemingly deleted the mediocre photo. She angled her phone higher than before. She directed her friend to bring her face closer to hers, turn her face to the right, and hold her smile longer. Click. They both looked at the image with a satisfied grin. Nova nodded approvingly, as if she had taken and seen the photo.

Before her, a couple, probably in their early twenties, was having an exchange that gradually appeared to intensify. Nova zeroed in her focus on their conversation. Yes, she was being a little nosey, but it sounded like something worth being nosey about.

"I feel like I have to force you to spend time with me," the girl said as loudly as she could whisper it.

"We are here, aren't we? You think that I want to spend

three hours at the mall? But I do it for you, and you don't even appreciate it," the guy replied, matching her volume.

"Oh. My. God. Heaven forbid we spend some time together doing something that I want to do. What a fucking sacrifice is it to spend some time with your girlfriend, dude. They should nominate you for the Nobel Prize!" Her pitch was a little higher but still low enough to qualify as a murmur.

"See, why do you always have to be so damn dramatic? Nothing I do is good enough."

"I just want you to want to spend time with me doing the things that I want to do too," she cried out.

"I can't do this right now." He got up and walked away.

Nova immediately looked down, even though she knew her sunglasses masked her eavesdropping stare. When she looked up again, the girl was sitting alone in tears. Perhaps it was the magic, or perhaps it was an organic feeling; but she felt a pull to check on the girl, to make sure she was okay. Why? This was none of her business. No, but she had to. Nova slid her glasses on top of her head and walked toward the young woman apprehensively.

"Hey, are you okay?" she whispered.

She was expecting the girl to give her a generic answer to shoo her away, but she didn't. "I just had a stupid fight with my boyfriend. I'm just tired of us arguing all the time." Nova sat down slowly to not startle her. She pulled her chair out in a manner that could only be compared to someone opening a fridge at 2 AM, after sneaking out of their room. "I feel like I'm not asking for much, you know. I go watch all the games that I don't really care about with him. I watch him play video games. Hang out with his friends. I spend time doing things that he enjoys with a genuine smile on my face," she continued, still in tears, "but every time I ask him to do things that I want to do, he acts like it's a fucking chore. I'm just tired of begging him to enjoy being with me no matter what we are doing the same way that I enjoy being with him."

It was a little more information that Nova was prepared for, but this was where her nosiness had led her. "How long have you guys been together?"

"Four years."

"Do you think he understands what you just explained to me?"

"Yes." She wiped her tears with the back of her hand. "I think he doesn't care enough about me to change. He doesn't love me anymore. I think that over the last couple of years, things have gradually gotten worse because he has wanted to end things, but he doesn't have the balls to do it. He just wants me to put two and two together, so that I could be the one to end it, that way, he can look like the good guy. Fucking coward." Her eyes were still red from the tears, but her tone was getting more assertive. "I was hoping that if I did more and compromised more, he would appreciate it and eventually meet me halfway. I was hoping things would go back to the way they used to be in the beginning. But deep down, I also know that it's time. It's been time. Four years is just a long time, you know. I feel like I just wasted four years of my life with someone who is not my soulmate."

"You haven't wasted your time," Nova said calmly. "During those four years, you have learned a lot about yourself. You have grown. You have experienced life, whether good or bad. You are who you are today because of the way life has shaped you over the past four years. Take the lessons from this relationship and work on becoming the best version of yourself."

Tears came back, running down the girl's eyes. She jumped to hug Nova. "Are you some type of fairy godmother or something?" They both laughed.

Nova looked at the time. 5:02 PM. Although she wanted to stay, she had to go. Or did she? What? Of course, she did.

"Maybe." She got up and winked at the girl who had this new confidence and resolve painted all over her face.

"Thank you so much." The girl waved goodbye to Nova.

"You're welcome. Take care of yourself."

Nova felt so satisfied on her drive home. She would have never dared to cold approach someone on the real side, but she was so glad she did *here*. The girl already knew what she wanted to do. She just needed someone to help her vocalize it, so she could act. Nova was glad she was that vehicle. It was empowering to deliver that speech; and how naturally it had come to her. She always had good advice and thoughts, but in reality, they mostly inhabited her mind. On this side, they jumped out seamlessly, like a rabbit out of a magician's hat. Except that here, it wasn't a trick. It was really magic.

Continue to work on becoming the best version of yourself, she had told the girl. What a hypocrite she was. Here she was advising someone to use their past experiences, good or bad, as learning lessons and tools for growth. She encouraged the girl to continue to work on becoming the best version of herself, whereas she was ready to throw in the towel on the real side. She was so close to staying on the magic side because, in this alternate reality, she didn't have to put in any work or effort to be the best *her*. To be fair to herself, she highly doubted that the mall girl had been completely shunned by her own family and disregarded by all the people she was close to.

Things had been a little more difficult for Nova, thus, the advice she had given the girl was not entirely applicable to herself. She had the right to indulge in a little bit of magic. She was owed that break by the universe.

She walked inside her apartment, straight to the mirror. She inhaled deeply as she faced her reflection. Staying on this side was irreversible. She was not ready to make her final decision. She still had some fight left in her. If she would choose to stay *here*, she wanted to make sure that she had given it her all *there*.

5:38 PM. Lips. Glass. Another chance, *to be?*

***

Back to reality.

Nova pushed the snooze button for the second time. A few minutes later, she felt her phone vibrate again. She slowly opened her eyes to find her phone on the other end of the bed. She checked the time. 8:09 AM. She stopped her alarm and slowly sat up. What would she not give for an extra hour of sleep today? She was not necessarily tired as much as she was dreading going to work.

First, it was the new sales representative's first day. And although she wouldn't have to train her because she was not the assistant manager on this side, she still had to introduce herself and put up a pleasant façade to disguise her having been robbed of the opportunity.

She would also have to deal with Paul's new managerial antics. Ugh. Then, Lily. She had to confront her and let her know that the jig was up. Whatever her plan was, she could stop the charade. Lily had her chance, and she blew it. It was Nova's turn, and she had no intention to give the mirror away. The only thing she was looking forward to was seeing

Hakeem. Though she was just his unremarkable coworker on this side, she could still look at him and daydream about their kiss on the other side to get through her day.

She walked into *Fit Gals and Pals* at 9:01 AM. Jeff looked up and gestured at her to come his way. She looked down and sighed as she walked toward him. What did he want to tell her exactly? She knew her role today. Do the same thing she had been doing for the last four years.

He skipped the greeting. "As you know, the new rep is starting today. Her name is Rose, by the way. Obviously, Paul will be training her. However, I know that you are the most experienced one, so I would appreciate if you could assist with any questions she might have that Paul may not know the answer to."

Then why the fuck did you promote him and not me? she said internally. Aloud, she said, "Will do." She made a lackluster attempt at a smile.

"Thank you, Nova," Jeff replied, then looked back at his computer.

She walked to her desk with a clenched jaw. Paul was not at his desk. Thank goodness because she needed a minute to exhale. Unfortunately, the moment she sat down, she saw Paul and someone dressed in their pink and blue uniform headed toward the sales cubicles.

Rose had a very amiable disposition which could be seen even from afar. Her short haircut complimented her chiseled jawline and sharp features. Nova could not hear Paul yet, but his dramatic hand motions were speaking for themselves. Rose was looking at him with a pleasant but slightly strained glance. It was clear she had already noticed Paul's antics and was just nodding and going along with them because she had to. Nova took an immediate liking to her then.

"Hey, Nova," Paul said louder than someone who was trying to have a conversation at the club. "This is Rose, our new sales rep."

Nova stood up and shook her hand. "Hey, Rose. It's nice to meet you."

"Nice to meet you too! I have heard great things about you." Rose held a pleasant grin.

Nova knew that it was the nice and professional thing to say, but the way Rose delivered it made her feel warm inside. Oh yeah, she would sell the hell out of those gym memberships.

"I hope so." She beamed at Rose.

"Yeah, Nova is great," Paul jumped in. He then directed his attention toward Rose. "So, do you have any questions about anything we just went over?"

"Yes, I have one question. What is the difference in commission between selling a new membership and an upgrade?"

Paul took a moment to think. "Hmm, good question. I believe it's fifteen percent more for selling a new membership versus an upgrade." He paused. "I might have to check with Jeff to make sure." After a moment of reflection, he reluctantly turned toward Nova, "Do you happen to know?"

It took everything in her not to stick her tongue out at him. "I do." She looked at Rose, "If you sell an 'unlimited' membership, the commission is sixteen percent higher than a standard upgrade. If you sell a 'select' membership, the commission is nine percent higher than a standard upgrade. The standard upgrade is basically having them go from the 'select' membership to the unlimited one, which is a six percent comm—"

"We went over what a standard upgrade is," Paul said. "Thank you for clarifying."

Rose focused on her. "Thank you, Nova. That was very helpful."

Nova tried to maintain her composure and ignore Paul's interjection. "You're welcome. Glad I can help."

Paul motioned at Rose to follow him, so they could finish her walk-through. She moved along behind him and gave Nova a sympathetic tight-lipped smile when she walked away. Great, the new girl was already seeing her as this pathetic person whom she could feel sorry for.

The next few hours went by slower than a severely dehydrated person in the desert, in search of an oasis. She looked around the floor a few times but could not find Hakeem. It was becoming increasingly difficult to predict his schedule and whereabouts. It almost felt like he was purposely trying to avoid her. She knew that it could not be the case. To try and avoid someone, one had to notice them.

Every time she took a glance around the gym, she saw Paul and Rose in a different area. A few times, she located them in spots they had previously been in. Rose looked a little more worn out every single time, which made Nova giggle uncontrollably. She felt validated for the way she had been feeling about Paul over the last few years.

The next time she looked over at the entrance, she saw Lily walk in. Finally! She was ready to deal with that situation. She immediately got up and fast-paced toward her. Lily stopped dead in her tracks the moment she spotted her.

"Hey, Nova, how ar—"

"Cut the crap! I know what you want," she said between

her teeth.

Lily's cheeks flushed. "What do you mean?"

"Carole told me."

Her face dropped. "I…Hmm…It's not…"

"Let's step outside. Follow me."

Lily nodded and followed her outside through the back exit. The second they were out Nova vomited her words. "I know what you are trying to do, and it will not work. You had your chance. It's my turn."

Lily squinted her eyes. "What do you think I'm trying to do exactly?"

"Can you stop acting oblivious? I will not transfer the ownership of the mirror over to you."

She bit her lip. "Oh. Carole did tell you."

Nova rolled her eyes. "So, what was your plan exactly? Signing up for a membership here, and then what? Between squats, try to convince me to give away the magic mirror that is allowing me to be the person I want to be. The mirror that is allowing me to start living the life I want to live." She stopped her speech for a second to catch her breath. "You had your chance. The mirror was yours, and for whatever reason, you decided to stop using it. And now you want me to give it away, so you can have it back? Sorry, it's not going to happen."

Lily looked down and away. "How long have you been using the mirror?"

"Nine to ten days, I think." A thought crossed her mind. "How did you find me, anyway? Did Carole tell you that I was the one who purchased the mirror?"

"No, she would never do that. I've been going to the café and dining across the street from *Magique Antiques* every day, waiting to see who will purchase the mirror. I saw you the first time that you came in. Then the same day, I saw the delivery guys get the mirror in the truck. I followed them to your apartment. Then, I followed you here. I'm sorry. I really need to get back there."

"This is insane."

Lily ignored her shock. "You are going to have to make a decision soon."

"I know that. Whatever my decision is, it's none of your concern."

"I would give everything to get back there."

"Then, why did you decide to stop using the mirror?"

"Things just got so crazy, Nova. I had it for eight days. I started confusing which events were happening between both sides. It got to the point where it started affecting me on the magic side. Don't get me wrong; the other side was still objectively better. However, because of my own mix-ups, I began to believe I could replicate the way I was there on the real side. So, I decided to stop using the mirror and give reality a shot. I was so wrong. Things went downhill quickly afterward. I almost lost everything here. I went back to Carole, and she reluctantly told me that the only way to get back to the magic side of the mirror would be to find a current owner who would willingly agree to do a transfer of ownership. The last three owners before you made their decision so quickly that I didn't have a chance to convince them. And then you. You have kept the mirror the longest out of all three of them. It's obvious that you are hesitant and want to stay in reality. And I think that you should."

Nova raised a brow. "Let me get this straight. You think the other side is so much better that you have tracked down the last four owners to try to hopefully convince them to willingly transfer the ownership back to you. But you think I should choose to stay here?"

"Yes, I think you should stay here. It would be in your best interest. Nova, the other side is not real. You know that."

"Please, do not patronize me. Don't act like this is genuine advice you are giving me. You do not have my best interest in mind here. Stop pretending. This is only for your own benefit. You gave up the mirror, and you regret it. Now you are trying to frame it as if you want the best for me." She shook her head. "If it's in my best interest to give up the mirror and choose reality. Why is it not in yours to do the same and stay here?"

"It's not that simple for me."

"Ditto."

Lily looked at the horizon like she was searching for something in the distance. "I'm battling some addictions here. Obviously, being on the other side is not a cure. But the best version of me has the strength to get the support that I need and not give up. There, I was so close to overcoming those demons just after one week. The moment I was transported there, I was equipped with the toughness and resilience that I have never been able to maintain here. I began to get clean there, and things just got better so quickly. I just had some hiccups and started confusing what was happening where. For a moment, I thought I could become the strong and resilient me on this side. I was so foolish to think that I could accomplish what I did on the magic side of the mirror in reality. I should have never given up the mirror. I have regretted it ever since. My life is falling apart now. The only thing that is getting me through is knowing I might have a chance to go back there." She took a moment to exhale. "I'm sure Carole told you that, in her opinion staying on the other side is essentially the equivalent of living in your mind. I think so too. But I'm okay with that. I can't stay here. I can't make it much longer."

Nova's original irritated look was gone. "Wow. I couldn't have imagined. Thank you for sharing your story with me." She hesitated, then said, "I mean, you are just so stunning; honestly, I didn't understand why you would have even needed the mirror in the first place."

"Unfortunately, looks do not treat addictions." She smiled faintly.

Nova looked down. She gently kicked a rock by her foot. "Although I very much empathize with what you have shared with me, I have my own struggles too. And the other side has been a safe haven. I'm sorry, but I'm just not ready to give that up."

"And I'm not asking you to. I understand you need more time, and I'm willing to wait. This is the only option for me. I have made up my mind to stay there forever. I just need to have the opportunity to get back."

Nova frowned to recall. "I remember Carole told me that if a previous owner went back to the other side after a transfer of ownership, the rules may not be the same as the ones that we know. Are you willing to take that risk?"

"Nova, if I stay here, I'm going to literally die soon. In all senses of the term. Or I can choose the magic side and only die physically." She air-quoted *die*. "There, I can have the opportunity to be the person I want to be, even if it's only in my mind…or some sort of alternate universe. I don't care. Whatever it is, I choose the latter."

She nodded in understanding. "I would love to help you now and tell you: *yes, let's kiss the mirror at the same time.* But I owe it to myself to take advantage of this and decide to make the decision that is in my best interest."

"I get it. I'll wait as long as I can. I don't have any other options."

Nova smiled softly at her before she turned around. "I have to get back to work." Lily nodded but did not come back inside behind her.

Nova walked back to her desk while trying to quiet her mind. She would have to sort through these thoughts later. Although Lily's story was moving and her reason for wanting to go back to the other side understandable and arguably more legitimate, Nova still had to put herself first. This was a once-in-a-lifetime opportunity. The fate of her existence was at stake. To be helpful, perhaps she would try to make her decision quicker so that the next owner would hopefully agree to yield to Lily's request. That was how Nova could help her.

Paul and Rose were sitting inside the sales cubicles when she made it back to her desk. Paul gave her an irritated stare. "Where have you been?"

She was surprised by both the question and the tone. "I needed to use the restroom."

"For twenty minutes? The phone was ringing when we came back. Try to stay at your desk until another salesperson comes back if you can."

She screamed internally. Paul had always been annoying, but now he was just plain rude. The phone ringing had never been an issue. It would go to voicemail, and they would leave a message for a callback. Big fucking deal. He was clearly trying to assert his new authority. Nova knew he was also upping the antics because Rose was there. It was clear that things would only get worse now that he could peacock in front of a new audience.

"Understood." She sat down and immediately stared at her screen. What was on that screen? A mystery. She couldn't see or think clearly. The only ray of light that shined through the void was knowing she would travel back *there* soon.

At half past five, Nova walked inside her apartment on the verge of tears. She was exhausted. She was tired of trying only to not have things work in her favor. She also felt so alone. She realized how much she missed her parents. To get them out of her mind, she thought about her best friends. She hadn't heard from Ana or Kameela in the last few days. To be fair, Ana had tried to contact her, and she had ignored her then. Kameela probably wanted to stay out of it. Or maybe she had picked a side and chosen the friend closer to self-actualization.

Nova picked up her phone. She dialed a number she knew by heart. She hung up at the first beep. She breathed in and out until she mustered the courage to dial again. As she had anticipated, after a couple of rings, her call was sent to voicemail. She paused for a moment. She took the deepest breath before she spoke.

"Mom, Dad…I really miss you guys. I love you. I'm sorry I have disappointed you. I'm sorry I was not able to be the person you wanted me to be. I love you. Please forgive me."

She approached the mirror with a redness in her eyes that embodied her sorrow. Yes, she felt for Lily; but she felt even more for herself. She felt immense sympathy for Lily. To a certain extent, she was even empathetic toward her. She tried to put herself in Lily's shoes to understand where she was coming from. But she just couldn't look away from her own worn-out shoes. She couldn't feel more sadness from someone else when her own heart was in pieces. When she couldn't figure out how to put her own life together.

7:08 PM.

She slowly closed her eyes and pressed her lips against the glass mirror. She gasped for air.

***

5:38 PM.

She opened her eyes. Their previous redness was washed away during the transport. Her heartbeat evened out. She was where she belonged: her safe place.

CHAPTER 17

Nova woke up the next day with a smile on her face. She was excited about what was ahead. She was looking forward to getting to know Rose better than she had gotten a chance to on the real side. She had a good feeling about her. She especially couldn't wait to watch Paul work his hardest to avoid making eye contact with her, as he had done since her promotion was announced. She was excited to see Hakeem as well. The one crucial thing was getting there a little earlier. That way, she could confirm Jeff was on board with her idea to go business to business, to drop their flyers. It was imperative he was. Her lips had to meet the mirror at 4:38 PM.

She walked into the gym at 8:50 AM. Jeff gestured at her to come his way with a smile on his face.

"Hey, Nova! First day as assistant manager. How are you feeling?"

"Great! I'm excited. I can't wait to meet Rose."

Jeff frowned. "I don't remember telling you her name."

Shit. Nova's eyes widened slightly. Thankfully, that fluid thing in the atmosphere helped her regain her composure almost immediately. "Oh, I'm not sure. I think I saw it somewhere." This was only her first mix-up, but she had to be more careful. She did not want to mess things up as Lily had done by confusing realities.

"Probably." He waved it off. "Anyways, she will be here in about half an hour. Just begin by showing her around. Then, walk her through the different products, how the commission works, and whatever else you think she needs to know without overwhelming her."

"Of course. I'll have her go through some of the Q&A cheat sheet as well."

"Perfect." He looked back at his computer.

It was now or never. "Oh, and one more thing, Jeff."

He looked back at her. "Yes?"

"I would also like to take an initiative starting today."

"What's that?"

"Over the next few days, I would like to take about an hour to go business to business to distribute our flyers. When I first started working here, we did that for a little while, and I remember that we noticeably increased our traffic. So, I'll have Rose work on the online training during that time, and I'll try to cover all the businesses in a five-mile radius for the rest of the week."

Jeff paused for a moment, tapping his index finger on the table. Oh god. What if he said no? She did not have a backup plan. She had assumed he would agree without hesitation. She was not ready to stay on this side forever. If he said no, she would have to leave and deal with the consequences. Her blood pumped faster and faster, in panicked anticipation.

"That is a fantastic idea," he finally said. "If you think of anything else, please let me know!"

She held a *phew* inside of her throat. "Thank you, Jeff."

Why did she still panic on this side? Things always

worked out in her favor. That was just how the gilded magic cards were dealt. She approached her desk, grinning. When she saw Paul, she wished she felt all the anger she had toward him on the real side; so that she could fully savor his fate *here*. But most of the negative feelings she had toward him were trapped *there*. However, she could still enjoy how much he tried to avoid meeting her eyes. She was entertained by how he kept himself faux busy to not have to engage in conversation with her. It was satisfying to an unreasonable degree.

"Hey, Paul! How are you doing today?"

"Hey," he said, turning the pages of a notebook with extreme focus. "I'm good. You?"

"I'm great! The new rep is starting today. She should be here shortly. Her name is Rose by the way."

"Great." He continued to aimlessly turn the pages of the notebook without looking up. What would he do when he got to the last page? Nova had to find out.

She tittered. "I will meet her at the front desk, then I will give her a walkthrough and introduce her to you," she said at a slow pace, as if she was explaining a new concept to a five-year-old.

She could see Paul scrambling to figure out what he would do next to avoid looking up at her. He was getting dangerously close to the notebook's tail. It was hilarious to watch. For an instant, she almost felt bad for him and considered ending the conversation. The poor guy was obviously having a hard enough time handling the fact that she was now his superior. Though she did not harbor the feelings she had toward him on the real side *here*, she still recalled that he had been an asshole to her when the shoe was on the other side.

"Do you have any questions for me before she gets here?" she said.

He was still looking down at the now-closed notebook. Was he going to open it again and act like he had missed one imaginary note? Was he going to write some meaningless words down? The possibilities were comically endless. After a moment of silence, he looked at the floor. He hesitantly leaned down and tied his already-tied shoes.

"No, no questions."

It took everything in her not to explode in laughter. She thought she was not handling his promotion well on the real side, but he was evidently having a way harder time than her in this reality. She took a mental screenshot of this moment, hoping she could refer to it when he would inevitably upset her in reality, for the nth time. When he began to tie the other shoe, she decided to put an end to his misery.

She walked to the front to wait for Rose. She giggled the entire way there. The kind of giggles that made the shoulders move up and down, like a cartoon character. When she was close enough to the front desk, she quickly skimmed the gym. Hakeem wasn't there. That was odd. He was always there at that time.

At the front desk, she discovered that they had hired a brand-new receptionist. The last one did not even last a week. The new front desk person looked as nonchalant and uninterested as the last few ones. He did not bother introducing himself and simply nodded at Nova, like, *'Sup?* They stood silently for a few minutes until Rose mercifully walked in. She had a huge smile on her face. She looked as amicable as Nova remembered.

"Hey, Rose. I'm Nova, the assistant manager." She shook her hand. "Nice to meet you!"

"Hey, Nova. Very nice to meet you!"

"Okay. I know that you already took care of all the paperwork stuff with Jeff." Rose nodded to confirm. "So, we will begin by doing the gym walk-through. Then, we will go over the different membership options and the commission structure. Sounds good?"

"Sounds great!"

She began the tour by walking Rose through all the areas of the gym. Hakeem was still nowhere to be found. He must have changed his schedule. Rose was watching and listening attentively. Nova noticed that she squinted her eyes to focus.

"Any questions so far?"

"So far, so good. You are very thorough, Nova"

"Well, thank you." She smiled, more moved by the compliment than she expected. "What did you do before this?" She led Rose to the sitting area.

"I mostly worked in the restaurant industry. I did some serving, bartending, and catering. I do have a passion for fitness and wellness. And I love talking to people. So, this is the perfect fit for me," she said as they sat down.

"That's awesome. Are you from Florida?"

"No, I'm from Tennessee. Nashville. I moved here a couple of years ago."

Nova knew she had to get back to the training, but she wanted to learn more about Rose. "Home of the hot chicken, right? I heard it's beautiful out there. Why did you move to Orlando?"

Rose kept a pleasant smile on her face. "That's right." Then, she slightly tensed up. "I moved here because there was some family stuff I had to get away from. It was just time for me to experience something else too. Change scene. Plus, I love being close to open waters."

Per Rose's slight rigidity, Nova understood it was time to stop asking personal questions. "Definitely. Well, we are excited to have you on the team." She upped her tone by an octave. "So, this is the plan for today. I'll go over the different memberships and the pay structure with you. Then, I'll have you look over some of the most frequently asked questions and answers." Rose was nodding silently while taking down notes. "Then, around four, I'll have you start on the online training."

"Sounds like a plan."

Nova went over all the details with her. She was flattered by how diligently Rose was writing down all the information she was sharing with her. Her knowledge was valuable. She was invaluable. She was important. She was not dispensable. She mattered...*here*.

Rose followed her to the sales cubicles, where Paul was quietly staring at the same notebook. She was amused by his shenanigans earlier, but she hoped he would put a halt to the circus to properly introduce himself to their new team member.

"Hey, Paul. This is Rose, our new sales rep."

To Nova and—most importantly—to Paul's neck relief, he finally looked up. "Hey, Rose. Very nice to meet you."

"Nice to meet you too, Paul. I have heard great things about you."

His eyes lit up. "Have you? Well, that's good to hear. How is it going so far?"

"It's going great. I feel pretty good about everything I

have learned so far. Nova is awesome and very thorough!"

A vein appeared on the right side of his poor neck. He met Nova's eyes. He exhaled without making a sound. "Yes, she is."

Paul was usually easy to read, but the look on his face would have been almost impenetrable to the layman's eye. It was hard to tell whether it conveyed admiration, envy, or sadness. It felt like a mixture of all three. The only reason Nova recognized that look was because she had sported it herself on numerous occasions. She had had the same look when Kameela announced that she was engaged to the love of her life, whilst Nova had woken up a couple of weeks prior to a nameless, unfunny, and unsatisfying one-night stand. She had had the same look when Ana announced that she had been promoted to the youngest brand manager in her company, whereas Nova was working what she felt at the time was a dead-end job. She had had the same look when she saw how Hakeem had looked at Lily when it seemed like he merely looked through her.

But that was then. That was *there*.

Here and now, she was causing someone else to feel the same emotion(s). And she wished she could have genuinely said that she gained no validation or feel-good feelings from being the culprit of someone else's envy. She could have said that, yes, but that would have been a lie.

A few minutes before the clock struck four, Nova walked Rose through how to begin the online training. Then, she grabbed a few of her cards and gym's flyers. She let Jeff know that she would be back in about an hour. He gave her a no-look nod and thumbs up as she stepped outside of the building. She immediately ran to her car. There was a plaza only a couple of miles away from the gym. Her plan was to walk in and drop flyers inside as many businesses as possible within a few minutes.

Thankfully, *Fit Gals and Pals* was well-established and had a good reputation. Almost all the businesses she went into did not ask any additional questions after she offered all their customers an additional free week trial if they stopped by for a walk-through. She also grabbed each of their flyers and offered to display them at their front entrance. In retrospect, she was glad the travel time conflict had forced her to come up with this idea. She was convinced this would increase their traffic. Jeff would be happy with her performance. He would be proud of her.

She walked inside the last business she could cover for the day, a small but always busy froyo shop. The moment she walked in, her eyes immediately recognized one very familiar figure and another vaguely familiar profile in the back corner of the shop. She did not need to squint or wipe her eyes: Hakeem and Emily were having a delightful conversation. Emily was leaning in, twirling her hair with her index finger, and laughing vehemently.

That man is not that funny, Nova thought to herself. She chuckled at her internal comment. Hakeem looked her way. He froze when he recognized her. Emily followed his gaze and smirked when she saw Nova. Crap. She literally did not have time for this. She waved at the both of them and walked toward the froyo rep to give him the run-down. He agreed without hesitation and gave her one of their flyers. She walked out without looking back at them. She could feel the heaviness of their stare on her skin on her way out.

She had driven like a maniac on the tollway, but it was

all worth it. She walked inside of her apartment at 4:33 PM. She sat on her bed for a moment to catch her breath. Carole and Lily were right; she would have to make a decision soon. She could barely envision doing this over the next few days, let alone months. Deep down, she already had made up her mind. It was just so hard to act on it because of the implications. The more time went by, the overwhelming pros continued to outweigh the cons from one side to the other. The little encounter she had at the froyo shop had not really fazed her or influenced her decision. She was convinced that if she wanted Hakeem, she could have him...*here*.

4:38 PM. Lips against glass. Static Motion.

***

There.

The instant she materialized back on the real side of the mirror, her eyes regained their redness and puffiness. When she walked toward the bathroom to wash her face, she heard her phone ring. She hoped with every fiber of her being that it was her parents calling her back to tell her they loved her and that they, too, had missed her. She paced to her bed to find her phone. The hope immediately evaporated when she recognized the name on the screen.

"Hey, girlie!" Kameela said.

"Hey."

"Are you okay? You don't sound well."

"I'm fine."

"Nova, what's going on? You know you can talk to me, right?"

"Yes."

"Then, do it."

Silence.

203

"I'm okay."

Nova could hear Kameela blowing something. Given the time, she guessed that it was her frankincense incense sticks. The thought softened her a smidge.

"Nova, I'm worried about you." She cleared her throat. "I know you weren't in the bathroom and left the apartment that night I decided to come back home. You don't have to tell me where you went. I just want you to know that I'm here for you if you need anything."

Nova's heartbeat sped up as if she had run a marathon. Perhaps she should just tell her everything now. She was the one person who would understand. She could use some support. Although she knew that Kameela would not even bat an eyelid at the discovery that a magic mirror that led to an alternate reality existed, she was certain that she would try to talk her out of her decision to stay on the real side. To be fair to Kameela's potential reaction, Nova would be gone in reality forever. Her body would remain, but she would be in a state of coma she would have no chance of waking out of.

Was it selfish of her? She had not taken the time to think of the impact it would have on the people who cared about her. It was not even that hard of a task. The only person who seemed to care about her was the one on the other side of the line. She loved Kameela, but it was not enough to make her choose this side.

"I promise I'm okay. Thank you for always checking on me; you are a good friend."

"Okay, I'm leaving it alone," she snorted. "You are a good friend too. You gave me great advice the night I left, about the situation with Josh. I think I was not ready to hear it then, but you were right. I should have definitely stood my ground more."

"Is everything okay?"

"Yes, but Josh and I had a serious heart-to-heart. I voiced to him that he could not just make all the decisions for both of us. I reminded him that we were in a lifetime partnership. Therefore, one person didn't get the final say on everything. I told him that I was his wife and not his employee. We both laughed at that comment. Then, we stayed up all night. We were just up talking and laughing about any and everything. Things are wonderful now, but that conversation was well overdue. Thank you for reminding me I needed to stand up for myself."

Nova teared up. "I'm so happy to hear that. You two are truly soulmates." She choked on the next words. "Anytime, friend."

Kameela paused before speaking. "Hmm, friend?"

Nova knew what she would say next. "Yes?"

"When are you going to return our other friend's calls?"

"I don't know."

"I've given the two of you enough time to come back to your senses, and I stayed out of it. But enough!"

"She was out of line!"

"Nova, deep breaths. I get it. You know I've had my own fair share of exchanges with her. I already talked to her, and she knows she shouldn't have said what she said. She didn't mean it."

"But she did, and you know it. It's okay. I just don't want to talk to her right now. I need more time. I'll reach out to her when I'm ready."

Kameela huffed. "Fine."

Nova giggled at her exasperation. "Well, I'm actually

going to run myself a bath, so I'll talk to you later."

"Enjoy! Love you, girl."

"Love you too."

She felt a tad better after talking to Kameela. Especially knowing she had somewhat contributed to bettering her relationship with Josh. She felt a pinch more valuable. Enough to make her smile and feel lukewarm but not enough to influence her decision. She had not taken a bath since Kameela had gone back home. She very much needed one tonight. She needed to dissolve her negative feelings, even if it only lasted for a fraction of an instant.

She lit a vanilla-scented candle and sat in the warm bubbly water-filled tub. She closed her eyes. She breathed in and out. Several thoughts made their way through her mind, but she didn't analyze them. She observed them without judgment. She let them occupy more space but didn't try to make sense of why they were there. She wanted to be in the moment. The only thing she tried to care about was how warm the water felt against her skin. The soft smell of the candle burning. The quiet sound of the bubbles bursting. She kept trying to ignore her thoughts. She succeeded for the most part. However, one fought harder and came to the forefront. She tried to dismiss it. She tried to focus on the warmth of the water enveloping her. But the water did not feel warm anymore. It felt like nothing at all. Just like her. She tried to find the delicate smell of the candle, but she couldn't identify it anymore. It was lost in the atmosphere. Just like her. And she couldn't hear the bubbles bursting anymore. They must have all become undone. Just like her. The thought became louder. She couldn't ignore it anymore. She couldn't fight it anymore.

The next time she went back *there* would be the last. Her mind was made up: she would stay on the other side of the mirror.

CHAPTER 18

Nova could have traveled to the other side the moment she woke up. She could have stayed there for twenty-four hours. She was assured of her decision, so why wait? It was her last day *here*. She wanted to stay in reality as long as she could until it was time to travel back to the other side. It was the last time she would experience this reality. It was bittersweet. Though sweeter than bitter, it was bitter still. Yes, she would have all the same people currently in her life *there*. Yes, she would get to live a better life because she was a better her. But she would still be gone on this side.

The people who cared about her (even though she only needed a finger or two to count them) would be left to grieve. Kameela would be devastated. And she knew that although Ana had meant what she said, she would be too. Her parents would probably find out way later or never find out at all. And if or when they did, they might be mournful for a short while, but it would eventually be a relief for them. Kameela would be sad for some time, but she would eventually get over it and continue to live her happily ever after. Ana would be greatly affected as well, but probably not as long and not as hard. The *Fit Gals and Pals* crew would be mildly impacted, but things would quickly go back to normal. Paul would not mind her absence. Rose would fill in. Jeff would forget her name within weeks. Hakeem would probably not even notice she was gone. Naveen crossed her mind as well. Their story only existed on the other side. He had already forgotten about her *here*. But *there*, they had a potential future together. So did she and Hakeem. And *there*, things were wonderful with her two friends. And she was already doing well as the new assistant manager *there*. Her life was so exciting on the other side that she didn't think about her parents as much. Maybe *there*, they would rekindle things. But whether they did or not, things would be so much better. She knew it for sure simply because they already were.

Nova drove to the gym in silence. She walked inside the building quietly. It was a strange feeling knowing that everything she was experiencing was final. It was odd being conscious of the end of something whilst undergoing its last moments. It almost felt like an out-of-body experience. It looked like everything was moving in slow motion. It sounded like all the words she was hearing were echoing, "Nova...Nova...Nova...Nova...Nova," until she could not hear them anymore. Everything looked blurry. The air felt heavier on her skin. Her last day in reality.

"Nova!" Paul yelled.

She snapped out of her thoughts. "Uh...yes?"

"What the hell? I have been yelling your name for like ten seconds. Are you okay?" he said, looking like he was holding a *what the fuck?* at the tip of his tongue.

She didn't care about his tone. There was no point in doing so. She wouldn't have to interact with him on this side much longer. "Sorry about that. What's up?"

He shook his head and sighed. "I need you to take all the walk-ins and my walk-throughs today. I only have three scheduled appointments. I saw that you only have a couple. I need to fast-track Rose's training, so she can start doing walk-throughs by the end of the week. Can you handle that?"

It's almost as if he unconsciously knew to prepare for her absence. "Yes," she said.

"Great. Thanks." He walked away so fast toward Rose that he might as well have run.

Nova absently scrolled through the list of appointments she would have to cover. Being booked up would keep her mind busy until it was time to leave. She walked to the front desk to welcome her first appointment. She was not sure if it was a new person or the same receptionist who greeted her. Her body was on autopilot. Her mind had already departed this reality.

The first prospect walked in at his scheduled time. She honestly wouldn't have been able to describe him if someone had demanded she did with a gun held against her temple. His answers were indistinguishable from the ones she had heard over the past four years. "Busy with work...blah blah blah...kids...blah blah blah...significant other...blah blah blah...life." The fifth one walked in a couple of minutes early. "Crazy schedule...blah blah blah...teenagers...blah blah blah...divorce...blah blah blah...life."

During the questionnaire with the fifth appointment, she saw Hakeem standing by the free weight area. This was her last opportunity to interact with him on this side. As she had done countless times, she walked the prospect toward him. He saw them coming and immediately smiled, recognizing his cue.

Her words felt so weighty as they came out. "Hey, Hakeem, I wanted to introduce you to our new member. She decided to join today, and she will most likely work with you to have a smooth start."

Hakeem gave them that impeccable dentist-approved smile. "Very nice to meet you. It's an honor that you have chosen *Fit Gals and Pals* to assist you in your wellness journey." He looked at Nova and gave her a pat on the back. He then looked back at the new member and ended with, "Welcome!"

Something was off about Hakeem's delivery. He was not as inviting as usual. However, she still felt those butterflies she always felt when his hand met her back. That feeling didn't really exist on the other side of the mirror. *There*, the feeling was becoming reciprocal. *Here*, there was something fun about crushing on Hakeem, knowing he probably didn't share the same feelings. The hope was suspensefully exciting. There was something thrilling about holding onto when her eyes met his and letting her mind wonder about what any exchange with him could have potentially meant. She knew he didn't feel the same way on this side. Yet, it was exhilarating to let her mind wonder. She would miss that feeling.

Later, Rose walked back toward the cubicles alone. Nova had not seen her all day. She looked strained; her shoulders were hunched forward.

"Are you okay?" Nova asked.

"Yes, but It has been a long day. Paul is trying to have me ready to begin walk-throughs before the end of the week, so we have been going over everything, repeatedly, since the moment I got in this morning."

"Wow. I'm sure you are exhausted. How do you feel about everything you guys have covered?"

"I feel fine about it. I just wish the pace was a little slower, but it seems like he really wants me on the floor asap."

"Yes, it seems like that's the plan," she said absently. Her mind couldn't help but wonder. Her last day in reality.

"How are things going for you?"

Nova took a few seconds to register Rose's question. "Oh, fine. I took Paul's appointments so that he could focus on your training. Five out of five signed up, so pretty good day."

"You are a beast! How long have you been working here?"

"Four years."

Rose furrowed her brow. "So, you have been here longer than Paul?"

"Yes."

She opened her mouth, then closed it. She sat down on the seat facing Nova and finally said, "I hope this is okay to ask, but if not, you don't have to answer. Were you not interested in the assistant manager position?"

"I was, but the offer was not extended to me."

Rose frowned. "Why? Paul is fine, but you are obviously more experienced and knowledgeable."

"I guess I didn't make my interest known soon enough."

"That's bullshit!" Rose immediately covered her mouth. "Sorry, I'm completely speaking out of turn."

Nova half-smiled. "No, it's okay. Thank you for saying that."

Rose grinned. "Well, I'm glad my big mouth could be of help. For the record, I'm looking forward to working with you the most."

Nova nodded but said nothing else. This interaction with

Rose was enough to make her smile and feel slightly understood. But, not enough to make her change her mind. She liked Rose. She was looking forward to building a friendship with her. It would just have to be on the other side of the mirror.

The front desk person strolled toward Nova. "Hey. There is someone at the front for you."

She wasn't expecting any walk-ins today. Her heart skipped a beat. Naveen was the last person who had come by unexpectedly. But that was on the other side. She walked toward the front with apprehension. When she recognized the silhouette by the entrance, she sighed. She was not expecting, "Ana?"

"Hey, Nova," she mumbled.

This was the last person she wanted to see today. She got closer to Ana and whispered, "What are you doing here?"

"Well, you have not returned my calls, and you are not giving me a chance to apologize, so I decided to come here."

"Don't you have to be at work?"

"Our friendship is more important, so I took the day off to come here and talk to you." Ana grinned. Nova folded her arms and looked at her like, *Bitch, please.* "Okay, the entire staff is off today, but I need to talk to you. I hate that things are not good between us. I miss you."

Nova gestured for her to come closer to the corner of the room. "I appreciate you coming here, but I'm working. I really can't do this right now."

Ana smiled and nodded. "I knew you would say that. Since you get off at five, let's do this: I'll go grab us some wine and snacks, and I'll meet you at your place around 5:30?"

"God, Ana. I don't—"

214

"Nova, please," she pleaded.

She had to travel to the other side around seven. She would have enough time to nod at Ana's compelled apology. She could still leave on time. Under different circumstances, she would have said no. But since it was her last day in reality, she would oblige.

She sighed. "Okay."

"Yes! So, I'll go ahead and—"

A voice rose behind them, "Hey, Nova, I'm so sorry to interrupt. Someone is on the line asking a question I'm not sure how to answer, and I couldn't find Paul."

They both looked at the owner of the voice. Ana gave it a double take. Nova noticed and moved closer to the voice, to block Ana's view.

"No worries. Thank you for letting me know, Rose. I'll be right there."

Before Rose could walk away, Ana chimed in with a beam. "Sorry for taking her away from her post, Rose."

Rose replied, grinning just as widely, "It's no problem."

The moment she was far enough, Nova glared at Ana. "Don't even try! She is really sweet."

"So am I!"

Nova ignored her answer. "I'll see you at my place at 5:30."

Ana ran out with a huge smile on her face. "Can't wait!"

Nova was genuinely moved that Ana had taken the time to come to *Fit Gals and Pals* on an off day to amend things with her. Although, she was certain Kameela had called Ana right after speaking with her last night to request that she reached out. Still, she appreciated the effort. If it was just another day, Nova would have probably told her she wasn't ready to talk to her and that she would contact her when she was. However, today was not just another day. It was her last day in reality. Ana showed that she cared enough about her to take time out of her—undoubtedly very busy—off day to talk things out. She wanted things to end on a good note between them. When her body would return in a state of coma in reality, she wanted the last memory that Ana had of her to be positive.

She slowly gathered her stuff when the clock approached five. She stood up in slow motion. She looked at Rose and even Paul with a tender eye. She waved both goodbye. She found Hakeem on the floor. Their eyes met. She didn't get flustered. She simply waved at him. He waved back. Before she stepped out, she said her last goodbye.

"Bye, Jeff."

Jeff gave her the same no-look nod he had always given her. She walked slowly to her car. She wanted to remember each step. She took one final look at the building. Why was she being so dramatic? She would be in this very same building tomorrow. Plus, things would be so much better. She exhaled loudly and motioned to open her car door.

"Nova!"

She looked back. Lily was pacing toward her.

Goddamn it! Did everyone get a notice that she had made her final decision? She did not want to deal with Lily right now. She hoped things would work out for her, so she could get back *there*. It would just have to happen without her help.

"I know that look, Nova. I've been watching you. You have made your decision, haven't you?"

She considered lying, but what was the point? "Yes. I'm

sorry."

Lily bit her lip. "Are you sure? Did Carole explain the consequences to you? I really thought you would choose to make things work on this side."

"I'm aware of the implications, and I'm okay with them. Lily, I truly empathize with what you have shared with me. But as bad as you want to go back there, I'm still struggling to understand how you want to convince me to not want the same thing."

Lily stared at her; her piercing gaze focused on Nova's face. "There is a light in your eyes that I lost even before the mirror. There is no hope for me here, and I have come to terms with that. I'm okay with ceasing to exist in reality, so that I can have a chance to live…even if it is only in mind, an alternative reality, or whatever the other side is. But if I still had that light that you have, if I felt like there was any chance I could have a shot on this side, even if it was miniscule, I would have chosen reality forever. I feel like you can still turn things around here. I feel like you are giving up too soon. I know this is rich coming from me, but I swear I mean what I'm saying. You can still live the life you want to live in reality, I can see it in your eyes. Don't give up just yet. I'm not saying this for me. I promise that I'm saying it for your sake."

Nova teared up. "I'm sorry, I have to go." She rushed inside her car and drove away.

As Nova walked inside her apartment, she continued to fight the urge to think about what Lily had told her. Thankfully, she heard door knocks behind her. Ana was here. She could distract her mind by listening to her contrived apology. Honestly, Ana didn't owe her one. Her delivery had been harsh, but the message was true. She wallowed in her

217

own misery. And she had done little to improve her circumstances over the past few years. She actually should have thanked Ana. She was following her advice and changing her state of affairs. It was poetic that the person who had told her the truth she was too cowardly to tell herself, which eventually had led her to choose the other side, was the last person she would interact with in reality. To Nova, it was a confirmation she was making the right decision.

She opened the door with a new resolve. "Come on in."

Ana strolled in, waving a bottle of wine in the air. "I got us something sweet and light to help with our talk."

"Okay."

They poured the drinks, laid out the snacks, and sat down quietly. Ana took a sip and immediately began. "Nova, I know that life has gotten in the way in the past few years, and we do not get to be together as much as we used to. But I don't know when the disconnect happened and you began to feel like I thought you were a burden or some loser." She paused then continued, "That could not be further from the truth. Not only do I love you and I consider you to be family, but I also have so much respect for you."

Nova's eyes widened. "You do?"

"Nova, do you understand how strong you fucking are? I know you don't like to talk about this shit, but you were x-ed out by your entire congregation, all the people that you grew up with, and your own parents. You basically had to figure this life shit on your own, start over. Unlearn and relearn everything, with no guidance. You could have given up then and it would have been completely understandable. But you didn't. You just kept putting one foot in front of the other and trusted that things would get better. Like, what the hell: you are a badass. I can't even imagine going through what you went through and being where you are today. I don't know how I've never told you this, but I admire the hell out of you."

Nova was at a loss for words. She had expected the standard, *I'm sorry I didn't mean it. I love you.* Not this. She was not sure what to say in response. After a moment of silence, she said, "You know after you say what you said, I sat on it and realized that the reason I was so hurt was because…you were right. A part of me does enjoy feeling sorry for myself. And over the last few years, I've just let life happen to me."

Ana moved closer to her. "Nova, you also have two amazing traits: you are self-aware and introspective. I did put my foot in my mouth a little bit, but I'm not going to bullshit you, I meant some of what I said. But I did sit on it as well and I realized that I was entirely too harsh with you. Some of what I said was unfair, and for that I am sorry. You have been through a lot, and you are still standing here today. For that alone, my hat is off to you. But I also know you have the potential to do great things no matter what route you choose to take in life." She took a breath. "On the other hand, I also understand there are different phases in life. It seems like you are in a sort of hibernation phase right now?"

Nova chuckled. "Yes, it's been a very harsh Floridian winter."

Ana laughed. "You know what I mean."

She replied, still laughing, "Sure."

"I've been in this go-go-go, no resting, no days off phase for years and honestly, I feel burnt out. I can take a page out of your book. It's okay to not do or not be as productive all the time. It's okay to just reflect sometimes. Hell, it's okay to just be. And in time, you will get out of the den; whenever you are ready to move to your next stage. I was wrong for trying to force you out of the den when you still needed to protect yourself from the very cold Orlando winter."

Nova's eyes watered. "No, I think I have been in the den past the hibernation period. It's warming up outside and I'm scared to step out. But I know it's time. I'm just scared."

Ana choked before her words could come out. "I want you to remember that when you do step out, you will not be alone," she finished, teary-eyed and hoarse.

They lunged into each other's arms and declared simultaneously, "I love you, girl."

Ana wiped her eyes. "Geez, I've never used the word *den* so many times in my life."

Nova laughed, still in tears. She suddenly sat up straighter. "Since we are opening up today, please be honest with me." Ana straightened up as well. "Why do you put so much pressure on yourself to never fail at anything?" Nova crossed her arms. "And don't give me the *I want to win* spiel. You have not stopped going since the first day I met you. I admire your drive, but it seems like it's deeper than wanting to be successful for you."

She took a breath. "Have you ever wondered why I prefer to go by Ana and not Tadhana?"

"I have always been curious about that, yes. I figured it was just a preference."

Ana sighed. "Yeah, it is a little more than that." She took a sip of her drink. "As you know, my parents migrated from the Philippines to this country when I was two years old. And as you obviously know, I'm the oldest of three. I have always felt a lot of pressure to be a stellar example for my sister and brother. And given what my parents have gone through to make it to the US, I feel like there is no complaint or excuse that I could ever have that would compare to what they have gone through for me to be here. It has been ingrained in me that as the oldest, I'm the one who has to set the standard for my family's legacy in this country. I prefer to go by Ana and not Tadhana because I don't want anyone to have any preconceptions of me based on my heritage. I have no room for unnecessary hinderance."

"Wow. I had no idea. That is a lot of pressure and expectations for one person," Nova said. Ana nodded. She continued, "You know how kickass I think you are, but I really think you should ease off on yourself. You have been an outstanding role model for your siblings. You have already set the standard for your family's legacy. And if you make some mistakes, it's okay. You will learn from them and come stronger on the other side. This will also give room to your sister and your brother to see that it is okay to fail sometimes. It's human. Give yourself room to be flawed."

Ana wiped a tear. "Thank you, Nova. I needed to hear that." She then got up to find her purse. "Okay, enough with the emotional stuff." She sat back down, hiding her hands behind her back. Then, she revealed a small glass pipe in her left hand and dried green leaves in her right hand.

"Shall we?" She winked.

Nova looked at the clock, 6:17 PM. The last time she traveled back at 7:31 PM. She could stay a little longer. For once, she wanted to stay *here* as long as she could.

"Let's!"

Ana took the first hit and reacted with a mild cough. Then, she melted into the couch. She passed the pipe to

Nova, who coughed intensely as the smoke traveled through her esophagus and rested inside her lungs. It felt like fire. Then warmth. Then tranquility. Ana was talking and laughing about something. Nova could hardly make sense of her words. She tried to keep her eyes on the clock. The more hits she took, the more difficult it became to understand Ana while simultaneously attempting to keep up with the time. She couldn't do both, so she focused solely on the time. 6:42 PM.

"That new coworker of yours is very hot." Ana giggled.

"Mm-hmm," Nova said with her eyes half-opened.

"I won't mess things up, I promise. Do I have your blessings?"

"Mm-hmm."

"I do? Are you sure?"

"Mm-hmm."

"You have no idea what I'm talking about, do you?"

"Mm-hmm."

"Well, I'll still accept your very inebriated endorsement."

"Mm-hmm."

Ana continued to laugh. Nova looked her way as her friend faded into oblivion. She felt incredible peace. Her mind was quiet. She closed her eyes for a moment. In that instant, for a second, she understood the meaning of life yet again. She understood the purpose of her own existence. She could not put it into words, but she felt it in her bones. She felt lighter. She opened her eyes. 7:12 PM. Time to go.

She looked at Ana, who had passed out next to her. She smiled at her sleeping friend. Before her talk with Ana, she was convinced of her decision. Nova was even assured that her talk with her would have sealed the deal. However, the opposite happened. It was not a one-eighty. She did not want to give up the mirror…yet. But she was now certain that she could not make her final decision today. The talk with Ana had breathed some life back into her. Some hope. Some strength.

She stood in front of the mirror as steadily as she could. She could almost see the light Lily had referred to earlier, shining behind her gaze. A fire still burned somewhere inside of her. It might have been embers. Whatever it was, it had survived inside of her over the last few years. And it had been miraculously revived today. However, she was not ready to stop using the mirror. She still needed a hideaway place, just in case.

7:22 PM. Eyes closed. Lips against glass. Uncertainty. Den.

CHAPTER 19

4:38 PM.

Nova rushed on the tollway back to the gym. She was only going back to *Fit Gals and Pals* for a final check-in with Rose and Jeff. She would have to leave again right after it. This additional back and forth was inconvenient. Though she had conceded to not make her final decision today, she still needed to make it sooner than later. She walked inside the building with a triumphant smile. She spread the flyers from all the businesses she had gotten into across Jeff's desk.

"Ta-da!" she sang.

Jeff looked up, with his eyes slightly widened. "You were able to get into all of them today?"

"Yes! It went very well. I offered the free week trial to draw them in, so I really think we should get an influx soon."

"Great job Nova, keep it up!" He high fived her. "And how is it going with Rose?"

"Good! She is picking up on things quickly. I think she's going to do really well."

"Well, she has a great trainer, so I think so too."

She walked back to her desk, still beaming. Paul was already gone. Rose was still focused on her online training. Nova gently tapped her shoulder. Rose jumped then looked back.

"Sorry, I didn't mean to scare you."

Rose smiled. "No, it's okay. I'm easily startled."

"How is the online training going?"

"So far so good. I took a ton of notes." She fanned the pages of her notebook to support her statement.

"Nice! You are all set for today. You can head home. We will pick back up tomorrow."

"Awesome! Thank you, Nova."

She felt good about her day. She felt accomplished. She felt like she belonged. Although *here* she couldn't feel all the emotions from her talk with Ana on the real side, she still could objectively recognize that it had convinced her to not stay on this side definitively, at least not yet. Given how great she felt at the moment, it was difficult to understand why she kept allowing herself to interrupt that feeling.

She walked to her car and heard her name being yelled from the distance. Hakeem paced toward her. Good grief. What was it with people waiting for her to leave work to accost her?

"Hey, Hakeem," she said as lively as she could muster.

"Hey…Hmm…Sorry to intercept you when you are leaving work. I just wanted to explain what you saw earlier."

"It's okay. You don't owe me an explanation."

"I know, but I want to."

"Okay." She leaned against her car. "I'm listening."

He moved closer to her. "I'm sure you remember Emily from brunch. If you recall, her and the other guy have been trying to convince me to go back to *Fitness Link*." Nova nodded. He continued, "So, Emily asked me to meet a few days ago because they have a new management position available for personal trainers. I was set on not going back there, but it is a really great opportunity. I love *Fit Gals and Pals,* but I decided to interview for the position. I met with Emily again today because she was able to get some intel, and I did get the position. They'll call me tomorrow to make the offer."

"Wow, that's great news! Congratulations." She hugged him. She was not as sad as she had anticipated to find out they would no longer work together.

"Thank you. It is bittersweet, though." He looked down. "On one hand, I'm super excited about this new adventure." He looked back up, directly into the brown of her eyes. "On the other hand, I'll miss seeing you every day."

"Me too."

"Don't think you are off the hook, though. I still need to take you on that bike ride."

She smiled and focused her gaze on his lips. He moved even closer and met hers slowly, then more passionately. She caressed his bottom lip with her thumb before she moved inside of her car.

"Ciao," she said. She blew him a kiss and drove off. She loved her dramatic exits on this side.

***

Hakeem stood there wordless. This would be a little more complicated than what he had expected. He had not really lied to Nova, but he had certainly omitted a portion of the truth. Part of his meetings with Emily had been about the management position he would be offered at *Fitness Link.* However, they were also talking about rekindling their relationship. He honestly had not expected his novel lust for Nova to be this intense. He had so much history with Emily. He had always known they would eventually find their way

227

back to each other. When he envisioned his future, Emily was the one he saw next to him. But this thing with Nova was so raw and fervent, almost primal. Hakeem had no intention of getting in a relationship with her, but he wanted to taste more of that new thing she had. And the sooner, the better.

***

Naveen had not planned on getting into a relationship, but he could not fight it. He liked Nova. The more time they spent together, the more he wanted to be around her. He could not wait to see her tomorrow. Hopefully, she felt the same.

This day had marked one year since he had ended things with Michelle. Naveen remembered because that Thursday he walked in on her cheating on him was also his father's birthday. He had called his dad earlier today to wish him happy birthday. His father was having a blast, celebrating with his mother and some other family members. They were still so in love with each other. It was beautiful to witness. Every time they spoke, his parents expressed how proud they were that he became the man they had expected him to become. How proud they were he had followed the path they had directed him toward.

Naveen paused his thoughts the moment he walked inside the restaurant. Golibe was already there, sitting at the bar. The place was almost empty. The conversation from the only other three patrons was covered by the house music playing in the background.

"What's up, bro?" Naveen said.

They pound hugged. "I need a drink," Golibe said.

"Uh-oh. What happened?"

Before he answered, Golibe waved at the bartender.

228

They both ordered old fashioned.

When the bartender walked away, Golibe spoke. "This girl is driving me nuts with this proposal countdown." He covered his face with both hands and shook his head. "She bought a calendar that she somehow glued to her fridge and mine. And now she is physically x-ing out the days until six months from the day she initially gave me her proposal ultimatum. That date is of course circled in bold with arrows pointing to it on my calendar, just in case I would not see it."

Naveen could not hold his laughter. "You two are hilarious."

Golibe sucked his teeth. "I'm glad my pain is entertaining to you." He stared directly at the mirror behind the bar and cried out, "Mirror, mirror on the wall, why did I end up with the craziest of them all?"

Naveen could not stop laughing. "You are definitely going to need a little bit of magic to help you on this one." He finally settled down. "You still don't know whether you are going to propose or not?"

"Eh. Of course not! I still have five months and twenty-four days according to my calendar, so, I'm good."

Naveen crossed his arms. "Seriously, Go. Do you really not know or are just cold feet? You two have been together for what, three years?" Golibe nodded silently, still facing the mirror. "I can tell she is making you really happy. I know you've mentioned not wanting to get divorced, but it is a risk when getting married. I know you, bro. The fact that she gave you an ultimatum and you didn't walk away tells me that you have already made your decision to stay with her. You are just running the clock."

Golibe turned his body in one swift motion to face

229

Naveen. "And I'm going to run it until the second before the buzzer goes off. It's my last six months as a bachelor after all. Damn. It's like, I'm simultaneously not ready and ready for this shit, you know? You are right though: she is the one. Fuck."

Naveen frantically gestured at the bartender to bring two shots. "Cheers to you finding the one!"

Golibe cheered in a faux reluctant manner. "Jesus of Nazareth, I'm about to be someone's whole fiancé." He grinned.

"I'm happy for you, bro. Love couldn't have knocked at a better man's door."

A tear rolled down Golibe's eye. "Damn you! I came here to drink, not to cry." They hugged each other and laughed. "Now that you have fixed my life, Iyanla, what's going on with you?"

Naveen sighed. "Dude, this girl…I don't understand. You know me. I don't rush into things. There is just something about her. Obviously, I can't say if she is my person yet, given that tomorrow will only be our third official date and—"

"They were some unofficial ones?" Golibe raised both eyebrows and pursed his lips.

"Not really. I just went to the gym where she works and signed up for a membership," he said, then facepalmed.

"What the fuck? Doesn't she work at *Fit Gals and Pals*? That's like forty minutes from your place. Wow. This girl got you getting on I-4 for a gym membership you don't even need, just so you can see her? Yeah, there is something about her, alright. And why didn't you tell me? My boy is really in love, oh." Golibe chuckled.

"Yeah, I didn't tell you because of this reaction right here." Naveen shook his head. "Anyway, I usually don't feel so strongly so quickly, but I do. I want to be honest and act upon the way I feel, but I don't want to rush into anything, you know. I also don't know if she feels the same way. The last thing I need is to put my heart on the line again, only for it not to work out."

"Wait, are you saying that you are actually in love with her?"

"Not yet, I am not that hopeless of a romantic." He took a sip. "But I do want to hopefully move toward becoming exclusive soon. I just want to focus on her and I'm hoping she feels the same way."

"Well, I'll give you the same advice you just gave me." Golibe followed with his best Naveen's impersonation, which was mostly holding an invisible ponytail with his left hand. "I can tell that she is making you really happy. I know you mentioned being afraid things might end up not working out, but it is a risk when dating."

Naveen smiled. "You just had to throw it back at me."

Golibe released his nonexistent ponytail to pat Naveen's shoulder. "Nav, you really like this girl. Stop trying to fight it. You can't let your past ruin your present. I think love is looking to knock at a better's man door." Naveen looked at him. They were both on the verge of tears. "God, what the hell is in these shots?" Golibe said. He quickly wiped his face. "I'm blaming all this emotional ass talk on the alcohol."

***

Had Nova merely been inebriated by his smile and good looks? The more she found out about him, the less she wanted to know. The more he shared, the less she cared. The more they kissed, the less…No, that one would be a lie. She thoroughly enjoyed kissing Hakeem. She enjoyed being inside his arms. She enjoyed looking at him. But she was steadily coming to the conclusion that her crush for him was more exciting when it was just that. A crush. She got her internal confirmation when he announced that he would accept the job offer at *Fitness Link*. She was not sad about it. Yes, she would miss his smile. She would miss seeing him because he was a visual marvel. However, she didn't feel gutted. She felt fine. This would actually make things a lot easier. She could now focus on the person who was roaming the streets of her mind.

"I'm looking forward to seeing you tomorrow," Naveen messaged her.

"Me too."

The next day went on as well as it always *did* here. To her entertainment, Paul was getting more ridiculous with ways to avoid making eye contact with her. The next one always more hilarious than its predecessor. His last maneuver had been to pick up a pen that had fallen on the floor the moment she had asked him a question. And he just could not pick it until he was done answering her question. Would he just never look at her in the eyes again? It was the right amount of bizarre and amusing.

Rose was learning quickly. She had a knack for fitness sales, which made Nova's job easier. As for Hakeem, she had not seen him all day. She figured that he was somewhere with Emily, celebrating his job offer. That thought incited no emotions within her. At three o'clock, she signaled to Jeff that she was leaving for her business-to-business promotion run. He looked up and gave her a thumbs up in response.

232

When she approached the mirror, she felt different. Although she could not wait to get back to this side to see Naveen, for the first time, she was equally excited to go back to reality and pick up where she left off.

3:38 PM. Lips against glass. Lukewarmth. Reality.

CHAPTER 20

7:45PM.
The lotus flowers turned back to their original side as Nova materialized back into reality.

"What in the actual hell? Did you just...come out of that mirror?" Ana gasped loudly.

Nova was caught off guard. Immobile. She had left reality as high as the heavens with Ana passed out on her living room couch. What could she do or say? Perhaps Nova could knock her over the head with whatever solid object was in her bedroom, so Ana would pass out. Pro: Ana might forget the whole thing, and if she didn't, Nova would at least have some time to come up with a believable explanation. Con: Definitely the fact it would be an assault, and she could cause some unintended harm to her friend. Yeah, no.

Maybe, she could fake it as if she were the one passing out. Pro: Ana would be so concerned about her well-being she would not be worried about what she had seen. Con: It was Ana, for Christ's sake. The moment she was confident Nova was feeling better, she would demand answers. Definitely a no. Dammit, all her ideas were terrible. She was still too inebriated to think or see clearly...Eureka!

"Girl, you are high as hell! What are you talking about?" Nova said.

"No, I'm not that damn high. You just came out of that mirror!" Ana paused. She shook her head and stared at the floor. "Or am I?"

She approached the gold-framed lotus flowers mirror with slow and careful steps. Nova didn't utter a word. Ana slowly grazed the glass with her index finger while looking away with one eye closed. It looked like she had anticipated that the mirror's portal would open and lead her to Narnia or some other fanciful place. However, Nova knew the glass was cold and sleek, as one would expect. Nova tittered. Then, Ana formed a fist and knocked on the glass with her two eyes now open. Nothing happened.

She turned to Nova. "Shit. I need to stop buying weed from strangers." She laughed, tears rolling down her eyes.

Nova joined her and erupted in laughter, attempting to hide the relief under her guffaw. This was more than a close call. It was a call to make her final decision.

First, the additional back and forth, and now having to further lie to her friends? She needed to put an end to this. She wanted to put an end to this. Before her talk with Ana, she was almost one hundred percent sure that staying on the other side was the right decision. At this very moment, she was every bit fifty-fifty. She could go either way. The better part of her wanted to choose reality. She just needed something to tip the scale in its favor.

"Oh my god, that was hilarious." Nova continued to laugh.

"I don't even remember why I walked in here," Ana said, still cackling. "Oh, right, I need to use the bathroom."

Before she could walk away, Nova spoke, "I just want to say this now because I'm afraid I'll forget within the next five seconds."

Ana turned around and began to swing her hips from side to side as if her body had also just remembered that she had to use the bathroom. "What is it?"

"You apologized earlier, and I also owe you an apology. I was completely immature in the way that I reacted, and for that, I am sorry. Thank you for all the times you told me what I needed to hear, even when I didn't want to hear them. It has impacted me in ways you cannot even imagine."

They embraced for a long time; the way Kameela had taught them. "Anytime, Nova. We are family." Ana resumed the swinging of her hips. "Now I really have to pee!" She ran to the bathroom under Nova's amused and loving gaze.

Somehow, Nova woke up just in time for work the next morning. The later part of last night was a blur. She was not sure when Ana had left. From the tightness of her stomach, she was confident that a lot of belly laughs had been involved in the wee hours.

The day went on as she had anticipated. She didn't speak unless spoken to. Nothing out of the ordinary happened, and she was okay with that. She had glimpsed Hakeem once, but later he was nowhere to be found. She wondered if he would even consider telling her he was leaving *Fit Gals and Pals* on this side. Paul was less frantic than the day before. Rose looked less overwhelmed. Jeff was...Jeff.

Rose approached her near the end of her shift. "Hey, Nova. You have been very quiet today. Is everything okay?"

"Yes, everything is okay. Just ready for the weekend, I guess."

"Same here."

"It looks like you should be ready for your first walk-through soon," Nova said while gathering her belongings.

"Yes, I should be." Rose picked up her stuff as well. "I'm about to leave too. Let's walk outside together."

"Okay."

They both waved goodbye to Jeff and received his standard no-look nod. They looked at each other, holding a chuckle.

"He has got to be watching porn," Rose said when they were far enough from the building. "There is no way his eyes are glued to that screen all day long, and it's not porn."

Nova laughed harder than she had expected. "You might be onto something."

Rose's laughter quieted down, and she looked at Nova with an even expression. "Are you sure that everything is okay? I know we just started working together, and I don't want to cross any boundaries here. But I can tell you were a bit off today."

"How can you tell?"

"Your eyes."

Her stupid eyes had been telling on her and oversharing with everyone who would listen. *Hey Siri, how do I silence my eyes?* "What are they saying?"

"They are saying that you are going through something and are thinking about what to do next."

Wow. *Hey Siri, silence my eyes!* "You are good at reading eyes." She half-smiled.

Rose hesitated, then said, "The reason I can read that look well is because I had a similar look a few years ago." She took a moment. "I don't know why I feel so comfortable being this open with you, but I just have the feeling you need to hear this. Whatever it is that you are going through, I want you to know that there is a light at the end of the tunnel. Even if it doesn't seem like it right now, things will be okay."

Nova could read the pain in Rose's eyes. "You don't have to share if it's too personal, but what happened to you a few years ago?"

Rose answered with no hesitation. "Long story short, my parents did not agree with my lifestyle." She air-quoted lifestyle, and Nova immediately understood what she meant. "They just could not fathom that I loved who I loved. They ended up kicking me out of the house when I was seventeen. I left Nashville. I moved from state to state for a while. I was essentially a nomad. The wind happened to blow me to Orlando, where I was able to find my tribe. I don't want to get into all the details, but I had a few very..." she looked down, then continued, "...dark years." She looked back at Nova. "I wouldn't be here today if it wasn't for someone pulling me to the side to share their story with me and let me know that there was a light at the end of the tunnel, that things would be okay."

Rose's story was somewhat similar to hers, yet Nova was too choked up to share hers. "Thank you so much for sharing that with me. I'm so glad you were able to find a supportive community and that you are here today. Thank you for checking in on me. I really appreciate it. I'm grateful that you did. It means a lot."

Rose's eyes had so much care and warmth that Nova could feel her body temperature rising. Rose could see her. She understood. She gave a damn.

"You're more than welcome." Rose turned around to head to her car. She made a swift one-eighty turn at the last minute. "By the way, your friend from yesterday is gorgeous."

A part of last night's conversation with Ana rushed back to Nova's mind. *That new coworker of yours is very hot.* Oh hell, why not?

"She also thinks that you are, and I quote, *very hot.*"

Rose did a little dance and then walked away with a grin. "I'll see you tomorrow!"

Nova typically drove off the exact moment she buckled her seat belt. She always looked forward to leaving work on the real side. But today, she wanted to sit still until her body told her it was time to drive away. A mixture of emotions rushed out with fervor.

She was overwhelmed by Rose's concern. By Lily's. By Kameela's. By Ana's. She was overwhelmed by how much effort and love they had all poured into her in their own ways over the past few days. She was overwhelmed because someone cared about her.

Rose was virtually a stranger still, but somehow, she knew. And she didn't have to check in on her and share her own story to uplift her, but she did. Why? Because she cared. Lily admittedly wanted to get back to the other side of the mirror. However, Nova could tell she had genuine worry for her. She gave her some encouragement and told her not to give up just yet. Why? Because she cared. Kameela had called to check on her, to make sure she was okay. To tell her she was a good friend. Why? Because she cared. And Ana. She told her she respected her and valued their friendship. She even shared something she had kept secret for as long as they had known each other. She affirmed that when she got out of the den, she would be there for her. Why? Because she cared. Someone cared. Nova could not hold the flow of tears that cascaded through her visage.

Over the past few years, she had been broken. At the core, she was a shell of herself because she believed no one cared about her. She was a burden. A nuisance. She knew that her initial trigger was the abandonment of her parents. The coldness of the separation. The lack of love. The lack of care. Her two friends had become her family. But at some point, she felt like they, too, would discard her at any moment because she was not good enough. God, how broken was she. She had given up on trying to put herself back together because she was certain no one would want something that was fundamentally damaged. No matter how hard she would try to piece herself back together, people would simply point at the scotch tape on her face and know that she was a broken thing masquerading as whole. It was true that she was broken still. However, it was not true no one cared. Oh god, they cared! She was someone worth caring for. She felt immense relief, almost like a literal twenty-pound weight had been removed off her shoulders. She was not a burden. She was not a nuisance. She mattered. And they cared.

She cried, unrestrained. The tears healed some of her unspoken wounds. She felt somewhat new. After a peaceful moment of silence, her body whispered, *You can drive away now.* So, she did.

She decided to leave reality earlier than usual. This time it was not because she was eager to go back to the magic side but rather because it would be her last day *there*. She was not sure at what exact moment she had gotten to this point, but this was where she sincerely was. The scale had been tipped. Reality had won. It was far from a flawless victory. However, Lily was right. There was a light she could now unmistakably feel burning behind her eyes, the window of her soul, within her deepest parts. It was a quiet fire, but it was lit. Perhaps, she would never get to be the *her* she was on the other side here. However, she knew that reality was worth her best try.

The only reason she wanted to go back to the magic side one last time was to see Naveen. Her friends, the people who cared about her, were preserved in reality where they belonged. However, her story with Prince Naveen was a fairytale that would cease to exist the moment the magic mirror went away. She wanted to indulge in that magic one final time. After giving up the mirror, she might not even remember much of it, or potentially nothing at all. But according to Carole, she might at least remember how she felt. That alone was worth one final travel.

6:05 PM.

Eyes closed. Lips against glass. Motion stillness. Once last, magic.

CHAPTER 21

S he drove back to the gym silently. Though her emotions didn't carry from one side to the other, she unequivocally felt different. She still felt like the better her *here*. She was still certain that the sun shined brighter on this side of the mirror. She still felt that fluid thing in the air, leaving confidence mist on her skin. Yet, she was assured of her decision to stay in the flawed reality forever after. Today was her last day in fantasy.

She walked inside *Fit Gals and Pals* with an unspoken air of finality. She inhaled longer, deeper, and exhaled softly. She secretly hoped she could store the magic air and smuggle it into reality. When she walked to her desk, Paul zeroed his attention on the screen. She knew this side only came to life when she was present, but she still wanted to end things on a good note with Paul. Though this Paul would cease to exist with her absence, she felt like talking things out with him would somewhat carry over into their relationship on the real side.

"Hey, Paul. Do you have a moment?"

The weight of his head seemed to struggle against gravity. At last, it won and he looked up. With his eyes still unfocused, he spoke lowly. "Sure."

Nova led him to a secluded sitting area toward the back exit. She spoke the moment they sat down. "Are you okay?

You haven't been yourself lately."

He did not look at her. "How do you mean?"

"For one, you have been avoiding making eye contact with me for the past few days. And you haven't been your usual energetic self."

It seemed to take everything in him, but his eyes finally met hers. "I…" he looked away again, then he looked back at her. "Off the record?" She motioned as if she was locking an imaginary door in place of her mouth and threw the imaginary key in the distance.

He smiled and continued, "I guess I might as well be honest." He took a breath. "I really thought I would get the promotion. I have been talking to Jeff about it since the first day I got here. I know you have been here longer than I have, but I have been going above and beyond. I've always made sure to remind Jeff of what my end goal was every chance I got." He sighed. "The thing that kills me is how much less effort you need to put in to get the same result that I get, when I have to work ten times harder. This shit is just natural for you." Nova was listening quietly, hiding her surprise with an even face. "I spoke to Jeff afterward just to get some feedback. He basically told me, in so many words, that you were just better at this job. I guess my ego was bruised. But I shouldn't have reacted the way I did. I guess I was envious and resentful of how easy things are for you."

"I had no idea," she said. "You know that I think you are a great salesman. I'm sure you would have done just as well or even better than me in this role." She truly meant that. And, she had reality as proof. She could have never imagined that Paul thought things were easy for her. "And trust me, I do not have it easy at all."

Paul gazed at her. "The first day I met you, I immediately noticed how much you undervalued yourself. That's why I felt confident that any leadership position would be offered to me first. I did notice that you have gotten more…confident over the past week or so. Good for you. But you have always done better than you think, Nova."

He had noticed her worth even before the mirror. The scale weighed down further on reality's end. She did not need additional reinforcement, but it was validating to get it. Especially from her former work's 'nemesis'.

"Thank you, Paul. Are we okay?"

"Yes. Expect extremely direct and intense eye contact moving forward." He laughed faintly. They parted ways with an amicable fist bump. "I'll see you tomorrow!" he said with a lively tone.

"Yes." *See you on the other side.*

Nova walked back to her desk. She sat in silence and breathed consciously, still storing the magic air in her lungs (hopefully).

"Hey, Nova, I'm about to head out for the day. Is there anything else you want me to go over beforehand?" Rose said, interrupting her conscious breathing.

"No, I think you're good for the day."

Rose looked at her for a moment. "Your energy is different today."

"How so?"

"You're usually very cheerful, but today you seem very…I don't know…tranquil."

"My eyes told you?"

"Yes! I was going to use those exact words. How did you know?"

"Déjà vu."

"Well, it soothes you. See you tomorrow!"

"Yes." *See you in reality.*

Around five, she gathered her stuff as she always did. On her way out, she waved goodbye to Jeff.

"Bye, Nova," he said, looking up. A vocal farewell paired with eye contact from Jeff. Things couldn't have ended on a better note with him *here*.

The one goodbye she had not accounted for at *Fit Gals and Pals* was Hakeem. She had not seen him all day. She was okay with their story ending with no further communication on both sides. She looked at the ocean-blue sky one last time. She closed her eyes to store more magic air passed her lungs, hopefully somewhere safe within her unconscious. She allowed the bright magic sun to get through her skin. The moment she turned to her car to get in, she felt that unmistakable tap on her shoulders. Well, there would be a final exchange after all.

She turned slowly toward the person she was expecting to see. "Hey, Hakeem."

"Hey!" He pulled her in for a hug. "I'm sorry I keep catching you when you are leaving. I came in to give my one week's notice." He grinned, then said, "I'm not going to lie, I did time it so I could get here when you were leaving. I wanted to see you."

"I'm glad to see you here." *For the last time.*

He leaned in for a kiss. She turned her head away to avoid it.

"It's okay, no one is around," he whispered in her ear.

"It's not that." She stepped back. She knew this dynamic would stop existing when she stopped using the mirror.

However, she felt like ending things here would somehow help her close the Hakeem chapter in reality. For good.

He blinked a couple of times, furrowed brows. "Then, what is it?"

"I know we haven't really started anything, but I think we should end things here. I obviously think you're a great guy, but I—"

"I told you, there is nothing going on between me and my ex. I want to pursue you. Especially now that we won't be working together, we can get to know each other freely." He looked at her lips.

"No, I believe you. I just don't think we should go down this road. I'd prefer if we just stayed friends."

He looked flabbergasted, eyes narrowing in apparent disbelief. "I know you might be a little nervous with the sudden interest I've shown you, but it's genuine. You can put your walls down, Nova." He smiled that smile that only he knew how to smile.

Her face remained even. "I'm not nervous, Hakeem. I'm just not interested in being more than friends."

His smile evaporated. His body stiffened. His features became somber. "Nova, I know that you've had a crush on me since I started working here. Now that I'm showing you some interest, I'm not sure why you're trying to play coy. Relax, I find you attractive. You are not dreaming." He ended his speech with a lingering smirk.

At that moment, she came to the realization that he believed he was completely out of her league. He thought he was doing her a favor by giving her the time of day. She should kneel and look up to praise the heavens because he had even considered looking her way. He had been generous

247

enough to rest his divine lips against hers, a mere mortal. He felt he was lowering his standards by engaging with her. God forbid, she was not interested. How dare she. She was not good enough to not want him and to have self-worth. Except that she was. Not only *here* but also on the real side of the mirror.

She sighed. "I'm very relaxed and very much aware that I'm awake. In this very serene and conscious state of mind, I can assure you I'm confident in the fact that I'd prefer to end things here. Just one correction, we don't have to be friends at all. Best of luck in your future endeavors."

He said something in response. She was certain they were words, but she did not hear them. She did not care to. She got in her car and drove away. She felt good. The chapter was closed. She was not regretful that it had happened, but she was content it was over. She hoped with all her being that this feeling would carry over into reality.

The evening finally came, bringing out the moon and the stars above her head. The moment she had been waiting for. The sole reason she decided to make her final travel to the magic side of the mirror: Naveen. He texted her at 7:30 PM.

"**I'm on my way there. See you soon!**"

She sent a text to her two friends. "**Date night with Naveen! I'll let you know how it goes. Love you guys, truly.**"

Kameela answered, "**Have fun, beautiful. You deserve it. Love you!**"

Ana followed. "**Nova, it's been 84 years. I'm worried about you. Please get some dick. Love you too!**"

She first laughed, then smiled, and finally pondered. It was her last day on this side. Perhaps she should indulge in some magically enhanced sex. After reflecting, she came to a simple conclusion: she would let the night follow its natural course. She simply wanted to see him and be with him…one last time.

Nova wore a cowl neck emerald dress. She walked inside of the restaurant, looking around at the bamboo plants lining every wall. She was neither nervous nor anxious. Though, a part of her was sad because it understood the gravity and the finality of the situation. Everyone else that she had said goodbye to would still be a part of her life when she returned to the real side. But things were different with Naveen. She had her shot in reality, but she had blown it. This side of the mirror was the only place where their story was alive. And soon, it would be over. She understood what tonight was. As much as she wanted to cry, she was also happy that she would get to spend a final evening with him. She hoped these memories would find refuge somewhere in her psyche.

Naveen rested his head on his palm. His hair was down, past his collarbone. He shook his head in awe when their eyes met. "Hello, beautiful."

She had missed him more than she had realized. "Hi," she said with the widest beam.

"You look stunning."

"Thank you. You look very handsome as well."

They hugged. Then their faces were right next to each other. Nova pressed her lips together and smiled. Naveen smiled, then leaned in. They kissed. Slowly. Gently. He exhaled under his breath. He pulled her chair out.

"Thank you." She sat down.

"Of course."

They ordered their food while holding hands on top of the table. He held her firmly but not roughly, like an egg outside of a carton.

"I'm so happy to be here with you," he said.

"Me too. I've been thinking about you…a lot." She usually wouldn't have been so forward, but today did not have room for holding back.

Nova could hear her heart beating faster inside of her chest, resembling the last few seconds of a drumroll. He looked at her as if he could hear it too.

"So have I, Nova," he said. "I usually don't feel so strongly so soon. But I do. I'm so relieved you feel the same way."

Their food and drinks arrived promptly, though the service was not as ceremonial as the last place they had gone too. They caught up for a little while, having to speak a little louder over the upbeat music. Naveen let her know that things were thankfully becoming less stressful at his job. He shared that every time he got stressed, he thought about her, and it felt a little better. That revelation warmed her entire body. She told him how well things were going at *Fit Gals and Pals*. She even shared the conversation she had with Paul.

"I completely understand the guy. I mean how could he ever compete against you," he said while caressing her hand. "I'm glad you two were able to talk it out, though."

"Me too." She smiled before asking, "Oh. How is your friend…Golibe, right?"

His eyes lit up. "Yes, you got it! He is great. In fact, the other day, he told me that he was going to propose to his girlfriend soon."

"That's awesome! I'm happy for them!"

"So am I! He is like a brother to me. I'm over the moon for them. They are soulmates."

Nova narrowed her stare. "What about your soulmate?"

"I can't say for certain yet, but I think I was able to track her down." He looked directly into the brown of her eyes.

She held his stare and smiled. "Now that you have done that, what is your next move?"

"Make sure that she is enjoying dinner." He paused. "How are you liking the food?"

She maintained his gaze and widened her grin. "I like the food, and I love the company."

Their desserts were served. Strawberry cheesecake for her. Chocolate mousse for him. Nova realized that she had not asked him how his family was doing. She recalled he had shared that they were all very close.

"How are your parents doing?" she said between bites.

His voice lowered. "They are doing well. Yesterday was actually my dad's birthday."

"Nice! Did he do anything fun?"

"Yes. He celebrated with my mom and some other family members. My brother and I facetimed them. We hung out for a little while. It was nice."

"That's lovely. It sounds like you guys are a tight-knit family. That's wonderful."

"Yes. There are pros and cons to everything, though."

Nova didn't want him to reveal more than he was ready for. However, she had a feeling he wanted to share. "What are some of the cons?"

He was silent for a moment. "Do you remember our last date?"

"Of course."

"You asked me if I would have preferred to have gone a different route career wise had my parents not advised I chose between the two options they thought would be best for me."

"Yes, I remember." She nodded. She held his hand gently, and she could feel his body tensing under her grasp.

"The unrefined answer to that question is yes. I was very passionate about cricket growing up. I was pretty good at it and my dream was to go pro. But my parents felt like my odds to become a successful professional athlete were slim." He took a moment to catch his breath. "Wow. I never shared this with anyone except my brother."

She caressed his forearm. "It's okay."

He continued. "I understand why they felt the way they did. My career is stable and secure. Making a living as a professional athlete would have been somewhat of a gamble. However, at the same time, that was my dream, you know. They just shut me down and never even thought about it twice." His voice broke hoarsely. "And I just agreed. I didn't put up a fight. I just went along with their wish and threw mine away."

Nova could see his eyes reddening. She wished she had the perfect answer to appease him, but she didn't. She pulled her chair closer to his and hugged him tight until their heartbeats sounded like one. Somehow, the hug knew the words that she did not know how to enunciate. The hug knew how to comfort him and reassure him he was where he was supposed to be. He said nothing for a while, but Nova felt his muscles relax inside their embrace.

"Thank you," he said at last.

"Thank you for trusting me."

"What about you, Nova? You never talk about your family."

The server came by their table to drop the check. He let them know not to rush and to stay as long as they needed. They both nodded in understanding. Nova looked back at Naveen. She had not planned on talking about her parents tonight. However, she was happy that this conversation was happening. She wanted him to know about her upbringing. Even though a few hours from now, this moment might not be discernable in her memory, she felt like it would matter in the ether scheme of things.

She cleared her throat. "I had a very strict upbringing." Naveen zeroed his focus on her. He tightened both of her hands under his grip. She immediately felt safe. "I was raised a Jehovah Witness, and my parents are fundamentalists. There were so many restrictions to what I could and could not do. How I should think. Who I could hang out with. Long story short, I started questioning some of the practices and beliefs, which led me to be disfellowshipped." Naveen was listening intently but looked slightly perplexed. "This essentially means that I was cast out of my congregation because I had dared to question some things. I was shunned by everyone, including my own parents." Her voice broke. "They have not spoken to me since the elders officially announced that I was disfellowshipped almost four years ago."

A tear rolled down Naveen's eye. "Oh my god. Nova, I could've never imagined. I'm so sorry you went through that." He opened his arms. She and her sorrow disappeared inside of them. "I'm sorry," he repeated.

"Thank you," she said, still choked up.

They stayed in the embrace and said nothing for a while. The music stopped playing. They both looked around them.

Everyone was gone.

Naveen covered the bill hastily.

"Let's get out of here," he said.

She followed behind him. When they made it outside, he said, "This evening was wonderful. It turned out to be a little more emotional than I expected, but I'm happy that it did. I just want to make sure that you are okay. Do you want me to drop you home? I can come to pick you up in the morning to get your car. I don't want you to drive home alone like this. What would you like me to do?"

She looked deeply into the brown of his eyes. She spoke with no hesitation. "Let's go to your place."

CHAPTER 22

Naveen opened his apartment door to let Nova in. She walked inside without saying a word. She could feel him right behind her, close and warm. All his furniture ranged from dark brown to black, except for the glass coffee table. Nothing was out of place. There were no dishes in the sink. All the paintings were hung at the right angle. There were a few statues of women with a multitude of arms seated cross-legged, with three eyes, with their bodies stretched out in incredible ways all throughout the living room. Across the entrance was a wall displaying his cricket trophies and medals. All the canvases were abstract. Colorful shapes, lines, and contrasting textures lit up the space.

"Your place is very nice," she said, looking at the painting above the black leather sofa. "I didn't know you were an art connoisseur."

"Thank you. And I wouldn't say that I am a connoisseur, more so an aesthete." He put his keys on the counter and then turned to face her. "I know a beautiful and unique piece when I see one."

She could feel herself blush, red below her deep mahogany exterior. She sat down and crossed her legs perfectly parallel. Did magic make her even more flexible? Or did her body intuitively know the moment called for it?

Either way.

"Let's say I'm abstract art; how would you explain me?"

He sat next to her. His legs were lined up with his shoulders. Closer. Warmer. "With abstract art, the point is not necessarily to figure out its meaning but rather to allow oneself to be taken by it. The thing with you is that I don't have to allow it. I'm taken without my own permission, and I'm loving every second."

The moment Nova heard those words, something she knew but could not name freed itself from within her. Her heart rate sped up, yet she could still capture every beat. She uncrossed her legs and wrapped them over his. She looked at his profile, biting her bottom lip. His jawline clenched. His chest was rising and dropping rapidly. He lifted her so she could rest on him, facing him. Their lips met, at first softly, then more passionately. She held his face. He wrapped his arms around her waist. Then, she could feel his hands promenading from the back of her neck, back to her waist, pausing on her hips and slowly finding rest at her bottom. She wrapped her arms around his neck. She breathed into his ear, then bit his earlobe. He moaned. She moved back slightly to remove her dress above her head. He was watching silently, leaned back with his hands behind his head, like a suspect caught engaging in some risqué behavior.

Before she could undo her bra, he opened his mouth slowly. His voice was shaky, struggling to let the words out. "I know tonight was very emotional, are you sur—?"

She moved her index finger to his mouth to stop his speech. "Be taken," she whispered like a spell.

He smiled and helped her out of her bra. "Yes, ma'am." He took his shirt off.

They lay on the couch, chest against chest. They kissed, him on top of her, then her on top of him. Their bodies intertwined as if they had always belonged together, like a puzzle put back together. They rolled around on the sofa until they ran out of space. They fell on the floor and broke into laughter. He looked at her as her laughter faded into a smile. He took his pants off. Then, they resumed their dance. She felt his fingers and his lips exploring her entire body. His tongue moved from her forehead to her lips, her neck, her breasts, more on her breasts, her belly button, then between her thighs. He stayed there for a while, letting his tongue move to the right place at the right time. She could hear herself gasp under his touch, helpless and not wanting to be helped. The gentle grip she had known was now firm on her breasts.

Naveen looked at her with a new sparkle in his eyes. He lifted her up: one arm under her legs and the other behind her back, like a groom carrying his bride to their honeymoon suite. She just looked into his eyes as they entered his bedroom. He gently lay her on the bed. He kissed her forehead. Then, he searched through the nightstand. He grabbed a condom and looked back at Nova. She caressed his chest and smiled. He unrolled the condom down his erected part. He paused for a moment to look at her. She was lying down, vulnerable and bare.

"You are so beautiful," he said at last.

He leaned in, parted her legs, and dwelled inside of her. She could immediately feel herself accept his presence under both of their uneven breaths and moans. She wrapped her arms and legs around him tightly, demanding more.

The next day, Nova rose with the sun. She searched the

bed with her hand to find Naveen, but he was not there. Was it all a dream?

"Good morning, beautiful." She heard behind her. Naveen was carrying two coffee mugs. He handed her one and gave her a soft kiss on the lips. "How did you sleep?"

"Wonderfully," she said with a wide grin. "What about you?"

"Amazingly." He looked at the clock next to his TV. He sat next to her. "Are you going to be able to make it to work on time?"

Nova pondered for a moment. She had just had the most amazing night of her life. There was a strong possibility the person next to her could be the one. They were in the genesis of forming a beautiful bond, one with the potential to last a lifetime. With her decision to stop using the mirror, she could lose it all: their laughter, their banter, his touch, his presence, him. It would all be gone. The worst part was that she might not even remember it at all. The cost of choosing reality was to lose a possible soulmate. But no matter how much she wanted to stay here and continue to live this dream, she now understood that it was just that: a fantasy. Naveen was not falling for the real her. He was enthralled by the mirror's version of her. She could not give up on reality just to live a fairy tale, no matter how happy the ever after promised to be. At least, she had a few more hours to enjoy the magic.

"I don't have to go to work today," she said. She placed the mug on the nightstand. She invited him back to the bed with her index finger.

A huge smile enveloped his face. He placed his mug next to hers. "I'm working from home today, and I don't have my first meeting until 11."

She sat back up and lunged at him. He fell on the bed, grinning like a willing victim. They laughed, kissed, then rediscovered each other with a passionate delight. Their bodies collapsed next to one another when they were done making love. Nova rested her head on his chest. Naveen tucked her in closer and rested a kiss on her forehead. She felt so unbelievably good. She was not sure how she would be able to leave now. The more time she spent inside of his arms, the harder she sensed it would be to go away. But she had to.

"I really like you, Nova," he whispered into her ear.

"I really like you too."

"Let's go to the movies tonight!" he said. She could not hold the tears that rushed out. The reminder that their love story was on its final page. "Are you okay?" he asked, holding her tighter.

"Yes." She wiped her face. "I'm just happy."

She kissed him gently. They stayed in a joyful silence for a while. Time no longer existed. She fell back into Morpheus' hands.

She woke up close to noon. She checked her phone. She had numerous missed calls from Jeff. She waved it off. It didn't matter. She stretched out on the bed. She did not have to go back to reality until 2:38 PM. She could stay a little longer.

Naveen walked back into the bedroom when he heard her movements. "Hello, sleeping beauty." He sat at the corner of the bed.

"I cannot believe I slept till noon."

"You looked like you were having the best sleep, so I didn't want to wake you up."

She crawled toward him and hugged him from behind.

"Thank you."

"Of course. I would hate for someone to wake me up when I'm sleeping like a baby."

She sat next to him, holding the tears watering her eyes. "No, thank you for everything. Last night. This morning. All of it. Thank you."

He furrowed his brow. "It's just the beginning." He smiled. "Let's do movies tonight, if you are free?"

She could almost hear her heart shattering. It seemed he heard it too, because his frown deepened.

"Yes, sure," she said. She attempted a smile, but her lips barely moved. "I have to go now," she said brusquely. She put her clothes on. Naveen gazed at her silently, immobile. She landed a kiss on his forehead. A tear cascaded down her cheek. "Goodbye, Naveen."

He nodded but did not speak. She looked back at him before she walked out. He was sitting still, staring at the floor.

Nova drove home with eyes full of tears. Why? Why did it have to end like this? She strongly considered continuing to use the mirror. But she knew the longer she stayed on the magic side, the harder it would be to leave. The one thing harder than feeling heartbroken was feeling heartbroken when staying in the situation that made one happy was still an option. She rolled down her window, hoping the breeze would clear her mind. She tried to recall everything she had experienced *here*, especially Naveen. If she could focus hard enough, perhaps she could hide her happy memories away from the erasing magic.

Perhaps Carole could let her know of a way not to forget. She immediately remembered that she had never interacted with Carole on this side. When she got closer to the location where the shop should have been, her eyes discovered its absence. *Magique Antiques* did not exist on this side of the mirror. Nova then recalled Carole had explained that someone who had previously owned the mirror could not be on the magic side after they had stopped using it. Damn it!

Perhaps she could go back to reality to see Carole and get some advice. Then, she could return to this side one last time and hopefully be guaranteed to preserve her memories. She just needed more time. More magic...No. She didn't. Getting back to this cycle would resume the back and forth she had miraculously talked herself out of. The one which had almost made her choose a fantasy instead of reality. She had to make her final move now while she still had the strength.

She rushed to her apartment and ran inside as soon as she parked her car. The mirror was standing inside her bedroom. It seemed like it was taking more space. It looked like its gold had a novel glow. The lotus flowers appeared to have expanded in size. Nova could have almost sworn that something was trying to talk her out of her decision. She was not sure whether it was her internal voice, the mirror itself, or something else. But some words echoed somewhere.

What are you doing? You know that you want to stay here.
It's better here, and you know it.
Think about how much better things are at your job. Think
about how much more your friendships with Kameela and
Ana will blossom here. You basically dumped Hakeem here.
He doesn't even glance your way on the other side.
It's better here, and you know it.
Think about Naveen. You two do not stand a chance on
the other side. It's already over there. But here, you two

261

could have the love story you have always dreamt of.
It's better here, and you know it!

2:33 PM.

The invitation to stay was powerful and overwhelming. It froze her muscles and clogged her throat. The mirror's gold frame was shining. The words spoken were convincing. Why was she fighting this comforting feeling? Perhaps she should just stay here. It was indeed better on this side, and she knew it. She had known from the first time her lips had met the mirror's glass. It was effortless. It was better. It was magic.

Fantasy.

In a lucid moment, she recalled her interactions with Lily, Rose, Kameela, and Ana on the real side. The flawed but real side. It was neither perfect nor effortless, but it was her reality. And her friends cared about her. She owed it to them and herself not to give up. No, she could not stay here.

She snapped out of the spell and yelled out, "This side is not real, and I know it!"

2:38 PM.

She forced her lips on the shiny glass. Eyes closed. She felt both still and in motion. Her heart paused. Her skin warmed up. The transport felt like it always did. Except this time there was an additional sensation during her crossing back to reality: release.

Eyes closed still. Tepidity. She exhaled, out of the den.

CHAPTER 23

Nova checked the time as soon as she appeared back on the real side. 6:28 PM. The accuracy of the magic still astonished her. She lay on her bed, motionless. She pushed herself to remember every single detail of her night with Naveen...*there*. Her emotions from the other side did not travel back to reality with her, as expected. However, she could objectively recall what had happened. Unfortunately, that silver lining might soon be a thing of the past.

She closed her eyes. She focused to recall Naveen's touch, his kisses, the sound of his voice when he was close to climax. She thought about the way he always looked at her, like it was his mission to make sure she felt safe at all times. She did not want to forget how he made her feel. She did not want to forget what they had. She did not want to forget him. The alternative was just too costly. She had to face reality, good or bad. No more escaping. It was time for her to garner the courage to be the person she wanted to be in reality.

Nova loved who she was on the other side: playful, vibrant, and bold. The mirror had created the version of her she wanted to be. As she thought deeper about it, she realized the reason she could not translate that version of her into reality was merely because it was not her.

Then, who was she?

She remembered one question from her job interview with Jeff: *What are three words that describe you best?* Then, she had given the three words that would help her get hired: hardworking, patient, and reliable. She chuckled at the memory. What a load of crap. It indeed helped her get the job. However, those were not the three words that described her best. She was not the most hardworking, patient, or reliable person like she had played up to get her job. She was also not the most playful, the most vibrant, or the boldest like the version of her on the other side.

Who was Nova Wright, then?

She thought about what Ana had said: *you could have given up then, and it would have been understandable. But you didn't.* She was resilient. Her last conversation with Paul on the other side flashed through her mind: *you have always done better than you think, Nova.* She was capable. At last, she recalled what Lily had cried out to reason her to choose reality: *you can still live the life you want to live in reality. I can see it in your eyes.* She was not done. Hope was alive. She could turn things around. She wasn't sure how to just yet, but she knew that she could. And that was enough to make her feel confident about her decision.

The thought of Lily lingered in her mind. She, on the other hand, had given up. The least Nova could do to thank her was to give her what she wanted the most: the portal back to fantasy. And maybe she could talk her out of it. She could let her know that she still had a shot on the real side. She could help. She wasn't sure how, but at the very least, she could be there for her. She could offer a listening ear. She could let her know things would be okay, that there was a light at the end of the tunnel. Frankly, Nova could hardly see the light at the end of her own tunnel, but she knew it would be there. And just like it would appear for her and blind her with shiny hopefulness, it would be there for Lily as well. Nova needed to make amends with reality. She would make a good deed offering. She would save both herself and Lily from the seductive fantasy.

Nova had slept a dreamless sleep. Or she didn't remember what she had dreamed of. Hopefully, the reason for her unanimated Morpheus' visit was that her subconscious had been too busy storing and hiding her memories from the magic side instead.

When she made it to *Fit Gals and Pals*, she immediately looked around to see if Lily was there. She wasn't there at nine. Still not there by twelve. Nowhere to be found at three. Lily came to the gym every day. Today had to be the day she would not show up.

Nova had to see her today. She would try to talk her out of her decision to choose the other side. But, if she failed to do so, it was imperative she made the transfer of ownership today. She didn't want to simply stop using the mirror, causing Lily to have to track down the next owner. However, she could not risk traveling back to the other side simply to hold onto the mirror for Lily. Today was the day. After pacing up and down the entire gym, she finally sat down.

"Are you looking for someone?" Rose said.

Nova was so focused on her mission that she had not thought about how it looked. "No. I just need to get ten thousand steps in today." She hated that she had to lie to Rose, but telling her who she was looking for would lead her to make up an even bigger lie.

"I got you." Rose smiled. "You look better today."

"Thank you," she began. "I—" Her speech was paused by Lily's entrance. "I'll be right back."

Lily grinned with all her teeth when she recognized Nova. "Thank God," she said.

Nova nodded. "Follow me." She led her to the back exit like she had done the first time, when she had confronted her about her intentions. The moment they stepped outside, she said, "I have decided to stop using the mirror and stay on the real side."

Lily's eyes lit up. "Oh my god. That's great! I'm so happy for you. You are making the right decision, Nova." She moved in for a hug but was halted by Nova's rigid stance.

"I don't think you should go back there."

Lily frowned. "Nova, we went over this. I appreciate the fact that you are trying to help me, but I'm hanging by a thread here."

"I know you are going through a lot here, and the mirror seems like a safe haven, but you and I both know that it is not real. It's a fantasy. I know things are hard for you here." She paused and exhaled. "I don't know how difficult it is to try to overcome any addiction, but I know my life is far from perfect on this side too. The other side is a seductive mirage, but I'd rather stay in reality and try to become the best version of myself here…even if it won't be the ideal prototype I had in my head. I'm not trying to lecture you, but I would hate myself if I didn't at least try." She took another moment. "Think about your loved ones. You would just leave them here. If not for yourself, choose reality for the people who love you."

Lily looked directly into her eyes. She did not blink for the entirety of her delivery. "I have no one here." Her voice came out deeper. "Almost everyone that I cared about has died due to the very demons that I'm battling. And the ones who are still alive might as well be dead. I don't want to be next, but if I stay here, I will." Her piercing eyes narrowed and darkened. "When I came in today, I was afraid I wouldn't find you. I was afraid that you might have chosen to stay there. Honestly, if you did, my days would have been numbered. I really appreciate you trying, but I cannot stay here. I have tried here, and it simply doesn't work. I understand all the implications. I know that it's not reality. I know that it's a fantasy." Her voice rose. "I don't care! It seems real, and it feels real. I have a shot there. I'm a dead woman walking here. The only way any part of my being can survive is by being gone in reality. Please, Nova, allow me to go."

Nova could feel her eyes water. "Lily, I just…" She wanted to try again. Perhaps her previous argument wasn't strong enough. It could have been her wording. If she tried again and argued harder, perhaps she could talk her out of her decision.

When she finally allowed Lily's words to settle in, she realized she was merely a few loved ones away from being in Lily's shoes. She had chosen reality because she had concluded that some people did care about her. She had not decided based on the sole realization of her self-worth and adequacy. That had been secondary. Lily was facing even harsher circumstances than hers, with seemingly no one who cared about her. And as much as Nova was trying to initiate a reset by "saving" Lily, she would be a hypocrite if she did not admit that she most likely would have chosen the other side if she were in her predicament.

Nova spoke again. "I understand where you are coming from. I just want to make sure you are fully aware of the gravity of your decision. Carole did say that any previous owner who went back to the other side after a transfer would be faced with a different set of rules."

Lily nodded. "I thought hard and thoroughly about this. Whatever happens to me, it's not on you. This is my decision. I'm willing to face whatever consequences come with it. I'm so thankful we met here, and I'm glad I was a part of your journey." Lily moved closer and held her hand. "It's okay, Nova. Let me go."

Nova's eyes watered. The tears flowed freely down her face. Though Lily was virtually still a stranger, they had a unique bond. The bond of two people dealt the worst set of cards and still expected to win the game, somehow. The bond of two people who had understandably given up at one point in time due to their extreme circumstances. The only difference was that one of them was rescued by loved ones when she was ready to jump off the ledge. The other one had the strength to remain still for a longer period whilst contemplating her decision, hoping that someone would come to the rescue. No one did, except a lotus flowers gold framed mirror. Nova had no right to get in the way of that.

"Okay," she said, choked up. "Follow me to my place when I get off work."

At the end of the day, Lily followed behind Nova's car. They quietly walked inside her apartment. Every step single they made felt as heavy as the moment soon to follow.

"Nice place. I like minimalism." Lily said, looking around.

Nova rarely thought about the décor—or lack thereof—

at her place. All she saw were white walls and empty spaces. She felt like it illustrated the *her* she had been trying to unbecome: unremarkable, banal, and forgettable. It was pleasant to hear that someone thought it was *nice* and even belonged in a category.

"Thank you." She smiled briefly. "The mirror is in my bedroom." She gestured at Lily to follow behind her.

When they walked in, the air surrounding the mirror was dense. It was so thick it was almost visible, undulating around the frame. The gold of the lotus flowers was the shiniest Nova had ever seen. Almost blinding. It was as if the mirror itself understood what was about to happen.

"I forgot how beautiful the mirror was." Lily gasped, staring at it.

Nova nodded. "Well, shall we?"

"Let's."

They both closed in on the mirror, and their steps aligned like they had choreographed it. Nova gave her a final pleading look. "Are you sure?"

Lily hugged her. "Thank you for giving me a second chance."

Nova wiped a tear. "So, we are just kissing it at the same time?"

"Yes."

"Then, you and the mirror will disappear, and so will potentially my memories of the mirror and everything related to it?"

"Yes." Lily nodded.

Nova walked backwards. She stumbled on her bed. She lay face up and eyes closed. She whispered something she thought was too low for Lily to register. However, she answered, "Take your time. Think about everything you want to remember. These memories might just survive somewhere in your unconscious."

Nova did as advised. She frowned harder as if the closer her eyebrows got, the higher her chance to recall every single moment on the other side. Memories of the moment she was announced at *Fit Gals and Pals'* new assistant manager made an appearance. Her interactions with her two best friends waved at her. She waved back with enthusiasm. Then, the ones with Hakeem. She smiled and waved goodbye to them. She felt at peace with leaving them wherever her history on the other side resided. However, the moment she saw Naveen's face staring at her, sadness rushed to the forefront.

She could not lie to herself; she was devastated at the thought of forgetting her love story with him. She tried to remember everything about him and the moments they spent together. She tried to relive every moment they shared a few times over. She smiled brighter every single time. Even though those memories would most likely be erased in the next few minutes, she was beyond thankful they had happened.

She finally opened her eyes. She looked at Lily. "I'm ready." She stood up at once.

"Whatever it is you had on the other side, you can have it here. It might not be the same, but I know you can make some magic happen without the mirror. I believe in you!"

"Thank you, Lily." Nova embraced her. "I wish you the best of luck there. I'm grateful we were part of each other's journey."

They held each other for a moment. When their bodies parted, they both knew it was time. Nova looked at her clock the same way she had done over the past couple of weeks. Only this time, she knew it would be the last.

6:16 PM.

They walked toward the mirror, holding hands. They released their grip as they stood closer to the luminous portal to fantasy.

"Are you ready?" Lily said.

"Yes."

"Thank you, Nova."

Everything quietened down around them. The only thing she could hear was the steadiness of their heartbeats.

"Thank you, Lily. Good luck."

They leaned forward, eyes closed. Their lips met the smooth glass at the same exact time. The lotus flowers opened widely. Nova saw the static motion of the transport as if she was looking from the distance at the sunset settling on the horizon. She felt warmth, but it was far away. She saw Lily disappear into the mirror. The sense of refuge she felt wasn't hers, but the release was. She felt detached. Apart. Anew, yet the same. Then, Lily was gone. The mirror disappeared. She opened her eyes for a few seconds. She couldn't keep them open for long. With no thought, she lay on her bed and passed out.

***

The mirror materialized in the storage room of *Magique Antiques* the next day. Finally, Carole thought. She had been very anxious that Nova would keep using the mirror longer than she had anticipated. The longer they kept it, the less their life force was worth. She got closer and narrowed her gaze. She caressed one of the lotus flowers. She looked through the glass, inside of the mirror. It was not who she had expected.

271

Lily was lying on her bed with a hopeful grin. Carole would have preferred Nova. Lily was her backup plan. She knew telling her about the transfer of ownership would eventually serve a purpose. Something was better than nothing. Although it was better when it was an original first-time owner, she could not afford to be picky. Reality had not given Lily a fair shot. They would make good use of her soul.

It was so tricky having to convince them to make a volitional choice whilst simultaneously acknowledging how dire the consequences of the decision were. But that was what she had to do as the gatekeeper. The bridge between the land and the waters. The faithful servant of Mother. They had to voluntarily make their final decision while being fully aware of the implications. It was the only way it worked. It was the only way their souls could count. Forty-plus years later, and it was now second nature for her. She could convincingly convey concern and appear sincere whilst subconsciously planting seeds for them to choose the other side of the mirror.

Somehow, Nova chose reality. Carole had been so certain she would pick the other side. Oh well, Lily would suffice for this cycle. She examined the mirror. To her relief, she identified a novel lotus flower at the bottom right corner. Mother would be satisfied. She gestured at the two delivery guys. They were sitting quietly in front of her, waiting for her directive. They immediately stood up. One hurriedly looked through a drawer and grabbed a price tag. They both ran to the sales floor. They cleared some space around the floor mirrors' section, in the corner of the shop. Carole looked at them silently to make sure they were completing their task correctly.

After a moment, she turned around to face the mirror.

She knocked counterclockwise on four sections of the glass, three times. The glass became fluid-like, resembling ocean waters. The lotus flowers did not move, keeping the gold frame intact. Carole swam through the other side. The mirror regained its solid form behind her. She disappeared into it with an enigmatic grin.

CHAPTER 24

Nova woke up feeling like she had been hit by a truck. Her forehead was pulsating. She could not think through her headache. She hated to do it, but she had to stay home and rest today.

"You never call off work, so I know it must be really bad," Jeff said. "Take the time that you need. I hope you feel better soon. Let me know if you need anything."

"I will. Thank you, Jeff."

She sat up slowly. She massaged her temples, hoping to appease the pounding of her head. The later part of yesterday was a blur. Her thoughts and memories appeared to be spread across her mind. She focused her hardest to gather them. To recollect what had happened yesterday after she left work. The last week or two seem to have a hole, a missing piece. She looked around her bedroom. She noticed something was missing.

"The mirror!" she said out loud.

She vaguely remembered a lady from a thrift store. She couldn't recall her name or her face. But she remembered a mirror, at least partially. She knew within herself how it looked. However, if she were asked for specific details, she couldn't describe it. What about the mirror question related to her life? She recalled that she had broken her other mirror

275

when she was cleaning her bedroom. She went to some thrift store and purchased another mirror, the one she could no longer describe.

She got up and walked to her kitchen. She grabbed a bottle of water. Hopefully, hydrating would lubricate her memory. She took a sip. She stood still, hoping her thoughts would do the same. She remembered vividly most of what had happened over the past couple of weeks. Kameela and Josh had a fight and made up. She and Ana had a little exchange, but they talked things out. Paul had been promoted as the new assistant manager. She could have done away with that memory. She was getting along well with the new hire, Rose. Hakeem was still not paying her any mind outside of their occasional exchanges during her walk-throughs. She immediately noticed she wasn't feeling the little tingles around her heart she usually felt every time she thought about Hakeem. Interesting.

The last person who came to mind was the guy from the grocery store. The one with whom she had gone on the one date at *The Route*. Naveen. She still hadn't heard from him and probably never would again. She felt extremely sad about that thought. She shook her head to snap out of the feeling. *It was only one date.* It just felt like there was a lot more there. It felt like somehow, they had a lot more history. The thought of him made her feel warm inside. She wasn't sure how, but she was convinced the missing mirror had something to do with it.

Or perhaps, she was making it all up. Perhaps it was all a coping mechanism to deal with rejection. She suddenly felt very lightheaded. Going back to sleep might help. She needed more rest. Hopefully, things would be clearer when she woke up later.

She rose again, moments later. Her headache was not completely gone, but she felt a lot better. Although she still couldn't determine what was missing from her memories, she stopped trying to force herself to. What was the point, anyway? It was probably just a minute detail. Honestly, she was probably trying to busy her mind because she was home on a weekday with no plans. She looked at her inviting couch in the living room. She could microwave some food. Then, she could lay on it until Netflix shamed her by asking if she was still watching. She could do that. She did enjoy that. However, a voice inside of her whispered that it was time to step outside, literally and metaphorically.

Nova opened the window in her living room. The sun rushed in and held her with a soothing embrace. It was a beautiful day. It suddenly dawned on her that she lived less than an hour from the beach. She did not take advantage of it. Today was the perfect day to spend beachside. She did a little twirl to express her excitement. She looked through her closet. After a fervent search which created a pile of clothes behind her, she found a severely unworn red and white one-piece swimsuit. In the corner, she discovered a beach bag and some sunscreen she had not used in months. She grabbed a heart shaped necklace she rarely wore in her jewelry box. She held the silver heart piece for a moment. She smiled and then put the necklace around her neck.

Her face lit up with excitement. It would be such a fun day! She could lay down all day and drink some cocktails. Why didn't she do that more often? The thought of being by the water was thrilling. She could hear Kameela's reaction from where she stood: *Well, you are a water sign, so it makes perfect sense.*

Ana would just sigh in the background. That picture made her heart swell. She missed her friends immensely. She was thankful for them. She knew that her relationship with them over the years, and even more recently, had saved her life. They had nurtured her back to functionality after she was shunned by her own family. She still remembered it so vividly. However, she wasn't sure exactly how they had done so over the past few days. She just knew that they did. After she got over this odd feeling, she would invite them out for drinks. They were the closest thing she had to a family. She needed them to know how much they meant to her. She needed them to know she might not have been here if it wasn't for them.

The breeze on her drive beachside was a caress on her face. Trying to find a parking spot was a slap. It took her close to a half hour to find a tight spot between two Jeep Wranglers. Everyone had agreed it was the ideal day to lay on a towel next to the waves.

She loved how the sand rested against her heels. After the pebbly walk, she found a quiet area to spread her towel. Whatever quiet meant when an aerial shot of the beach would have revealed almost no hint of the golden sand. Earlier, she had stopped by a convenience store to purchase some margarita mix. She had poured the drink into an opaque container before stepping on the shore. Alcoholic beverages weren't allowed on the sand—yet almost everyone was tipsy, at the very least. She sat down cross-legged and sipped her cocktail.

The other beach attendants were providing her with some free entertainment. Kids were running around, throwing things, building sandcastles, then destroying them. It was so interesting how much fun they had destroying what they had taken such careful effort and time to build. They only took a moment to admire their work. Immediately after, their grin widened as they raised it to the ground. The most fascinating part was how they quickly moved on, did other things and came back later on to rebuild a new sandcastle. Like it was their first. Bright-eyed and bushy-tailed, like nothing happened.

Nova wished she had their carefreeness. She wished she moved as lightly as a child discovering the world. A child excited to learn and not afraid to start over. A child who enjoyed life for its moments, with no attachment to mundane expectations. She wished she could take things as lightly as them. She wished she could be as spontaneous and free as the children before her: building, destroying and rebuilding their sandcastles.

Teenagers were walking around in their developing bodies, somewhere between childhood and adulthood. Some were focused on their phones, squinting hard to shield their eyes from the glaring sunlight. Many were taking photos, converting their experiences into digital memories. Some were staring at others, too nervous about making the first move. The *others* were choppily looking back at the *some* to let them know that it was okay to. Nova smiled, amused by the intricacies of flirting.

She recalled her teenage years had missed some of the fun and awkwardness of the pre-adult years. She couldn't date casually because she needed to exclusively date to marry. Her parents had made that clear. She took another sip to shoo the thoughts of her parents away. Unsurprisingly, she still had not heard back from them. As much as she wanted them to be part of her life, she resented them for not fighting to keep her in theirs when she needed them most. She was their only child, for Christ's sake. She had wanted them to forgive her so badly that she had suppressed the feeling of resentment she was harboring toward them. However, the more she noticed how some parents held their children near while others made sure their offspring didn't get too far from the shore, the more she let herself acknowledge that she detested her parents for letting her get away from their sight, deep into the ocean, at the mercy of life's currents.

She lay down on her towel. She adjusted her sunglasses and closed her eyes. She still felt like something was missing from her memories. However, the harder she tried to recall what it was, the blurrier her thoughts became. It was probably best to stop trying to remember altogether. What was even the point of that exercise? She could recall the last couple of weeks almost entirely. With time passing, she could not remember every single occurrence seamlessly. But what about that mirror? She still remembered breaking her old one when she was deep cleaning a couple of weeks or so ago. However, she was certain she had purchased a remarkable replacement. When? She was not sure. Where? She had no idea. How did it look? She could not describe it.

She began to strongly question if she had ever purchased the mirror that only existed in her faint memories. If she did, where was it? And why wouldn't she be able to remember anything about it? She shook her head from side to side a couple of times. Why did she even care about some stupid mirror anyway? The only logical explanation was that she had never replaced her broken mirror. Perhaps she had a vivid dream. She was confusing Morpheus' tales with reality. Yes, that was it. Or at least, it's what she told herself.

It was time to let this go and focus on what she remembered. First, she was at a cul-de-sac at *Fit Gals and Pals*. As much as Paul being promoted instead of her had helped her get to this conclusion, she knew she would have eventually gotten there regardless of the circumstances. She was not sure what her next step was, but she knew for certain it was time for a change. Second, she needed to move on from her non-reciprocated crush on Hakeem. Somehow, this felt like the easiest change she had to make. She was not sure how or when it happened, but her heart now remained even when she thought about him. She figured her heart had its reasons, which she would not question.

Then, she thought about her parents…again. What was it about the sound of the waves crashing that made her think about them? She longed for a family, a sense of belonging. She thought about Kameela and Ana: her chosen family, her tribe. She belonged somewhere. Yet, she still felt a void, which she was convinced only her parents could fill. Perhaps it was her fate to have a couple of empty spaces at the center of her chest. As long as her heart continued to beat, she decided that she was at least functional.

Her back suddenly felt too warm against the towel. She sat back down and took a sip of her warmer beverage. When the liquid was down, she stood up. She stretched on top of her towel. She could hear her bones crack, seemingly shocked by her sudden movements. She walked slowly toward the water. The sound of the waves became more melodious the closer she got to the shoreline. It sounded like a song.

The warmth of the water and the voice of the waves made her think about a conversation she had with Kameela a while ago. A conversation about some African goddess named Mami Wata. It was not really a conversation, but rather one of the monologues Kameela usually went on about spirituality, goddesses, and astrology. Nova typically tuned her out. Instead, she thought about the latest show she had been watching. However, the Mami Wata story had grabbed her attention at some point.

"Her name means Mother of Waters. Her origin traces back to West, Central and Southern Africa. She is one of my favorite deities," Kameela began while lighting some sage in her living room. Nova was thinking about the fact that *Walter White* was slowly but surely becoming a villain. How he could have prevented *Jesse*'s girlfriend from choking to death in her sleep. "It is said that her beauty is mesmerizing. She has beautiful deep dark skin, dark kinky hair and very full lips. She is a half woman, half fish. A gorgeous mermaid." Poor *Jesse*. He didn't even know who his partner was becoming. "She usually has her serpent around her neck and often admires her own beauty in her golden mirror." *Walter White* had enough money now. It wasn't about the money anymore; it was about his ego and pride. "Whoever survives their encounter with her could become more attractive, more successful, and more fulfilled. Some people simply get the healing that they desire. These individuals would essentially heal their deepest wounds and become content with the state of their existence."

For whatever reason, that part made Nova snap out of *Breaking Bad*'s universe and get back into her own. "How does one survive their encounter with her?"

Kameela perked up at Nova's interest. "It's essentially her choice. She has to be pleased with you. Some people bring her offerings: food, jewelry, mirrors, combs, and a lot of other random stuff to satisfy her. But at the end of the day, she

282

decides who is worthy."

"What happens to the unworthy ones?" Nova air-quoted *unworthy*.

"They drown in the deep waters and are never seen again. I personally believe that she collects their souls to sustain her beauty and immortality."

Nova gasped. She knew these stories were merely myths and legends, but it was still shocking to the layman's ear. "What happens to the worthy ones?" She did not air-quote *worthy*.

"They receive what they've always wanted most. Some people want riches and good fortune. Some women wish for fertility. And others just want to mend their broken souls."

"She does all that?" Nova raised a brow.

Kameela rolled her eyes. "Yes." She continued with a deeper voice. "You'd just need to swim far enough into the ocean, make your offering, and hope that she finds you worthy. Proceed at your own risk."

Nova laughed out loud at the advice, which seemed directed at her. As if she would swim into the ocean and give up something that she had paid for, to offer it to some mythological goddess. Worst of all, the offering might not be good enough for her taste.

Who the hell would knowingly and willingly put their existence at risk for a chance at a better life, with such dire implications as a plausible outcome?

"Yeah, no, thank you," she said. She then traveled back to *Walter White,* aka *Heisenberg*'s fucked reality while Kameela pondered about how the upcoming fullness of the moon would affect her then new relationship with Josh.

Nova looked at her heart-shaped necklace as she walked

further into the ocean. It was not a valuable item, but she liked it enough. Perhaps Mami Wata would too. She laughed hysterically, resting her hands on her knees. The people around stared at her with confused expressions. Parents tucked their kids closer, away from her. That margarita mix must've gone straight to her head. She wasn't drunk, though. She was not tipsy anymore either. She had to be something to even consider throwing her necklace in the water.

What was even the procedure for this? She looked back. She was not that far from the shore, but she was distanced enough to have to squint to clearly identify her belongings. The water was up to her waist. She knew this mother of waters person did not exist. She had no doubt about it. However, she felt a pull to humor the legend. Honestly, she had nothing better to do.

"What the hell am I doing?" she said out loud.

The few people that were still around her looked at each other and walked back toward the shoreline. She knew how insane the whole scene must have looked. She shrugged it off. She swam a little further. The water had now formed its perimeter under her breastbone. She figured that she was far enough. She took her necklace off and threw it as far away as she could. Nothing happened. Her necklace was shining further away, still floating on the horizon.

She hated to admit it, but a small part of her had hoped that a dark-skin kinky-haired mermaid would have jumped to catch her necklace, and perhaps proceeded to speak to her in perfect English. Or better yet, Nova would have intuitively understood the tongue of the sea. She was disappointed. She had secretly wished the goddess of waters would have risen to deem her worthy of redemption.

The moment she turned around, she felt an undulating movement and sensed a presence behind her. She turned back around, equally quick and fearful. Nothing was there. She looked at the horizon. Her necklace was no longer shining. It must have sunk. This was getting a lot spookier than what she cared for. She turned back toward the shoreline and began to swim as fast away as she could. She still sensed that something was behind her. It was probably a fish. What was wrong with her? Of course, it was just some documented sea creature. Not a water goddess.

Nova continued to swim away, too afraid to stop or look back. Suddenly, she felt something very close. It gripped her ankle tightly. She heard a hiss. Then another one. Oh my god! The grip tightened. She could not get away. She had to face whatever was holding her back. She turned around and saw her: the most beautiful creature she had ever laid her eyes on. Powerful, captivating, deadly, yet healing. The mermaid woman looked at her and spoke. It was not English. It was not any human language. Nova's earlier guess had been right. It was the language of the sea. And she somehow intuitively understood it.

Nova, it's okay. Let go. The mirror has served its purpose.
You no longer need it. You are enough. You have always
been worthy. You just have to believe it.
Let go of your hurt. Let go of your doubts. Let go of your
fear. Forgive. Dare. Release. Love.
I will always watch over you.

"Mami Wata!" Nova yelled out.

She woke up in sweat and tears. Her heart was beating so fast she was afraid it would get out of her rib cage. She was not sure whether she should have been happy or sad that it had all been a dream.

Nova sat up on her bed, still dripping in sweat. She controlled her breaths until her heartbeat evened out. That was the most vivid dream she had ever had. She still could almost feel the tightening around her ankle. She shook her head until she felt fully awake. She still did not remember the entirety of the last couple of weeks, but after her dream, she was now certain there was indeed a mirror. She didn't understand how, but she knew it was not just an ordinary one. Nova concluded that she didn't need to remember everything that had happened to move forward. She had to change her life regardless of what her memories were keeping secret. And she knew where to start.

She picked up her phone and dialed. "Hey, Jeff, I'm not feeling well today, so I won't be able to make it."

"You never call off work, so I know it must be really bad," he said. "Take the time that you need. I hope you feel better soon. Let me know if you need anything."

"Well, there is something."

"Yes?"

"I also wanted to give you a heads up. I will send out my two weeks' notice tomorrow. I really enjoyed working at *Fit Gals and Pals* over the last few years, but it is time for me to move on."

Jeff was silent for a moment. "Is there anything that I can say or do to talk you out of your decision?"

"No," she said calmly. "I'm so thankful for my experience over the past years, and it's nothing against the company. It's just time for me to make some changes."

She could hear his voice soften behind the line. "I

completely understand. It's going to be hard to fill your shoes, but I know even greater things are ahead for you."

Her voice became uneven. He had valued her after all. "Thank you, Jeff."

"No, thank you, Nova. I'll see you tomorrow."

She felt so much lighter. She was not sure what her next professional move would be. But thanks to her frugality, she had enough cushion to take some time to figure it out. She had no clue what else she wanted to do. She had not drawn a plan yet. And who said she had to? She would move as freely as the children from her dream. She would take chances, explore, try, fail, and start over when needed. She would enjoy life for the moments it offered.

Nova knew that as vivid as her dream was, it had just been a dream. However, she wanted to be sure. She found her jewelry box and searched vehemently through it. The heart-shaped necklace had to be in there, somewhere. She untangled all the necklaces and bracelets which had become one, for worse. After every item regained their individuality, Nova could still not locate the necklace.

She could only think of three options as to the item's whereabouts. First, she had simply misplaced it, and she would find it later. Second, she had lost it. The first two were the most logical and plausible explanations. The last one was not as rational. What if her dream had been more real than fanciful? Between the missing mirror and her "dream" encounter with Mami Wata, Nova concluded that there was peace and contentment in unresolved mystery.

CHAPTER 25

She walked into the gym for the last time. She was more emotional than she had anticipated ending her journey at *Fit Gals and Pals*. Since she had given her two weeks' notice, her shifts at the gym had been predictably uneventful. Except for Ana, who had come by the gym a few times toward the end of the day to supposedly see her. Ana had always been a terrible liar. She walked in again as Nova was thinking about the fact that today would conclude a chapter of her life.

"She's in the back," Nova said to Ana the moment she saw her.

"Who is in the back?" Ana replied, flushed.

"Do not fuck this up! I really like her." She wagged her finger.

"O ye of little faith." Ana winked at her. "So do I."

Nova could not maintain her rigid expression. It was obvious how much Ana was smitten by Rose. And vice-versa.

She softened her tone. "I've never seen you like this. If I had no preconception of you, I might have even described it as cute."

"I'll take it." Ana chuckled. "Last day, huh? How do you feel?"

Nova gathered her stuff. "I feel amazing. I'm excited to figure out what's next for me."

Ana nodded, beaming. "I'm excited for you too. I'm proud of you for taking a leap into the unknown."

They hugged. "Thank you. I don't think I could have done it without you."

"Save that speech for the Oscars." Ana wiped a tear. "Please, could you walk me to staff room in the back? I'm not sure where it is."

Nova rolled her eyes, then shook her head. "Shocking, given how many times you have been here over the past couple of weeks to see me." She air-quoted, *see me*. "Follow me," she said in a faux reluctant tone. She could hear Ana's giggles behind her.

When they walked into the rest area in the back of the gym's main floor, Nova was surprised to find the lights off. They were never off. She searched for the switch. She turned the lights on the moment her index finger found it.

"Surprise!" The word echoed like a chorus.

Her eyes and ears were blinded and deafened at the same time. Balloons! Confetti! Jeff, Paul, Rose, the latest front desk person, the entire staff…and Hakeem, who she had not seen over the last week. They were all standing there with the brightest smiles on their faces. Tears ran away from her eyes like they were being chased in a horror movie. She looked next to her. Ana winked at her, the corners of her mouth almost meeting her ears.

"You bitch!" Nova hugged her. She heard laughter behind her. She turned back to face the crowd, her *Fit Gals and Pals* family. "You guys…I don't know what to say. I had no idea. Thank you!"

"Of course." Jeff's voice rose above the crowd. "We could'nt let you go without celebrating you." He walked up to her. "You have been such an outstanding team member. A true pleasure to work with. And although I'm sad to see you go, I'm even more excited for what the future holds for you, Nova." Then, he did the unimaginable: he hugged her.

She could not control the resilient flow of her tears. "Thank you, Jeff."

Then, she heard another voice above the mass. The voice she had dreaded hearing every morning when she walked into work for the last few years.

"Nova, I don't even know where to start," Paul said. "I don't know what we're going to do without you." She could still point out the performance in his delivery. However, under it was a hint of sincerity. It had always been there. And that was good enough.

She opened her arms for an embrace. Their first. "Thank you, Paul. I'll miss your amazing energy." It was a surprise to herself that she meant it.

Rose stepped forward. "I know we have not known each other for a long time, but somehow it feels like we have. I'll miss working with you, but I'm so excited for you, Nova."

They hugged tightly, like familiar souls. "Thank you, Rose," Nova said. "I'm so happy we'll continue to be in each other's lives." She looked at Ana and back at Rose. Ana grinned at them.

"My turn," a deeper voice came from behind them. She had almost forgotten about him. "I had to come to say my goodbyes when I heard the news," Hakeem said.

Rose stepped aside. Nova narrowed her focus on Hakeem. "I haven't seen you in a while."

"I know." He scratched his head. "I don't work here anymore. I found a better opportunity."

"Oh."

"It was pretty abrupt, so I didn't have time to say goodbye. Sorry."

The news was surprising. She was waiting for a rush of sadness and disappointment to flood in response to the fact that he had not cared enough to let her know. But nothing happened. Her blood continued to pump at the same pace.

"No worries. I'm glad you found a better gig. Did you come by just for this?"

She could see a crinkle form between his eyebrows. "Well, not exactly. I just needed to grab a piece of equipment that I forgot last week. But then Jeff told me about your surprise goodbye celebration, so I decided to stick around for it."

That answer was the only one that made sense, given their history. Her emotions were now clearer than the waters from her dream. "Thank you for staying around to say goodbye." She patted his back. "I have enjoyed working with you, and I wish you the best in all your future endeavors."

She sensed a déjà vu. She let it pass, unchallenged.

He nodded with that impeccable smile. "Likewise."

She walked back toward the crowd. She thanked everyone again. She was truly grateful that they had cared enough about her to have a send-off. Although she was assured of her decision to end her journey there, she would miss *Fit Gals and Pals* more than she had expected. Jeff and Paul gestured at her to grab some cupcakes. Ana and Rose were next to them, holding hands. She caught Hakeem standing still, looking her way. He waved goodbye when their eyes met. She waved adieu at the closing chapter.

CHAPTER 26

Naveen finally felt like himself again. He had not expected the encounter he had with Michelle to affect him as much as it did, but it did. It was not because he had any unresolved feelings for her but rather because it shined a light on something he had been trying to hide from himself. It was hard to admit, but he knew that he had to face the truth. And the truth was, more often than not, he had stayed silent and accepted whatever was happening to him. Too many times, he had just kept his own desires quiet. He had done what he was told or expected to do, whether it was what he truly wanted or not. Too many times, he had watched life happen to him as if he were a non-playing character in a video game. He had witnessed his own words and actions play out like he had no control over his own destiny.

He remembered the little voice inside of him he had silenced whenever his parents had told him that becoming a professional cricket player was not a viable option. He had even convinced himself that it was the logical route to take to kill that voice for good. And then, that voice somehow came back to life. She whispered that she knew he did not feel appreciated in his relationship with Michelle. Naveen stabbed her repeatedly with the knife of denial. He tried his hardest to convince her that he was content, to hopefully shut her up forever. But more recently, the voice somehow resurrected from the dead, yet again, to let him know that he had given up too quickly on his potential relationship with Nova. Yes, the first date had not been perfect. But neither was he. He knew deep down he had regretted not reaching out to her afterward. Now, too much time had passed. He wanted to contact her, but he was either too proud or too afraid to get rejected or ignored.

You know you want to see her again. Just admit it and contact her, the voice told him. He wished the voice would just mind her business. And perhaps, she was. Perhaps, he was her business. He knew, deep down, that the voice was his. He had been trying to suppress his own voice for years to avoid feeling disappointment and hurt. However, he could no longer do that. He had to take chances, regardless of the outcome. He owed it to the resilient voice inside of him to experience the unexpectedness of life.

***

What now? It had been three days since she had stopped working at *Fit Gals and Pals,* and she still had no idea what she would do next. She wanted to live her life to the fullest; but what did that even entail? She had no clue. Her weeks had been the same for the last few years: she woke up, drove to work, worked, sparingly worked out, drove back home, watched TV, occasionally hung out with Ana and Kameela, went to sleep, and started over the next week. She had stuck to that script for most of her adult life. And now that it was time to write new lines, she was drawing a blank.

She needed clarity and discernment. She remembered that Kameela always found it after meditating. Damn it, why not? She did not have a better alternative anyway. At the very

294

least, she would get to relax. She searched for some guided meditation online. She found one with the most positive feedback. She read the comments, both amused and comforted.

> *To whoever is reading this, you are strong and beautiful. Things will get better. You'll be fine.* – ZenW34.

> *This meditation is incredible! Did anyone else feel the tingles around their hands?* –Dvinebae.

> *This is the first time I tried to meditate. I'm actually sobbing right now. So powerful and healing!* – SamChills!32.

> The last one sold her. *I was so lost before this. I feel so at peace and confident on what my future holds after getting through this meditation.* – Hope2BeHappii.

She sat on the floor, cross-legged, with her hands following the length of her thighs. She had watched Kameela enough times to know the proper posture for a successful meditation. Visually, she knew what she should aim for. However, all the feelings and tingles those people referred to were a different story. For one, she rarely meditated. And when she did, it was not to get clarity but more so to feel relaxed, especially before bedtime. Yet today, she was hoping for discernment.

It had been three days, and nothing had happened. She wasn't sure whether she was too understanding with herself or not understanding enough. She wasn't sure whether her current state required patience and gentleness or urgency and tough love. She had never attempted to make these changes. She didn't know what the typical timeframe for a breakthrough was. She reread *Hope2BeHappii*'s comment. She closed her eyes, hopeful.

She followed the guided meditation precisely. She inhaled when she was told to. She exhaled when it was required. Thanks to Kameela, she knew where all the chakras were supposedly located. She focused hard to visualize her heart chakra at the center of her chest. She felt like it required the most attention. She tried to picture a glowing green light where her heart was in place. However, when the voice told her she might feel some warmth at the center of her chest, she had to call bullshit. She just wasn't sure which chakra she should direct her bullshit awareness to. She kept going anyway. She moved her focus between her brows, the location of her third eye. She could use an additional eye since the two she had rarely saw things coming. She pictured a glowing indigo light and hoped for the best. She focused hard, hoping for clarity. However, when she opened her eyes, she felt like the most relaxed and calm…confused person. As she had expected, she only felt zen for a brief and finite period. She would have to find clarity without the guidance of a random online meditation. *Hope2BeHappii* had oversold the whole thing.

She remained seated, cross-legged. She opened her eyes. The freedom of unrestricted possibilities now seemed more frightening than liberating. There was something comforting about knowing what was next, what every tomorrow would look like. Initially, the thought she could do whatever she wanted was attractive. However, now that she was sitting in her living room with not even a single clue on what to do next, she considered calling Jeff to tell him never mind.

She had obviously gotten ahead of herself. She had left her common sense behind. It would be different had she quit her job to follow her dream. But that wasn't her situation. She had essentially left a decent-paying position in the hopes of figuring out what her plan was. She had absolutely put the cart before the horse, and now that it was time to move forward, she understood why it wasn't practical. She should have thought about what she wanted to do next before quitting. Fuck. She could only survive about three months without working. How could she potentially figure out something she had given up trying to understand for most of her existence in such a limited period of time?

Nova recalled how effervescent she was when she was just Little Nova. She remembered that a variety of things excited her then. When she was younger, she couldn't keep still. She loved to move. She especially loved to dance. At first, her parents observed her quietly. When she grew a little older and her movements grew to become more passionate, her mother sat her down. "You should only dance in a way that honors Jehovah," she advised. Nova wasn't sure what she meant exactly. She was not motioning her body in a way that would have been considered inappropriate or suggestive. She would have never dreamed of doing that. She was simply allowing her hips to sway more vigorously and her feet to stomp more fervently. Then, dancing had been the only space where she could freely express herself. The strong movements of her body were the vehicle for the words she was not brave enough to say. But after her mom talked to her, she filtered her expression to appease her parents and Jehovah. And as her dance moves became more and more subdued, so did her spirit.

Eventually, she stopped dancing. She preferred not to do things at all instead of doing them in a non-satisfying way. She still felt that fire within her that she only knew how to keep alive with motion. So, she ran. At first, she ran with no direction. She ran whenever she had some downtime after school, before she went door-to-door to spread the good word, and mostly when her parents were too busy to keep track of her whereabouts. She felt amazing after every run. The part she was looking forward to the most was when it felt like her lungs were on the verge of quitting their job. That fraction of an instant when she wanted to stop but didn't. And when she got through that moment, it felt like she was levitating. She felt light and euphoric. She ran more often, almost every day, chasing ecstasy. Her parents eventually discovered her new interest. They were glad she had found another way to be physically active.

Nova began to time her run time. She was finishing her runs faster and faster. She eventually consistently completed her 5k runs around the twenty-five-minute mark. She wanted to see how well she would fare against her peers. So, she approached her school's cross-country coach and asked him if she could try out for the team. She did not win the race, but she placed in the top half against trained athletes. The coach advised that her technique needed improvement, but with some training she had the potential to become one of the district's top runners. She was over the moon. She could not wait to share the news with her parents. To her dismay, they did not share her excitement.

"It's one thing to run for fun and to maintain your health," her father said. "However, to do it competitively is a different story."

Nova had not expected them to have any negative feedback. She was just running, for God's sake. How could that possibly be bad?

"Dad, I really enjoy running. And the coach said that with training, I could become one of the top runners in the region," she pleaded.

"And that is exactly the point I am trying to make," he interjected. "I'm glad you like running, and I don't want you to stop doing something that you enjoy." Nova was looking down, waiting for the *but.* "However, competition breeds vanity, envy, greed, and rivalry. You are already talking about wanting to be the best runner. This is a worldly concern. It will stir your focus away from what matters." He got closer to her and gently rested his hand on her shoulder. "What matters is serving Jehovah." He paused, then said with the softest smile, "Do you understand?"

She could hear herself screaming inside. She could sense the words that she wanted to say clogged up inside her throat, leaving her mute. She could sense her voice giving up, tired of fighting. At last, two words escaped, only to betray her.

"I understand," she heard herself say out loud.

What Nova eventually understood was that none of her interests would please her parents or Jehovah. So, she eventually stopped trying to determine the things she liked altogether. It was more bearable if she did not know what she was passionate about; instead of falling in love with it, only to have to stop and walk away broken-hearted.

Although she eventually left the witnesses, she never mustered the strength to dig into who she was again. She knew she no longer needed her parents' approval. Yet, she felt like the moment she would figure out what she really wanted to do and the type of life she truly wanted to live; the other shoe would drop. Even though her parents were hours away, with their silence creating an even larger distance, she still believed that the moment she decided the path she wanted to take, they would materialize from the ether to convince her she was going the wrong way. Even after all these years of silence, she did not want to disappoint them more than she already had.

Nova got up from her meditative position. She grabbed her laptop and logged into one of the job search accounts she had used in the past. Hopefully, an opportunity would just stand out, and she would instinctively recognize that it was what she was meant to do. Her only relevant job had been at *Fit Gals and Pals*, so she knew she would be better qualified for another sales position. However, she wanted to be open-minded to her unknown heart's desires. She searched for all the jobs in a twenty-mile radius. Most of the ones that were suggested were still in sales.

She slowly scrolled through all the descriptions. She was amused by the boastfulness of a few:

Do you hate your job? Are you sick of clocking in? Do you want to make your own schedule and be your own boss? Do you want to change lives and make a difference in the world? Do you want to have unlimited earning potential? You are in the right place!

Almost all had an extremely vague pay structure:

Compensation: 25k to 100k.

Compensation: Unlimited.

Compensation: Based on experience.

Compensation: Pay per performance.

Compensation: Will be discussed in person.

When she read the post to find out more about the job that would allow her to change people's lives and potentially make up to six figures, she always ended up underwhelmed:

At Plume Paper Inc., we are committed to provide quality paper to our clients.

Sip and Shine's mission is to deliver beautiful and affordable wine glasses to our customers.

BearFoot socks are comfortable and durable to meet our clients' needs.

She logged out of the site, unresolved. She laid her laptop on the couch. She would try again later. If she was being honest with herself, figuring out her career path was just the tip of the iceberg. Under the water was the absence of knowing the life she wanted to live, what made her happy. She turned her TV on and selected a random acoustic playlist. At first, she stood still, quietly taking in the sound. She closed her eyes to visualize Little Dancing Nova. She recalled how she used to move, free and raw. She turned the volume to the maximum and danced.

She let her arms and her waist follow the waves of the sound. She slowly swayed her hips. She accelerated her movements to match the music. She could hear her heartbeat fastening with the drumming sounds. She saw Little Nova within her as she began to rhythmically stomp her feet. She whipped her head from side to side. She spun around endlessly until her living room conceded to join her. And when she stopped and stood still, everything around her continued to dance. She laughed hysterically while she struggled to regain her balance. She let her body embrace the ground. She lay down, still laughing. The living room eventually stopped spinning. Yet, she couldn't bring herself to stop laughing. She wasn't even sure what was so funny. She didn't want to understand. She didn't want to ruin the magic of the moment.

She closed her eyes and let her mind wander freely. She saw her present self walking toward Little Nova. She approached cautiously to not startle her younger self. But Little Nova did not look frightened. In fact, she was the fearful one. She halted her thread. Perhaps it was a trap. Then, Little Nova smiled brightly and opened her arms. Nova immediately felt safe. She ran toward her. She held her close, tight under her grasp. She cried both in her mind and in reality. With the embrace, she felt that Little Nova was sharing her grit, her unbrokenness, and her fire with her. Little Nova pulled her closer and spoke. She did not sound like her younger self; she sounded like a dream. Her voice echoed:

Let go of your hurt. Let go of your doubts. Let go of your
fear. Forgive. Dare. Release. Love.
I will always watch over you.

Nova couldn't recall when or where, but she was certain she had heard those exact words before. Though, this time they profoundly resonated within her, living imprints. Then Little Nova disappeared, and it was just her. She stood still. She felt warmth. She felt peace. She still didn't know what she would do next, but somehow, she knew she would be okay.

CHAPTER 27

Nova opened her eyes and exhaled deeply. It was time to let go of her past and release into her present. She picked up her phone and dialed. Last time, she felt nervous when the phone rang. Not today. She waited quietly as the voicemail greeting picked up.

"Greetings, brother or sister! You have reached John and Sarah Wright's line. We apologize for missing your call. Please leave your name, number, and a brief message, and we will make sure to return your call at our earliest availability. And always remember, Jehovah is with you!"

"Hello, Mom and Dad. I hope that you guys are doing well. I'm not sure how brief this will be, but here we go," she began with an even tone. "I know that we will never speak and be together again. I have now accepted it. I know you both have always done what you thought was best. I will forever be thankful for the way you took care of me and protected me growing up. However, I do not agree with your decision to cast me away and abandon me when I needed you the most. I understand why you did it, but I do not agree, nor do I respect it." Tears quietly fell down her cheeks, but her voice remained even. "Nonetheless, I forgive you. I have been holding this mixture of resentment and hope for our relationship since I was disfellowshipped. And I have been

303

stuck in this mental space for years. It has held me back from figuring out who I am and how I want to live my life." She wiped her face, though tears were still flowing. "I have been hoping that we would reconnect down the road. I truly did not realize I was letting life go by while I was waiting for you to agree to continue to be part of my journey. I felt like only you two had the key to unlock and set me free from this state of paralysis." The flow of her tears lost steam. "Honestly, I also used you guys as a scapegoat to not try and stay stagnant. Don't get me wrong; you guys really fucked me up." She gasped at the realization that she had never sworn while speaking to her parents. A feeling of liberation rose from within her. "Excuse my French; I'm not fluent yet." She chuckled. Her voice was lighter. "However, some of it is on me. I have to be accountable. I have to take the steps. I have to move on." Her tone was now confident and assured. "Although I was hoping to meet you guys along the way, I understand it will not happen. I'm at peace with it now." She paused for a moment. "Sorry, I'm rambling. I guess what I'm trying to say is that I will always love you, Mom and Dad. Always. However, it's time for me to completely and unapologetically go my own way. I will not call you again. I sincerely wish you the very best in this lifetime. I will always love you. Goodbye."

Nova felt like she could float away when she ended the call. She knew things would never be the same. She ran to her bedroom and grabbed her fluffiest pillow. She covered the entirety of her face and screamed loudly into it until her voice fainted back into her throat.

Finally, she had done it! After all these years, she had put her gloves on, and she had figured out how to wipe her slate clean. She had to share the good news with her loved ones.

"Hey ladies! Cancel your evening plans! Let's meet at our usual spot. My treat!"

She immediately saw bubbles forming in response.

"Your treat? Oh, I'll be there!" Ana wrote.

"Ditto!" Kameela followed.

"Let's look extra cute too!" Nova added.

"Duh!" Kameela answered.

"I'm not even sure what the other options would be?" Ana texted with a wink emoji.

"I've seen you in the other options," Kameela wrote with the same wink emoji. **"I can remind you when we get there!"**

"We haven't forgotten your fedora and belt on top of the t-shirt phase," Nova replied, giggling.

"Oh God, I blocked that shit out!" Kameela wrote.

"Screw y'all, that was hot!" Ana texted with a laughing emoji.

"See you guys soon!" Nova ended, laughing out loud.

Nova was the last one to walk in. Kameela and Ana beamed the moment they saw her.

"Speaking of the devil," Ana said.

She ran to hug them. She kept them tight in the embrace. "I'm so happy to see you guys!"

"We are, too," Kameela replied with a wide grin.

"We already ordered your strawberry margarita." Ana handed her the drink. "What's up with you, girl? You are looking rejuvenated. The unemployed life is treating you well, I see." She grimaced. "Catch us up!"

"I will, but I want to hear about you guys first." She directed her gaze toward Kameela and took a sip.

"I guess I'll start then." Kameela raised her glass. "I don't think this is that interesting of news, but I did get a part-time job offer at a yoga studio."

"What the hell do you mean this is not interesting news," Ana said. "That is great, congratulations!"

"Thank you," she said. "I mean, it's not a big shot job like yours or anything, but it's work."

"Kameela, stop." Nova chimed in. "You know you wouldn't stand being in an office. This is perfect for you!"

She cracked a smile. "True. I'm actually so excited about this. I can't believe I will get paid to do something that I enjoy!"

Ana nodded, then said, "And now you can talk about the benefits of Downward-Facing Dog and Warrior One to people who actually give a shit."

They all roared with laughter.

Kameela composed herself. "But on a serious note, thank you guys. I wouldn't have stood my ground and had that conversation with Josh if it wasn't for you two. We are still working on some things, but our marriage has tremendously improved since our talk." She grinned. "I can't wait to start working!"

"Aw, I'm so happy for you!" Nova teared up. Ana nodded in agreement, teary eyed. Nova looked at Ana. "Since we are on the subject of working. Ana, do you like work at *Fit Gals and Pals* now? Because my last week there, we basically had the same shift!" She raised her brow and held a smirk.

"Yeah! Someone got you leaving work only one hour after your scheduled time? This is major!" Kameela seconded. "Please, tell us more about this exceptional being."

"You two are actually the worst." Ana shook her head. Her cheeks were flushed. "Fine, I like her. She is cool."

"Kindly elaborate," Kameela said.

"Jesus. Okay, okay!" Ana looked away and then back at her friends. "She is amazing! She is witty. She is kind. She is empathetic. She is nurturing. She is patient. Oh, and hot. I could go on. Aside from you two, she is the only other person I can be my true self with." She took a breath. "She just gets me."

"Aw!" Nova and Kameela said in unison.

"Do you think she might be the one?" Nova asked, her hands covering her mouth in excitement.

Ana took a moment. "Actually, she just might be." She gasped at her own words. "God dammit. Cupid strikes again."

"Oh my god, I cannot believe my ears!" Kameela yelled out. "Let's fucking cheer to that!"

They clinked their glasses. After they all took a sip, Kameela and Ana immediately stared at Nova.

"Your turn!" they said at the same time.

Nova spoke with no hesitation. "I called my parents today."

"Did they answer?" Kameela asked, clenched jaws and frown face.

Ana was waiting for her answer with a similar look. "Did they?"

"No," Nova said. She saw the tension lingering around their shoulders. "But this call was different. I didn't expect or need them to answer. For a long time, I thought I did. I thought I needed a response from them. But turns out I just needed to say my piece. And after all these years, I finally garnered the courage to do it. It was weird. It felt both overdue and timely." Her friends were listening attentively, nodding in understanding. "I told them I will always love

307

them, but at the same time, it's time for me to move on with my life. I let them know that I would not contact them again. I will no longer put living my life the way I want to on hold in the hope that they decide to be part of it. I no longer have any resentment toward them. It's just time to let go. I owe it to myself."

"Wow, Nova," Ana said. "I'm beyond proud of you. I know this has weighed heavy on you for years."

Kameela squeezed her hand and held it. "We are proud of you, girl. We love you. And know that we will always be here for you."

"Words cannot express how thankful I am that you two are in my life. You guys have been my rock. I don't know if you know this, but you have literally saved my life. I don't know where I would be if it weren't for you two. I love you so much. Thank you for being my friends. My sisters. My family."

They lunged into each other's arms, forming an impenetrable circle. They stayed inside of the embrace until time physically felt like a construct. They let their tears roll freely. No words needed to be spoken out. Love was loud enough.

***

Nova felt her phone vibrate in her purse when she walked outside the restaurant. She immediately recognized the name on the screen.

"Hey Nova! It's Naveen (hopefully you remember me). I hope you've been well. I know it's been a while since we met. Hopefully this doesn't come off as cliché, but I just had a lot of stuff to sort through. I still should have kept in contact with you in the meantime, so I apologize. I can explain further in person, if it's not too late. You've been on my mind. I hope the door is not closed?"

She couldn't hold her smile while reading his message.

"Shit happens," she replied with a smiley emoji. **"What do you have in mind?"**

She grinned at the text bubbles forming in response.

***

Nova sat in her car. The silence was warm. She played her favorite feel-good song: *Feeling Good* by Nina Simone. The moment begged for it. It would have probably taken her a lifetime to count how many times she had listened to it. Though, the words never penetrated her as they did in that instant. It was a new dawn indeed. It was a new day. Yes, it was a new beginning. A fresh start. A new life! Oh God, how good did she feel! How free did she feel! How alive! She was not sure what was next. She was not sure what the future held for her. She still had not figured out what she wanted to do next. But she was not worried anymore. She knew that no matter what life had in store, she would show up. She would give it her best shot. She would give this reality the authentic and unapologetically flawed version of herself, no matter what it looked like. She would make Little Nova proud.

Eyes closed. Inhale. A smile. Exhale. Eyes opened. Bliss.

ABOUT THE AUTHOR

BIANCA PENSY ABA was born on May 27, 1993, in Yaoundé, Cameroon. She lived in her native country until she turned eighteen. She graduated from Graceland University in 2017. She was a college athlete who played sports most of her life. Her second love was basketball. Her first was writing. Her debut novel *Across Both Sides of the Mirror* is a story that she initially imagined when she was in her early teens. After over a decade of finding her way back to her passion for writing, she finally fleshed out the concept to tell *Nova*'s story. She lives in Allen, Texas where she enjoys picnicking, reading, hiking, watching terrible dating shows, sipping a glass of wine on her balcony, and doing whatever else she is in the mood for. You can learn more about Bianca and her upcoming projects at *www.biancapensyaba.com*.

Connect Online:

- www.biancapensyaba.com
- biancapensyabawrites
- Bianca Pensy Aba

Thank you for reading *Across Both Sides of the Mirror*. I hope you enjoyed it. If you have the time and inclination, please leave an honest review on your chosen platform(s) and tell a friend about this book. Thank you so much for the support!

Bianca Pensy Aba

Made in the USA
Middletown, DE
22 October 2023

41260459R00191